Grave Misgivings
by Kristen Houghton

© Copyright 2015 by Kristen Houghton

ISBN-13: 978-0-692-42310-3

Library of Congress Cataloguing-in-Publication Data
Houghton, Kristen
Grave Misgivings: A Cate Harlow Private Investigation crime novel/Kristen Houghton-1st. ed.
1.Cate Harlow (Fictitious character)-Fiction 2. private investigator 3.crime
4. female sleuth
5. mystery 6. detective 7. New York City

All rights reserved. No part of this publication may be reproduced, stored in a retrieval system, or transmitted in any form or by any means – electronic, mechanical, photocopy, recording, or any other – except for brief quotations in printed reviews, without the prior written permission of the author.

This is a work of fiction. All the characters in this book are fictitious, and any resemblance to actual persons, living or dead, is purely coincidental. The names, incidents, dialogue, and opinions expressed are products of the author's imagination and are not to be construed as real.

Published by
HH Skylight Publishing

175 Fifth Avenue
New York, NY10010
Skylightbooks.com

in association with
◣ köehlerstudios™

Books by Kristen Houghton

CRIME and MYSTERY
CATE HARLOW PRIVATE INVESTIGATION series
For I Have Sinned
Grave Misgivings
Unrepentent: Pray for Us Sinners

FANTASY
THE TEDDY JAMESON CHRONICLES
Welcome to Hell, Teddy Jameson
Life in Hell

HISTORICAL ROMANCE
The Anchoress: A Romantic Tale of Terror

ANTHOLOGY
*No Woman Diets Alone-There's Always
a Man Behind Her Eating a Doughnut
And Then I'll Be Happy!*

Grave Misgivings

A Cate Harlow Private Investigation

Kristen Houghton

"I always count it a plus when no one gets killed."
CATE HARLOW

Kristen Houghton

For Alan, with love and thanks always...

CHAPTER 1

"CATHERINE, YOU'RE LATE for your nine-thirty appointment," says the prim and proper voice of my part-time secretary Myrtle Goldberg Tuttle. "Your client, a Ms. Jennifer Brooks-Warren, has been waiting here in the office for twenty minutes. Where are you?"

"On my way, Myrtle. There's a garbage truck with a blown-out tire that's holding up traffic. Can you believe this? What a hot mess! Anyway, tell her I'll be there as soon as I can. Get her coffee or tea or whatever and tell her the truth about why I'm late. Give her one of Harry's pastries. They always make waiting easier."

"All right, tea or coffee, but I don't think the young woman wants one of Harry's double-stuffed cupcakes. She doesn't seem like the type who eats those. The older man with her might take one, though. By the way, you didn't tell me we had a modeling agency as part of our clientele."

"We don't. Why do you say that?"

"You'll see what I mean when you get here." Pause. "How are you dressed this morning?"

"The same as usual, jeans, sneakers; you know what I wear."

"Pity you didn't dress up. Are you wearing makeup at the very least?"

"A little. Why the sudden questions about my appearance, Myrtle? What's up?"

"Never mind. Just make sure your hair is neatly brushed before you come upstairs."

≈

She is one of the most beautiful women I have ever seen. There is no way to describe her other than breathtakingly beautiful or drop-dead gorgeous. Next to this incredible porcelain doll I feel like Raggedy Ann. I completely understand why Myrtle had thought this woman was a model. But as beautiful as she is, I am certain that her beauty isn't the reason she has come to *Catherine Harlow, Private Investigations*. I am right. The lady needs help of a protective kind. Someone has hired a professional hit man to kill her.

A well-dressed, distinguished-looking man with a meticulously trimmed beard sits next to her on my couch and a brief introduction lets me know that his name is Edward Penn, and that he is her fiancé. He is pleasant enough but he lets her do all the talking.

"This was me before the cosmetic surgery, Ms. Harlow," says my prospective client.

I tell her to call me Cate then look at the several photos she hands to me. They're the kind of "before" pictures plastic surgeons take of their prospective patients. I try not to change expression as I look at them but I do glance from the beauty in front of me to the beast in the pictures with surprise. Jennifer Brooks-Warren smiles at me and shakes her head.

"Unbelievable, right? But that really *was* me two years ago."

She's obviously waiting for me to say something so I do. "It is an incredible change, Ms. Brooks-Warren, um, Jennifer. May I ask what you had done?"

"Yes, of course. I had a brow lift, cheek implants, nose remodeling, jaw shaping, ear pinning, liposuction, extensive dental work and caps, and breast augmentation. I also lost forty pounds and regularly worked out with a trainer. I still try to work out every day even now. I've made myself into a completely different person." Her eyes hold a small glint of triumph.

"Quite a metamorphosis. You don't look like the same woman at all. And you say you think someone has put a contract out on your life?"

"Not think, I *know*."

"It's obvious that you wanted to put your past behind you so I have to assume that the person who wants you killed is someone *from* your past. Do you have the name of that someone?"

I am poised with a pen and small notebook.

"Y—y—yes, I do. But, you see, that's the problem. The person's name."

"I don't follow. You're hiring me to help you. If you do know who wants you dead it's in your best interest to tell me. Can you do that?" I pause. Something's not quite right. "You do know the person's name, right?" She nods her head yes.

"Okay, then tell me. It helps to spell it so I have the correct name to research."

She sits up straighter and holds her head up. I wait for a few moments. She sighs, looks at me and says, "Brooks-Warren, B-r-o-o-k-s-W-a-r-r-e-n."

I look up. "A relative? Can you give me the first name?"

"I can give you the whole name. Jennifer Brooks-Warren."

I put my pen down and look at my prospective client before speaking.

"Let me get this straight, Jennifer. Either you put a contract out on yourself or the person who wants you killed is a relative with the same name. Or, and I certainly hope this is not the case, you're some new celebrity with a reality show due to air soon, looking to pull some type of stupid scam for publicity's sake. If the last one's the reason that you're here, I have to tell you that you came to the wrong place. I don't do scams."

"No, no, it's me all right. I hired the hit, isn't that what's it's called? Anyway I put the hit out on myself."

"May I ask why? But before you answer, let me give you some advice. If you are indeed the one who hired the killer, you should be able to cancel the contract, minus a retainer fee of course. I mean, I don't condone hiring assassins and such, but if you pay a fee to this person to cancel out the hit then everyone's happy. Get in touch with him or her."

"Him. And I can't; I can't get in touch with him. The number I have for him is no longer in service. He seems to be unreachable and I'm scared."

"What about the police? Have you contacted them? Maybe they can protect you."

"Edward filed a report with them, he spoke with them several times; I was too upset to talk to them so he did so on my behalf. But I don't think they fully believed him. Edward felt that I should get private protection."

"All right, let's get some information about this hit you ordered. When was the last time you spoke to this man?"

"Over two years ago when I needed his services."

I look up from writing her info on my notepad and sigh deeply. Shit! "I'm sorry, but did you just say that you ordered the hit over *two years* ago, Ms. Brooks-Warren?" She nods. I'm getting a little annoyed. "Well, as far as I can see you're still alive. Again, I have to tell you that if this is some type of publicity scam, I absolutely do not…"

The man who was sitting so quietly on my couch that I had almost forgotten he was there suddenly speaks. "My fiancée, Jennifer, made the deal to have this professional hit man eliminate her on her twenty-fifth birthday." He pauses and rises slowly. "Her birthday is two months from today, Ms. Harlow."

⁂

My client-to-be looks out the window of my office, staring for a while at the flower-pot-cum-doves'-nest on my fire escape. The doves have been gone since last year; babies grown and all. The parents will be back in a week or two to begin nesting again and make new babies or so I've read. I hope so; they're family.

"Ms. Harlow, have you ever been ugly?"

Her question surprises me. I don't know how to respond

but my curiosity is piqued. Certainly at certain points in our lives, everyone feels ugly; that's usually just because we're going through a bad time. It's temporary until we feel good about ourselves again. Looking at Jennifer Brooks-Warren, I get the feeling that the before pictures of my new client tell more of a story than I had realized. When I don't answer, she continues.

"I mean truly ugly? Oh I know we women have a way of saying we look horrible or are having a bad hair day and silly things like that but that's *not* being ugly. I *know* what ugly really is and how cruel people can be about it. I was ugly all my life. Look at the pictures of me back then and look at me now."

I do as she says, glancing from the beautiful woman in front of me to the pictures taken of her a few years ago. Genetics had not been kind to this woman and so she had taken it into her own hands, or in this case, the expert hands of a top-notch plastic surgeon and become the woman she wanted to be. Nothing wrong with that. Whatever makes you happy is my personal motto on that score. I let her talk. Listening is a key component for being a good private investigator.

"My parents and I lived on a farm in Culpepper, Virginia about seventy miles from Washington, DC . I have no siblings but that's only because my mother had three miscarriages; one before and two after I was born. She was not a well woman and the miscarriages took a real toll on whatever health she had. Even though I know they loved me, there wasn't a whole lot of attention expended on me and there was very, very little money. My mother was always sick and depressed; she died when I was ten. All my father did was work that farm morning to night and save every dime, every penny, he could.

"He wasn't cruel or indifferent to my unhappiness; he was a farmer used to hard work and the misery that life can dole out. He'd had a hard life as a child. His family had lost their own farm to foreclosure. My dad felt that you had to suck up the bad things that happened in life and tough it out. Dad wasn't the type to show emotions; he was just distant because he was exhausted all the time, poor man. He worked himself to death."

She sighs and stops for a few minutes. Patience is a skill; I wait, allowing her to collect her thoughts.

"My school years were pure torture. You've seen in the news how some bullied children choose suicide over living in fear and torment? I understand that feeling all too well. I thought about it, believe me, but naively I continued to hope that maybe things would change. I was really naïve and possibly a fool to think that way, because the cruelties continued all through elementary and middle schools. I never had friends. I was always the target of bullies. But in high school I found a way to be...popular."

She walks toward the window.

"In high school I became something of a, I guess the only word to describe it is, a slut." Her fiancé, who has resumed sitting on the couch, gives her a sad smile.

"I thought that having sex with boys would bring me some type of acceptance, that someone would like me. Oh, believe me, they all wanted it and I gave it to them, *whatever* way they wanted it." She laughs bitterly. "An older girl, who I guess felt sorry for me, took me aside one day and told me I should stop what I was doing. It wasn't making me popular, she said, the boys were using me. Then she reluctantly repeated what the boys were saying about me. She told me that they said, 'If you put a bag over Jenny's head and close your eyes, fucking her isn't so bad.'"

I wince at the cruelty of teenage boys. In my freshman year of high school I punched a guy in the stomach hard enough to make him vomit. This was after he unexpectedly grabbed my breast in a dark corner at a homecoming dance and remarked loudly, "Wow! Harlow's got melons! Anything more than a handful is a waste." High school can be tough.

"I wanted to die after she told me that. I prayed to die. I didn't want to live anymore but I just kept on going." She stops and I hand her a box of tissues.

"I had worked all through my school years as the clean-up girl in a bar called the K & K. The owner, Kevin, didn't say it but I knew he didn't think I was attractive enough to be a waitress. The pretty girls who served the customers were good for business and he knew it.

"After graduation, I continued working there because it was a place to hide. At the bar, we had a lot of just regular folk come in, but occasionally there'd be some stranger who got lost or someone just traveling through who wanted a quick beer and burger. One night we were short-handed and Kevin actually asked me to be a waitress. And that was the night this man sat down at one of my tables. He was a hit man except I didn't know it then. You could see that he was someone who exuded power. I mean he was polite to Kevin and very well-spoken but he had the kind of bearing that made other people steer clear of him. Usually the people in the bar are friendly and talk to strangers and all but no one spoke to this man. His eyes were hard, almost cruel. He sat in a booth in my section of the bar near the back door and ordered beer and a burger just like anyone else. He didn't bother anyone."

I interrupt her to ask her to describe this man.

"Tall, definitely over six feet, very short blond hair, and he looked like an athlete."

"What color eyes?"

"Oh, cold, so cold, blue." She shivers.

This Jennifer Brooks-Warren seems to be reliving that night in her mind; it is almost as if she is talking to herself and has forgotten that I am sitting there. The man on my couch simply sits there with his eyes on Jennifer and says nothing.

"How did you find out that he did murder for hire, Jennifer?" I asked. "Certainly he didn't just mention it in polite conversation."

She smiles and shakes her head. "I found out about his...line of work accidentally. He got a call on his cell phone."

"Do you remember his part of the conversation?"

"I only heard a little of what he said to whoever called him. He said, 'You wanted it, you got it, it's done. I have the evidence you requested.' Even though his voice was low and polite, his words were frightening. But he was nice to me and gave me a twenty dollar tip for a twelve dollar bill."

"Can you tell me how you found out he was a killer for hire?" I press.

"From a business card."

"He *gave* you his business card?"

"Not exactly." Jennifer Brooks-Warren paces back and forth in front of the windows then comes to a stop in front of my desk.

"A woman came in shortly after his phone call and sat at his table. She ordered two drinks in a row, then a third one. It was as if she wanted to get drunk really fast. We had a lot of people do that on Fridays; you know, bad week; get drunk as fast as you can to forget it."

"Describe the woman if you can," I tell her. "Age, hair color, weight, and height; every detail helps me."

"She was maybe in her late thirties. I think her hair was a dark brown or black and very short. She was wearing some sort of exercise clothes, as if she'd just come from a gym. I guess she was about my height, five foot three, and she was very skinny. She was wearing glasses with black frames. That's all I can remember."

"You're doing fine, Jennifer. Go on. Tell me what happened next."

"After she finished her third drink the man motioned to her and then both of them got up from the table and stood talking. It got real loud suddenly because someone started up the old jukebox we had in the bar. The man looked annoyed.

"I had to take out the empty bottles for the recycle bins and that's when I saw both the man and the woman come outside. I kind of hid when the man looked around to see if anyone was nearby because he scared me. I heard them talking, though. She said, 'It's really over then? You did it? I'm free?' The man nodded and said to her really low, 'You're free. I get paid to do a job, it gets done, one way or another. You paid for this. Here it is.' I saw him take something out of his jacket that was wrapped in some type of foil. He unwrapped it and it was a, it was a... finger with a fancy ring still attached to it. He handed it to the woman. She took it and gasped then quickly handed it back to the man. I heard her say, 'Yes, this is proof, all right. That's his. Did he...suffer?' The man put the ringed finger back inside his jacket pocket and smiled coldly. 'That's what you paid for, isn't it? That's what you got. The elimination is complete.' Then he walked away toward the parking lot. The woman went back inside.

"I was afraid but I was also intrigued. The realization hit me that the woman had had this man kill someone. Why would he use the word eliminated? How else would he have a finger? I waited outside for a good twenty minutes after the man left and then went back through the kitchen.

"An hour later, when I went to clean up my tables I asked the woman if she wanted anything else, maybe a cab to drive her home; she was pretty drunk by then. She had had quite a few more drinks. 'No,' she said, 'There's nothing else I want.' She laughed a little crazily and whispered 'Especially not my father back from the dead. I'm finally, finally, finally free.'

"As I said she was pretty drunk but she looked at me and laughed again; she was giddy. I must've looked upset or something. I was thinking about how someone could have their own father killed. I mean your own *father*; he must have done something terrible to her.

"Anyway she misunderstood the look on my face because she said, 'Honey, you look like someone has screwed you over royally—some prick of a guy? Married or something?' I just stood there and looked at her. 'Hey!' she said to me in a confidential whisper. 'Cheer up! Listen to me; no one deserves to be treated like shit. My father was a monster, a monster! And I finally did something about it. If you ever want to...dispose of someone, I know just the man you need.'

"She began laughing again and I saw her take out a business card from her wallet. She scratched out the name and address of the business on the front, and wrote something on the back. 'Here, this is for you. Call this number and do it soon. The man who was in here before with me? He is the devil himself when it comes to eliminating people but he gets the job done.'"

Jennifer hands me a card with some writing scrawled on it in an unsteady hand. *Professional Eliminator* followed by a phone number. The information on the front of the card has been scratched out heavily with pen but I should be able to get some details from it.

"Three days later I called the number and ordered the hit. I figured it was the best thing I could do. I was so depressed and sad. If anything happened to me, my father would get a small payout on a life insurance policy I had." She laughs bitterly. "I was worth more dead than alive."

"Jennifer, I need you to tell me a few things about that call you made to the hit man. How was the phone answered? What was said and how long were you on the phone?"

"I guess the hit man answered; it was a man's voice but I don't know if it was the same voice as the one in the bar. There was no hello or any other greeting. All he said when he answered was, 'The price of a standard elimination is ten thousand dollars. You have twenty-four hours to think it over.'

"Then he told me to call him back with details of the subject to be eliminated, he said those exact words, I remember, and where to bring the money. He wanted cash, nothing larger than hundreds. He said that if I wanted proof of the elimination or anything extra, it would cost an additional five thousand dollars. I thought of that horrible cut-off finger. I told him no proof was necessary and I told him I wanted the death to be quick, no suffering. The whole conversation lasted less than two minutes."

Two minutes—most criminals are careful to keep their phone time short. Even though a trace does take time, police don't need a person to be on the phone for three minutes or more any longer. Computers can trace much more quickly today. Then there are burner phones that are hard to trace. But old criminal habits die hard. The rule that criminals go by is two minutes or less, phone time.

"The next day I called him back and said that I needed a week to get the money but that I was sure that I wanted to hire him. I wanted to work a little longer and save as much money as possible for my father so I asked the man if he would wait two years until the person he was to ...eliminate... turned twenty-five. I never told him I was taking the hit out on myself. He laughed and said, *'Giving this person a birthday present, huh? Sure, no problem.'* Then he said that he would call *me* when the week was up to confirm the deal. I gave him my cell number.

"When he called back he told me to include a picture of who I wanted eliminated in the envelope along with the money and any instructions. I was to come alone and leave everything in the town park under a mailbox." She stops and looks at her hands. "He said he would be watching me. He...told me...he told me something else too, Ms....Cate."

"Yes? Go on."

"He said once the money had been paid, the contract was set. When he said that I knew there was no going back for me but I didn't care."

"You never met him personally to give him the money?" She shook her head no. Asking her if I can keep the card, I also ask Ms. Brooks-Warren how she managed to come up with the ten grand.

"I stole it from Kevin, the owner of the bar. I knew where he kept the cash in a hidden safe in the cellar of the bar. Like a lot of people in farming communities, he didn't trust banks. I'm not proud of it, Cate, but I was desperate. I didn't want to live anymore and I saw no other way out. Before the week was out, I followed the hit man's instructions and left the money with a picture of me in an envelope. That picture you're holding is the one I left for him."

I look from the picture to her. "You've had extensive cosmetic surgery, Ms. Warren. Was the money for that stolen also?"

Suddenly my new client begins to cry and the cries turn into hysterical sobs. I get her a bottle of water from the small fridge and Myrtle comes over with a box of tissues. Her body shakes with her emotions as her fiancé holds her in his arms. She controls herself in a few minutes and looks down at her hands. "That's the cruelest part of this whole thing! When my father died unexpectedly of a massive heart attack two weeks later, I found out why he was so frugal. He had saved almost every cent he could in case of crop failure or if he wasn't able to work anymore." She pauses and takes a shaky breath. "My father left me nearly twenty-five thousand dollars and a life insurance policy worth over a million dollars. More than enough to start a new life and return the money to Kevin."

"And you tried to contact the hit man with no success?"

"I tried desperately to find him but I had no idea who he was or where he was! He never returned to Kevin's bar. I drove around for weeks to out-of-the-way bars and burger places praying that I might see him. I put ads in several major papers and on the internet via social media, along with pictures of me back then. I put up a description of that man who was in the K & K in Culpepper, Virginia stating the date and the time he was there and begging for information to find him. I said that I was desperate for him to contact me immediately. But nothing worked; it was as if he simply vanished into thin air. I've never heard from him again.

"You know, Cate, two years ago I thought that if I ran away from my small town and began a new life, I wouldn't have to worry about anything. I used the money to remake myself and for a while I felt safe. I met Edward," she gestures to the man she had introduced as her fiancé, "a year ago, and truly felt as if I could bury the past. But now..."

"What about the woman in the bar? Ever see her again or know where she might live or work?"

She shakes her head. "I never saw her again. From the way she spoke, I don't think she was from around Culpepper. I mean, even with the cursing and her being drunk, I could tell her speech was very proper."

"Jennifer, you paid this man his money, right? Maybe he took it and has forgotten about you. Two years is a long time to wait and you do not look anything like the woman in the pictures you showed to me."

Jennifer Brooks-Warren sat down next to her fiancé and

took his hand. He turned to me and spoke again in a clear and concise voice. His eyes focused on me alone as he spoke.

"He hasn't forgotten, Ms. Harlow." He hands me the type of card you'd find in a gift box. "Ten days ago someone sent two pictures to our condo. One was the picture of Jennifer as she looked two years ago and the other was one of her walking with me in Central Park. That was bad enough but last night Jennifer received a bouquet of flowers with that note that says, 'Can't wait until your birthday. Twenty-five is special.'

He pauses then says, "And, as I told you, my fiancée Jennifer will be twenty-five in two months' time."

~

The flowers Jennifer received were an order that was placed by phone; it had to be a burner one since I can't trace it. The dictated note was written by a clerk who works in a local florist shop and the credit card used to place the order was a pre-paid, untraceable Visa. All I can find out is that the card was purchased in Arizona but when I call there with the number, no one seems to remember who purchased it. "We get a lot of people, miss. Bad credit and such, that's why they get pre-paid credit cards. Most only go up to $200. Hard to remember who bought what." Obviously this hit man knows how to cover his tracks really well.

For the rest of the morning Myrtle and I work quietly together; me reviewing previous cases and updating my website and Myrtle fending off telemarketers and making an appointment for me to meet with the CEO of a limo service. She puts the company's owner on speaker so I can hear him say that he wants to hire 'a female dick, you know, one of those woman detectives to surveille our drivers. Ya got one who can look like a hooker so the guys don't get suspicious?' Myrtle assures him that something can be arranged and takes down his information. She looks over at me and says, "Still got those hooker heels from that pole dancing case last year?"

"Back of my closet just waiting for a chance to emerge."

At one o'clock I decide to leave my office with the express purpose of getting something to eat at Enzo's Trattoria. I haven't eaten anything since six a.m. and I am starving. Having spoken with Jennifer and her fiancé Edward for almost three hours has added to my hunger; I think better on a full stomach.

I ask Myrtle to come with me but she says she's too busy and then adds that she's not hungry. "Got to watch my weight," is what she says. I raise my eyebrows. Myrtle is a nicely built older woman who does ballroom dancing twice a week and plays golf in the warmer weather.

There's nothing wrong with her weight but I don't say anything.

Before they left, Ms. Brooks-Warren and her fiancé had signed the necessary papers that hired me as their investigator then wrote a nice check for my retainer fee. I gave those, and Jennifer and her fiancé, to Myrtle to handle while I made a phone call to a trusted and discreet security company and hired professionals to keep surveillance on Jennifer. The security company's owner has top-notch people working for him so I feel we're pretty well covered. I also make a mental note to do a background check on her fiancé Edward Penn. He's probably innocent but I wouldn't be doing my job if I didn't have him checked out.

I promised Jennifer that tonight I would introduce her personally to the woman from the security team who will shadow her every move whenever she leaves her condo. Finally I sent Ms. Brooks-Warren and Co. to a sketch artist I know so I can have a reasonable idea of what the hit man looks like. The hit man case is officially a go and I go out the door.

Outside my office building I see Bo the homeless man who washes car windows whenever someone stops at a light. He knows that I'm good for a twenty each Friday night when I tell him to get some food and not spend my hard-earned money on booze. Most times he does get food to go along with his beer. I live on hope with him.

Today he's accompanied by his buddy who inadvertently

helped me on my last case concerning the priests' murders. He still seems to have no name other than "Bo's friend" or "Hey" as Bo calls him. I walk over and surprise Bo by handing him a twenty. Today's Tuesday but I'm feeling generous.

"Get lunch for both of you, okay? But no beer." I look at his friend. "Hi Bo's friend."

Bo smiles a lopsided grin and says he'll get them pizza. Bo's friend hunches deeper into the oversized sweater he's wearing and doesn't look at me. I experience a twinge of guilt. I once broke his ribs and bloodied his nose when I thought he was a mugger or rapist trying to get into my car. Sighing I pull a ten out of my pocket. "This is only for you, Bo's friend. Get some ice cream from that woman over there," I say pointing to an ice cream vendor. He quickly grabs the ten and nods at me without looking up. I sigh again and continue on my way. Another Cate Harlow attack victim.

The walk to Enzo's always makes for an interesting insight into the differences in people. At this time of day I see moms in yoga pants running, holding on to special jogger-strollers, babies inside them either lulled to sleep by the rhythm of the run or wide awake looking ahead at the view in front of them. There are business people, men and women, both in suits and carrying attaché cases, cell phones glued to their ears deep in conversations, presenting a danger to themselves as they navigate crossing the busy streets. I watch construction workers, laughing, sitting on beams opening their lunches and coffee containers, relaxing for a while. And then I see the street people every city has, the ones who are homeless and sad depending on the rest of humanity for life's very basics, like food. I think of Bo.

My cell buzzes as I'm entering the small outdoor courtyard of the trattoria. It's from my ex-husband and sometime sex partner Will Benigni.

"Hi Will. What's up?" I laugh at the innuendo of my innocent greeting.

"Oh you'd like what's up, baby." God! The man never misses a beat. "Where are you?"

"Going into Enzo's for some much-needed nourishment. What are you doing?"

"Just finished taking a statement from some punk we busted on cocaine possession. We think he's a witness to a murder." He says this so matter-of-factly. "Anyway I'm going over to the law library later. You going to be home tonight? I need you to help quiz me on some questions."

Will's studying for the New York State Bar exam once again. The exam is in a few months and he's been driving me crazy about taking it. I hesitate.

"Listen, I really do need you to quiz me. What, did you think it's an excuse for me to come jump your bones? I don't need an excuse for that do I?"

"No, you don't. That's not it though. I was figuring on doing research for a new case and I don't know what time I'll get back to my brownstone. What time were you thinking of coming over?"

"Not 'til around eight or so. I've got paperwork up my ass here."

"Okay. I should be home by eight. Pick up Chinese food from P.F. Chang's and you've got a date and a meal."

"Right. Gotta go." His call abruptly ends but I'm used to that if he's at the precinct. I pocket my phone and enter my favorite Italian trattoria. Ordering a large antipasto salad with dressing on the side, I sit at a table by the window and wait, letting my mind wander.

By all accounts I consider myself a lucky woman. I have my own fairly successful business, *Catherine Harlow, Private Investigations,* am healthy, have some good friends, and have survived having my head bashed in during my missing person case last year. I put a pedophile priest in prison and reunited a sister and a brother. It was a satisfying ending to a convoluted case.

My ex, Will, and I have a kind of friends-with-benefits relationship meaning that we probably could not ever live together again as husband and wife but we can still enjoy the highly charged sex part of it. Then there's Giles Barrett, ME. We had a nice thing going for awhile and I still see him but we've decided to cool any intimacy between us for now. I think that Giles is waiting for the "Will rush" to run its course and feels that after that, we, Giles and I, will get back together. Who knows really? Will is like a drug but, as any addict will tell you, no matter how addicted you are you still know what you're doing is not good for you.

In my life, Will, my drug of choice, can be wonderful as well as dangerous. I know he's not really good for me but I love the rush I get from how expert he is at pushing my erotic buttons. I know the risks but I am with him *Will-ingly*, so to speak.

My lunch is brought to the table and I forget about the people in my life for awhile and concentrate only on the pleasure of eating.

CHAPTER 2

THE INFORMATION ON THE FRONT of the business card Jennifer gave me has been deeply scratched out. I can make out a word here and there. It's a crème-colored vellum card that you can buy over the Internet. I erase as much ink as possible and then gently blot the card with baby oil. The letters *h-o-l*. Maybe holiday? They're followed by *b-t---*. I know that if I work on it I'll get something good but it is tedious work. It's almost seven o'clock at night and I'm still working my new case. I spent a few hours checking police records for any homicides that occurred two years ago in the area where Jennifer met the woman who supposedly had her father offed. I check for police reports of a body found that was missing a finger. Nothing pops except a stabbing death of a teenage boy and a murder of a woman by her estranged boyfriend. No mention of a dead body with a missing digit shows up. How the hell was it covered up? Did this mysterious woman have connections in the coroner's office? Was the severed finger put back on the hand?

The sketch artist faxed me the image of the hit man about an hour ago. Jennifer and her fiancé must have gone there as soon as they left my office. I look at the sketch. He has a Nordic-looking face. He appears to be somewhere in his middle to late forties and he looks like a man who spends a lot of time outdoors. Sandy colored short hair tops a rugged, chiseled face. It's almost like looking at a face from some online dating site for professional eliminators.

> "Nice looking male professional eliminator, forty-ish, seeking sexy female companion for romance, travel, and murder-for-hire joint ventures. Must be willing to carry out eliminations quickly and cold-bloodedly."

The term hit man is an interesting one. No one advertises the fact that he or she is a paid assassin. Sometime a hit man is someone who you'd never suspect. The kind of person who has a day job as in the case of a St. Louis dentist named Glennon Edward Engleman. He moonlighted as a hit man for over thirty years and no one, not even his wife, knew about his after hours activities. Or Helene Connors, a social studies teacher in Florida, one of the best "hit men" in the business.

However, most people think of a hit man as someone who resembles a character from *The Sopranos*. Certainly organized crime has its share of hit men but what a lot of people don't realize is that there are men and women who are called professional eliminators, just as the handwriting on the back of the card stated. They're not doing a job for a mob boss, they don't hang around in groups or strip joints and talk about their "goomahs"; they're real, authentic, hired guns, killers and loners who will eliminate someone for a lot of money and who, once the job is done, disappear as if they never existed. Those in law enforcement call them ghosts. No names, no addresses, nothing. They appear and disappear at will. This man is more than likely one of those ghosts.

I fax the picture to a woman I know, a top-notch hacker. She's part of that group of individuals who are virtually untraceable, the ones who never leave any tech footprints. This type of hacker works off the Tor, more commonly called the Dark Net, which offers total anonymity and protection. This is done by bouncing your communications around a distributed network of relays run by volunteers all around the world: it prevents anybody who is watching your Internet connection from learning what sites you visit, and it prevents the sites you visit from learning your physical location. My contact has asked me several times if I want her to hook me up on the Tor and I am seriously thinking about it.

What she does is illegal but using someone who operates off the grid has never stopped me. If I think what the person does can help me on a case, I'm fine with it. I text her and tell her to run it through photos of known hired killers to look for a match. If this professional killer is really good, I don't expect she'll find much but you never know what info will pop up in any area. You've got to make sure you cover all parts of a case and get as much info as possible.

The clock says it's past seven thirty and I promised Will I'd meet him at my brownstone at eight. I leave what's on my desk and go check on the doves' nest on my fire escape. A nice surprise awaits me. The parent doves have come back unexpectedly and seem settled down for the night. They're a peaceful diversion in my life and I whisper good-night to them. I put my gun in the back of my jeans and hit the double locks as I pull closed the heavy old oak door to *Catherine Harlow, Private Investigations*.

Will is waiting on the steps of the brownstone with two large bags and the aromas hit me sweetly as I walk toward him. From across the street I can see he's not in the best of moods.

"I don't know *why* you won't give me the key to your place," is his greeting to me.

"It's personal, Will. This is my private haven, I already told you that. If you have a key, then it's not mine anymore." I put the key in the lock and open the door.

"That's not logical, Cate," Will says as he walks through the door in front of me heading to my kitchen.

"You do logic your way, I'll do it mine. Anyway, you're a detective, you know how to break and enter."

He looks offended. "I would never do that. Not unless I thought you were in trouble. I just think that it would be so much easier if I had a key, that's all." He looks all put out and everything. "I mean, come on now, we do sleep together although the word sleep is a misnomer for what we do. But, hell, Cate, making me sit outside waiting for you to come home was a royal pain in the ass tonight. Just give me a damn key."

"No. Subject closed." I smile sweetly at his scowl. "What'd you get us?"

A bit unwillingly he smiles back and with his mind on the food in the bags, tells me what feast he bought while I open a chilled bottle of merlot. A nice Italian wine with Chinese food—great combo.

After dinner I sit back on the couch and quiz Will on torts and criminal law, New York State style. He's good on some answers and hesitant on others. I don't think his heart is really in the lawyer thing. Other people, me included when we were married, have always encouraged him to pursue law. His mother, the elegant art historian Francesca Sutton Benigni, has always hoped that he would take up law someday; her father was a lawyer. Even his superiors in the precinct had given strong hints about him becoming a lawyer and then a tough DA.

And to be honest, Will did envision himself as a crusading DA type. He liked the idea too and that's why going through night school wasn't the drudge for him that it seems to be for most people. His dreams of being a lawyer turned DA were just that; dreams.

Dreams are good for all of us but then reality has a habit of smacking you in the back of the head. Take my line of work for an example. Everyone thinks that being a female PI is somehow glamorous. You know, you always look great and sexy, you're fearless in getting the job done, and then you have fantastic romantic encounters with some hot guy you met on the job. I admit I daydreamed those thoughts myself.

But the truth is much different than what is portrayed in movies and on TV. I rarely look great and sexy on the job except when I've had to play the part of a hooker, I have a healthy fear of the dangers that can happen to me on a case, and my romantic encounters never evolve from any guy I do meet while I'm working. Dreams vs the reality: reality wins every time.

Will and I go over tedious law terms until almost one in the morning. The boredom is palpable. I've been up since five thirty and I'm having a hard time keeping my eyes open. I keep nodding off. Will comes back from a bathroom run to find me with my head slumped against the back of the couch, eyes half-closed. He sits next to me and blows air toward the ceiling in frustration. In another minute he closes his eyes and is out. I nod off and a muffled snore wakes me.

"Hey," I touch his arm sleepily. "We need to stop for tonight. Go home and sleep. Or, better yet, sleep on the couch. I don't want you driving if you're too tired."

He opens his eyes and nods toward my bedroom door. "What, I can't sleep in the bed?"

I stand up feeling wobbly and lean against the couch. "Will, I am exhausted. You come into that bed with any thoughts of a sexual escapade..."

"Who, me?" He smiles that hot smile I know too well then gives away his own exhaustion in a loud yawn.

"Yes, you. I'm so tired that, if you even attempt to do anything, it will be as if you're having sex with a dead woman. Seriously, not tonight. Tomorrow, absolutely, but tonight I am wiped."

Another yawn. Looking at me he says, "Well, God knows that *I* am not someone who is into necrophilia so I'm taking the couch just for tonight."

He gives me a tiny smirk when he says the word necrophilia. It's his nasty little way of getting a dig in at my former love interest, Giles Barrett. Giles is the best medical examiner in New York State and being with him was sweet. For Will to make that crack about "doing it with the dead" is unworthy of him and I tell him so.

"Look, smart-ass, that was so uncalled-for. Giles is very respectful of the bodies down at the morgue. He's a doctor, he's a professional. You are such an..."

"Whoa! Hey! Did I say *Giles*? Did you hear me say his *name*? Seriously, would I really insinuate that *Giles* would do something unnatural with a dead body? Oh, Cate, you really are tired to think I meant Giles when I said I wasn't into necrophilia. I'm hurt, seriously hurt."

I *am* tired and my only retort as I head toward the bedroom is, "Go to Hell."

To which my ever-sarcastic ex-husband says innocently, "Hell will have to wait, babe. I'm going to sleep first."

CHAPTER 3

I WAKE UP TO a loud purring and soft meows from my cat Little Guy who is sitting next to my face on my pillow. His cat buddy, Mouse, is at the bottom of the bed looking intently at me. They're hungry.

And next to me, sleeping the sleep of the justly exhausted is Will wearing only the Rolex watch I gave him on our second anniversary together. Something inside me is glad he still has it; it took me a year to save up for it. I gingerly lift his wrist to check the time. 6:02 a.m. Damn!

Will mumbles "Baby" and grabs my thigh. The man does not ever change. I push his hand away and quickly slide out of bed.

"What the hell time is it?" he mumbles, eyes closed.

"Shhhhh. I'm just going to the bathroom. Be right back," I lie smoothly. "Go back to sleep."

He mumbles something else unintelligible and I sneak out of the room grabbing a shawl draped over a chair. Mouse and Little Guy run ahead of me as I open the door.

In the kitchen I put on coffee and then fill small bowls with cat food. I take a quick shower while the coffee brews. When I come out of the bathroom wrapped in a towel, the two cats are the only ones who greet me; Will must be more exhausted than I thought.

I pour cream into the bottom of a mug, add coffee to about an inch from the top, and then more cream. The first sip is perfect. Carrying my coffee into the corner of the living room where my laptop lives I check my e-mails. The Hacker has gotten back to me. She's one of my best sources.

"Hey Harlow. Long time. Zero matches on pic yet but working on it. No sweat. Soon."

I smile; she's known only as TRUST, all caps, and she is very reliable. She'll let me know where to send her fee when she's ready.

I am pouring a second cup of coffee when I hear movement in my bedroom. The door opens and Will sleepwalks into the kitchen muttering, "Coffee," then goes to sit down on the window seat overlooking the street. The cats make room for him and head-butt his shoulder and arm. They adore him.

"What time are you going to the precinct?" I hand him a steaming mug of coffee with just a drizzle of cream.

"Nine or so. Your office?"

"Not 'til after ten. I have a few stops to make before I go in. Why?"

Will has his eyes closed and his head resting against the curtained window.

"Will?" No response.

"Hey! Will? You awake, baby?"

"Huh? Did you say something?" He answers me without opening his eyes.

"Yes, I said that I have a few stops to make before I go to my office and asked why you want to know." A slight snore is the only answer I get and I rush to grab his coffee mug just as it starts to slip from his hand. "Will?" Not getting a response I nudge him gently, then not so gently.

His eyes open to slits. "What? I'm, yeah, just let me get started. I'm okay," he says as he closes his eyes and lolls his head against the window.

"Will, how much sleep are you getting? You are zonked!"

He opens his eyes, which are bleary and swollen with exhaustion. "Not a helluva lot. Working non-stop and studying for this bar exam is going to kill me." He stretches his arms toward the ceiling, rubs his eyes, shakes his head, and stands up a bit unsteadily.

"Go back to sleep," I say and begin to lead him toward the bedroom. "It's only just after six thirty. I'll wake you up in an hour, I promise." He doesn't protest, just stumbles along and falls into my bed. As I close the door, I hear a sigh and then steady breathing.

I arrive at my office close to eleven and am surprised to see that Myrtle isn't in. She's a stickler for that nine thirty arrival time. A quick check of her desk, and the un-straightened files on mine, tells me she hasn't just ducked out for a few minutes; she hasn't been in at all. A little odd. I've noticed that lately she hasn't been acting like her usual self. Probably nothing, but my professional experience tells me that when someone isn't acting in their usual way there's some type of personal issue going on. I'll try talking to her later. Right now, I need to get busy finding the Brooks-Warren hired killer.

Most people don't realize how simple it is to hire a professional killer. It's really easier than you think. It may seem weird to some people but there was actually a website called *Hire-a-Killer.com*. It was supposed to be a just-for-fun site that posted fake assassins along with virtual scenarios and clients. There were even bogus testimonials from these "clients" and people who visited the site started to write about it on Facebook. Everyone, and I mean everyone, thought the *Hire-a-Killer* site was something similar to other interactive sites such as *Grand Theft Auto* or *The Living Dead*.

Even law enforcement didn't take it seriously until a young cop, home at the end of a maternity leave and getting antsy to be back at work, decided to contact this site she'd heard about just for something to occupy her time. She wanted to see what the big fuss was all about. Once there she toured the site and in the spirit of interacting, pretended that she was a woman who wanted someone to off her husband. Then bored, she signed off. Fifteen minutes later, she got an untraceable e-mail that stated that it would cost fifteen thousand dollars and gave her a place and time to meet. She got in touch with her superiors who in turn called the Feds.

Needless to say, when the FBI tried to investigate the site's owners, they found a highly sophisticated system, untraceable people and e-mails, and so were never able to make arrests. The site was part of a very elaborate, completely pro operation. They were way off the grid.

The man Jennifer Brooks-Warren hired seems to be off the grid too. I can only hope that TRUST is able to use her formidable hacking skills to find him. Sitting at my computer I read through the e-mails that have accumulated. I am amazed at the e-mails that are sent at all hours; 12:35, 1:17, 2:52 all in the a.m. Doesn't anybody sleep? I remember a client I had last year who was actually very annoyed that I hadn't answered his 2:00 a.m. e-mail within an hour of receiving it. Go figure.

The door opens and I see Myrtle coming in with a bag of Timothy's coffee. She looks tired and slightly disheveled. My heart skips in my chest. Oh, God! I hope she's not sick.

"Hey! You okay?" I ask getting up from my chair.

"I'm fine and dandy. Here's your coffee and a bagel from Timothy's," is all she says as she goes to put on water for her tea.

"No goodies from Harry?" I ask slightly disappointed. Harry makes wonderful pastries. In the past year since he started seriously baking, I've had to hit the tennis practice wall an extra day a week to work off the added delicious calories. It was all worth it; Harry can duplicate any pastry recipe he sees on the cooking channels with ease. He's even had a small professional baker's oven installed in their kitchen.

"No," she says testily, "no goodies today. Harry didn't make anything because he *didn't come home* last night until *very late. Then* he went right to sleep."

That's strange in itself. Usually Harry and Myrtle are joined at the hip at night. They do everything together. Their whirlwind social life of Broadway shows and dinners at upscale restaurants is something to be envied. The only time he's not available at night is during tax season, January to mid-April, when this semi-retired accountant turns his and Myrtle's spare bedroom into a temporary office.

This is almost May. Harry out without Myrtle?

"Oh, really? Where was he? Some accountants' get-together or something?"

"I do not know *where* he was or with *whom*," is all she says. Her look tells me to mind my business.

The electric tea pot dings a tinny sound to announce that the water has boiled. Myrtle grabs her cup and turns away from me. I take the hint: subject closed for now.

In my business I can ask all the questions I want but if a client or suspect doesn't want to give me information the Q & A session hits a dead end. So it seems is the case with Myrtle. I'll try talking to her later. Getting through to her now is not going to happen.

I work the rest of the morning trying to clean up the business card Jennifer gave me to see if I can get some information about the woman in the bar. Just before noon, my wünder-hacker, TRUST, sends me a text.

> "Harlow- face has aka name but no address. Intel attach. Code-Red this one, Harlow. Mean Mo Fu you got here. Bonus for torture. And he's what we call a White Death so watch ur ass. Checking more. Soon."

White Death is a term for a killer who comes in like a white fog, gets the job done, and leaves without a trace. No need for any personal interaction from clients except the contract to kill. Job done, he disappears. I open the attachment to see that the hit man's face really does have a name to go with it. The name is Marc Croft. This can be an alias or not. It's a common enough name. The intel on him is short but definitely not sweet. He was a soldier of fortune from 1995 to 2008, a man who offered his services in any conflict to the side that paid him the most. He had no allegiance; his killing skills were sold for a hefty price. His code name is Duchovny, which makes me laugh. That name is Russian for ghost or spirit.

Croft seems to have been quite a busy bee and an expert in his profession. As TRUST intimated in her e-mail, some of the murders are particularly gruesome. From the descriptions of the kills, this eliminator was paid extra for having his victims suffer. And he's been active all over. Seems as if he has had a hand in border wars in Africa, blood diamond trafficking, drug cartel wars in South America, and "taking care" of politicians in countries where running for office is hazardous to your health. In those countries sudden-death syndrome is a daily possibility. His last professional hit seems to have been a political rival who was stirring up trouble for the government in Colombia. While he does do torture if required, his specialty seems to be a quick kill then getting rid of the body through various means. No evidence left. A true White Death.

Starting in 2008, after the kill in Colombia, he appears to have been incommunicado and unreachable for almost two years. There is no information on his whereabouts or activities. He surfaced again in February 2010 and several eliminations over the next few years in Mexico, Arizona, and Florida were attributed to him but never quite proven. The victims were not well-known or high-profile people. Some were wealthy, some were not. Seems as if my professional eliminator had come down a notch in whom he was hired to eliminate. From Soldier of Fortune to a simple murderer for hire is a demotion in the hit-man profession. Maybe it has something to do with those missing two years.

I go to work on the card again and actually get some results. Now I can see a word that looks like *b-a-t-h* coming into view. Bath what though? A place for bathroom fixtures, a Bed, Bath, and Beyond type of store? I sigh and put the card on my desk to dry a bit. If I keep rubbing it the card may just flake apart. I order lunch in and wait for an e-mail from TRUST while I check through the Yellow Pages online for any business in the Washington, DC area that has the word bath in its name.

At four o'clock I call my friend Melissa. Together we're going to transform me into a high-priced call-girl. It's going to be a long day into night. I'm working undercover for the limo service who requested a "female dick."

CHAPTER 4

I STUMBLE INTO my brownstone wearing my "hooker" heels, five inches of killer stiletto that could easily be used as a weapon. After all, the word stiletto is Italian for a long, narrow-bladed dagger designed as a stabbing weapon. In the fourteen hundreds, assassins would conveniently hide the stiletto up their full-sleeved shirts and strike their victims without warning.

My silver lamé dress barely covers my butt and the false eyelashes I am wearing make my eyes feel itchy. I survey myself in the mirror hanging over the fireplace. I look like a hooker who has had a hard night, no pun intended. My hair is teased and piled high on my head accenting the huge silver hoops on my earlobes. Tendrils of strategically placed hair frame my face. Fake acrylic nails applied by my Melissa are a startling shade of deep blood red and my make-up is what I call "call girl special"; heavy smoky-eyed sultry, deep red lip cream, and perfectly placed blush; way too much of everything. I think back to late afternoon and Melissa helping me make the transformation from PI to hooker.

"You look the part of the lady-of-the-evening," Melissa says grabbing her handbag and jacket after she finishes. "Very professional."

"Thanks...I think. Aren't you going to see me make my grand exit onto the street?"

"I can't. I'm going to a memorial for a friend who passed away last week and I don't want to be late. Sorry, Cate."

"No, I'm sorry. I didn't know. Close friend?"

Melissa looks at me and smiles sadly, "Very. He was a generous man and good to me."

I don't ask any more questions. I sense that this man was one of her well-heeled "clients." I don't question her line of work. That's part of our friendship. She air kisses me and goes out the door. I hear the click of her key fob unlocking her brand-new Jaguar.

It's been a helluva night. I had to punch one insistent would-be client in the gut to get him away from me. Another whack-job, who grabbed me in a very personal area, got stabbed hard in the foot with one of my stilettos. Happy to say that both men decided I was not their type and looked elsewhere for their hapless victims.

I did manage, however, to find out what the owner of the limo service wanted to know; his drivers are definitely on the take, ripping off high-on-the-latest-drug college boys and heavily intoxicated businessmen, over charging them the fare by three times what it normally would be. They also demand "a substantial tip" from the higher quality ladies of the evening who use the limo service to ferry them to their appointments around the city. I'm out seven hundred bucks, three-fifty a pop, for two rides from the Theatre District near Times Square to the Cipriani hotel downtown. You can be sure that that money will be included in my bill to the limo service owner.

A little after two in the morning I take a cab back to my brownstone. Taped to the dashboard of the cab are pictures of Jesus surrounded by angels. There is a sign that says, "Jesus loves you. Believe in Him and you will be saved."

I sigh. The driver stoically faces forward the whole ride and looks sad for what I'm sure he thinks is my downfall from grace. I'm positive he thinks he is dropping me off for a late-night sexual encounter when he pulls up in front of my brownstone. I don't care; I am tired and feel dirty.

As I reach into my oversized bag to get money to pay and tip the driver, my hand brushes against my gun and I feel its reassuring weight. I wearily wonder if any real call girls carry a gun for protection. I'm betting that they do.

"Hey, miss?" he calls hesitantly as I'm walking toward my steps. "I can drive you back to your own place, no charge. You don't have to do this for a living, you know. It's dangerous."

"That's okay. This *is* my place. Thanks anyway."

But he seems intent on saving a fallen woman. "Seriously, miss, you can get an honest job. Maybe a waitress or cleaning lady? Something safe."

"I'll think about making a life change," I say as I walk back to the cab and give the driver an additional hefty tip for his concern.

Inside I stand a bit shakily. How the hell do they do it? How do hookers walk in these heels all night? I wear heels for a night out but my night out usually consists of being dropped off in front of a restaurant or club and not doing much of any walking. I'm about to slip my shoes off when I hear a banging on my door.

"Open up! NYPD!" The voice has a strong authority. Police? For what? Did the neighbors next door have one of their occasional yelling matches?

"It's late. What's the problem, officer? I think you might want to check the brownstone next door," I call through the door.

"No, miss, this is the right address. We got a complaint from some guy you assaulted on Fifty-Third and Broadway. Says you stabbed him in his foot for no reason at all. He's limping. Short, beefy guy? Remember him? He's a cop from Philly. Followed you here in a private car. He's filled out a complaint against you so you better open up now."

"What?!" I yell through the closed door. That little creep followed me? A cop? Shit! "No, he, whoever he is, grabbed *me* and I jammed the heel of my shoe into his foot so he'd let go. Listen," I say as I open the door, "I'm a private detective. My name is Cate Harlow. I was undercover working a case for..." I stop cold when I see the two men in front of me. Damn, damn, damn! Standing on my doorstep are Will and a patrol cop, both of them barely able to conceal big, shit-eating grins.

"Thanks, Danny," says my ex. "I owe you one."

"Any time, detective, any time," laughs the cop walking back to a patrol car I see parked across the street. "Pretty lady ya got there."

"You bastard!" I start to slam the door in Will's face but his cop reflexes prevent it. He's an expert at stopping suspects from slamming doors on him. He pushes it open and walks in.

"Christ, Will, did you think this was funny?"

"No, baby, just doing my duty. Heard you did some damage to a Philly cop on vacation with his wife and kids. Bad girl, Cate, very bad girl."

"Really?" I'm pissed as hell right now. "His wife know he was looking for a hooker at the Cipriani Hotel and that his hand got caught going up my dress? I hope he's in a lot of pain. Hell, I hope I crippled the bastard!"

I look at Will. "What are you doing here, anyway? You're off-duty tonight. How'd you find out about what happened down near the Cipriani?"

"I got a call from another detective. He thought it was hilarious. By the way, he's on your side; thinks Mr. Philly got exactly what he asked for. We'll make sure the charges are 'lost'. All we have to do is mention his wife. Believe me that complaint will not see the light of day, Cate." He winks at me. "You're pretty well-known around the precincts in New York City, babe. I get calls about you all the time. Usually I don't pay much attention; I know you're working a case. But when I hear you're role-playing being a 'working girl', well, I have to come and see you."

The wink gets me every time. I want to kick him but I can't stay mad. I so *want* to stay mad but it has been a long night and I need some love, comfort, and personal attention; all the hot things that my ex knows exactly how to give me. Not to mention that Will looks so damn good and he's got that sexy smile I know all too well. Desire for Will struggles with my anger but the desire wins out. Damn!

"So, what do you think?" I give in to desire and strike a sultry pose, hands on hips, chest forward. Will walks toward me and pulls me close to him pinning my hands behind my back. "How much do you charge, bad girl?"

I pull away and walk backward toward the bedroom. Continuing the role-play, I say in my best sexy voice, "*That* depends on what you *want,* darlin'. Got the handcuffs?"

CHAPTER 5

TENNIS IS MY SALVATION. Up at five-thirty, I made it to the tennis courts by six-fifteen. There's only one other person who's there at that time. Her name is Ani Choi and she likes to hit the practice wall before going to her classes at NYU. We've partnered up for a quick game on the courts a few times and I have to say Ani is a formidable opponent. I have a better backhand but in all other moves she's pretty much my equal. She sees me and smiles a welcome.

"Hi Cate. Want a quick match? I have a class at nine so I'm free until eight-thirty."

"Sure. I need the exercise," I say dropping my tennis bag and taking out my racket and the balls.

Thwack! The rhythm of the ball against the rackets is a calming sound for me. I react automatically to the back and forth of the game. This allows me time to think about my cases. The card Jennifer gave me. The word that looks like *bath*. I wonder how many businesses there are in the Washington, DC area with that word in their logo? Thwack! I backhand the ball toward Ani making her really run for it. Thwack! We're getting a good workout, Ani and I. Besides being good physical exercise, the back and forth running clears my brain.

As I slam the ball hard with my racket I decide that there's only one way to go about finding the mysterious woman with the business card. Myrtle and I are going to have to cold call every business in a certain radius around Washington, D.C. that has the word 'bath' in its name and describe the woman who gave Jennifer the card. It has been almost two years, though, and there are a lot of ifs to consider. *If* she's still in the area, *if* she's still working there, or *if* she has the business; hopefully I'll find this mysterious woman and see if she knows how to contact the hit man.

Ani and I play three sets and I am exhilarated by the high the exercise gives me.

"Hey, great workout, Cate. How about Thursday? Nine o'clock okay?"

Thursday is two days away. If my idea about finding the mystery woman pans out I may be in the Washington, D.C. area. Reluctantly I decline and tell her next week is better for me.

"Sure, okay. Maybe next Tuesday, same time?"

"Sounds good, Ani. See you then."

Going home to shower, I stop and get a bagel with Taylor Ham and cheese from a vendor. I figure I burned off enough calories to compensate for the ones in the bagel. I'm starving so I eat it on the way.

Back at the door of my brownstone I put what's left of the bagel in my mouth while I hunt for my keys. It's a bad habit on my part. Will always tells me that I should have my keys out and ready. His theory, and it's a sound one, is that while I'm trying to find my keys anyone could grab me and then force their way into my home. I hate to agree with him. It is a careless mistake for someone in my profession who's supposed to be attuned to safety precautions.

Inside I finish eating the bagel, grab a bottle of water from the 'fridge and plan my day. It's just after eight o'clock. I can be at my office by ten, get a list of businesses in the areas surrounding Washington, D.C. with the word *bath* in their titles, and begin my phone calls by eleven. If I'm lucky, it will take a half-day of concentrated work, if I'm not, maybe an additional day.

Sighing I strip off my clothes and head to the bathroom for a cool shower and to wash my hair. Will hasn't been over for three days, which means he's busy as hell with his job and studying like crazy for the bar exam. It's good that we haven't seen each other for a few days; we're great in bed, we can even be friends, but when we're together too much, we tend to rub each other the wrong way, no sexual pun intended. Even the incredible sex isn't enough to take the edge off certain ways we annoy each other. He'll start complaining about my being domestically challenged; the place is cluttered and I do more take-out than actual cooking. Then *I'll* say that just because I was born with a vagina doesn't mean I'm genetically engineered to cook and clean. He'll come back with some nasty response that any *normal* person should *want* to live in a neat home and eat good food. It usually ends with my throwing something at him and him walking out the door. Time apart is good for us.

I get lucky outside my office; there's a space near the building and I park my Edge quickly. The day is warm, which I like; winter is not my happy season. I breathe in the odor of the New York streets, an interesting blend of car fumes, ethnic foods, and what I call City Perfume. It's home.

Myrtle is sitting at her desk when I open the door. She looks as if she hasn't slept well but she greets me with, "How did the female dick job go?"

"Great. I got the evidence the limo company owner needs. His guys are definitely gouging customers. The expenses are in the computer under Mercury Limo. Send the bill out as soon as you can. I met with him yesterday and the case is done."

"All right, will do."

This isn't like Myrtle at all. She likes to talk and normally she is interested in my cases. We discuss them over coffee or lunch and she is always fascinated by what people do or say.

"Myrtle," I begin. "Look, it's none of my business but I get the feeling something isn't right. Are you..." I take a breath, "are you sick? Do you need to go to see a doctor for a check-up or something? What about Harry? Is he sick?"

She doesn't look up but answers me curtly. "I just had a check-up a month ago, Harry too. A little high blood pressure but other than that we're both as healthy as wild stallions. Don't be concerned for me." Then, looking up, she says, "And you're right, Catherine. It *is* none of your business."

I know when to keep my mouth closed. If, and when, she wants to tell me, I'll be here. As the morning quickly goes by we work in peaceful, if non-communicative, association.

My morning has an unexpected surprise. My thinking about Will must have jogged the universe and made him appear. He makes one of his infrequent stops at the office. Will comes in every once in a while if he's near *Catherine Harlow, Private Investigations* and both Myrtle and I are usually glad to see him.

Myrtle especially likes Will and sometimes I think she and his mother Francesca are in cahoots to get us back together as a legally married couple. That, however, is not going to happen. We simply cannot be husband and wife. Ever.

⁂

"Myrtle, how's my special girl?" This is Will's favorite greeting to Myrtle who laps it up like a kitten licking cream. Today, though she smiles at him and offers her cheek for his kiss as usual, I sense something is off.

"Had to check out a witness to a possible shooting a few blocks from here so I figured I'd stop and see the office of my favorite private 'D'." He opens the small refrigerator to check for any of Harry's famous homemade pastries and there's nothing there but store-bought doughnuts.

"Did you have a lot of clients come in or what?" he says referring to the slim pickings. "There are none of Harry's pastries."

I notice the scowl on Myrtle's face, put my finger to my lips, and shake my head at Will to let him know he shouldn't ask any questions. Shrugging, he grabs a box of sugared crullers and goes to sit near my desk.

"Will, can you come with me to check under the hood of my SUV? There's, uh, like a funny sound when I start it up."

"*Now?*" he looks surprised. He has just sat down and has the cruller halfway to his mouth.

"Yes, *now*," I say getting up, grabbing his hand and practically pulling him with me to the door. "I'm concerned about what it could be." He stuffs the cruller in his mouth.

Down the stairs and outside I tell Will that something's not right in the life of Myrtle Goldberg Tuttle and that I think it has something to do with Harry.

"Financial problems? One of them sick?" Will runs through the possibilities.

"Well, not sick anyway. I never thought about money troubles but I doubt it. They're pretty well off."

"Stop being a detective with friends," says Will dismissing my concerns. "It only destroys friendships. Remember Phil Hayes, my buddy down at the precinct?" I remember. He and Will had a solid friendship but I haven't heard Will mention him in quite awhile.

"He and his girlfriend were going through some serious shit; she was a selfish little tart and I asked him one too many times why he didn't break it off with her. Phil felt I was sticking my nose in where it wasn't wanted; he was crazy about her. We almost came to blows over it. Now, unless it's work-related at the precinct, we don't talk. He's still with her, she still drives him nuts, so go figure." He stops. "Hell, didn't you tell me that Myrtle and Harry are married over forty years? People married that long, they have problems, they work through them. Let it go." He sounds firm and positive and walks over to my Edge.

"Now what's the problem with your car?"

"Nothing. It's fine. I just wanted to talk to you away from Myrtle."

He nods casually toward the building. "You might want to pretend we're checking it out. Myrtle is looking out the window."

"Oh, sure." I walk over to where Will is standing and for fifteen minutes we pretend to check my perfectly performing Edge.

After saying good-bye to Will, I run up the stairs to my office. Myrtle is still standing there at the window watching Will walk back to his unmarked police car.

"Car's fine," I say as I settle at my desk. "Will got a call from the precinct so he didn't have a chance to come back up here. He says he'll see you soon."

Myrtle continues looking out the window. "You know, Cate, maybe you were right to divorce him." I'm shocked; Myrtle loves Will. She turns and looks at me. "A cheating man doesn't deserve a good woman."

The first day of cold calling yields nothing. We are at it from ten in the morning until eight at night. The second day I work through lunch and so does Myrtle. We call number after number of any business that has the word bath in its name. It's tedious and frustrating. To make it less so I play a little game with Myrtle. For every call that does not produce results we put a mark on a sheet of paper; each mark represents a quarter. By two-thirty we take a break and count the make-believe money. Thirty-five calls and no mystery woman brings our total to eight dollars and seventy-five cents. Woo-hoo!

I take a break while Myrtle continues her calls. Walking to the fridge for some water I practice my tennis backhand swinging at an imaginary ball. This is going to take longer than I had hoped.

"Cate!" Myrtle stage-whispers my name while holding her hand over the phone's mouthpiece. "We've got something." I hurry to her desk just as she puts the person on the other end of the line on loudspeaker.

"Yes," Myrtle says reading from the description on her computer screen. "Very slender woman, dark brown or black hair. She used to wear it very short a couple of years ago. About five three in height. In her thirties. Works out a lot? Uh-huh."

"That sounds like Moira," says the squeaky voice on the other end, "the owner. She's out today at a crafts bazaar. I can give her your number and she'll call you back."

Myrtle shows me the name of the shop, Hollis Bath Boutique. It's located in Rosslyn, Virginia. The owner's name is Moira Michelle Hollis.

The speaker sounds as if she's a teenager and I step forward with an idea. "Hi, my name's Cate. Moira and I went to school together. My mom? The woman to whom you were speaking? Well, she was helping me contact Moira. See, I'm getting married in a couple of months and would so love to have Moira in my wedding party. The thing is that I wanted to surprise her and come down for a girls-only weekend, sort of a bachelorette fun thing. You know, reliving our girl days from school. We were kind of close in college, but I haven't seen her in person for about three years, you know how that is."

"Oh, so you're one of the boss lady's Kappa Alpha Theta Sorority sisters."

"Yes, I am," I say, grateful that young adults who grew up on the social networks have no reservations about giving out personal info to strangers. They don't realize how dangerous it can be. "Kappa Alpha Theta all the way!" I say.

"Moira keeps telling me to pledge that sorority next year when I go to college, but I don't know. I'm not really into all that. She says it's a wonderful group, though."

"Oh seriously, you should pledge," I say wanting to keep her talking. "We're a great sorority. Moira's right about that."

"Yeah, maybe." I hear her yawn; short attention span. "Anyway, I won't tell Moira you're coming if it's a surprise. You're going to love her new condo."

"Oh? You mean she's not at the...wait I have her address in my cell phone..,damn, where is my phone? Mom, do you know if I left my phone in the living room?" I stall for time hoping the woman on the other end will give me the address. "Can you hold for a sec?" I say trying to sound rattled and frustrated. I hear her sigh.

"Well, I'm supposed to be working so I really can't stay on

too long. Look, don't go crazy looking for your phone, okay? Um, listen, you probably have her down at the Regent Street address, her father's old house, right? But she lives at Barron Court now, I forgot the number but she bought a luxury condo there eight months ago. She was on a waiting list. Did you know her father died a couple of years ago? Real tragedy."

"Oh, I'm sorry," I murmur. "So sad."

"Yeah, I guess. He left her the house but she said it had too many memories. Anyway, between you and me, she certainly can *afford* the condo; her father was pretty well-off, so I hear."

The gods are looking out for me today; this is too easy.

"Yes, fairly well-to-do. But thank you so much for giving me her new address! I'll find her. I know where Barron Court is."

There's a pause on the other end. "You do? You said you hadn't been down here for awhile. They just built the place eleven months ago. It wasn't even named. Are you *sure* you know where to go?"

Shit! I should have just said thank you! Come on, Cate, think fast! A good PI is able to think on her feet and come up with a good lie when she's caught making a mistake.

"Oh, I'm so silly." I giggle as if I'm a sorority airhead. "I was thinking of *Brandon* Court near our sorority house." I sigh heavily. "This wedding has gotten me all giddy, I don't know whether I'm coming or going. Sorry!"

There's another pause then she says, "I know how that can be. My sister went totally insane during the two months before her wedding. She was forgetting details left and right."

"Oh that is so true! Anyway, I'm sure I can find it once I'm down there."

We girl-talk for a few more minutes and then I hear a bell ring as if a door had been opened.

"I gotta go now; customer came in. Nice talking."

"Oh yes, me too. Bye."

And with that out of the way I head to my computer to check out the whereabouts of Hollis Bath Boutique in Rosslyn, Virginia and calculate how long it will take me to drive there.

CHAPTER 6

IT'S TWO HUNDRED THIRTY-ONE miles to Rosslyn, which is near Arlington, Virginia. I left my home at 5 a.m. and am wide awake thanks to a large thermos of Timothy's coffee and a breakfast sandwich of Taylor Ham, egg, and cheese. You need fuel when you drive.

Truthfully I don't mind driving by myself. I play my music, make sure that I have snacks and water in the car, and just drive. I feel relatively safe in my Edge and don't fear the eighteen-wheelers roaring down the interstate next to me.

There's been no word from my trusty hacker TRUST about the hit man Duchovny, but I'm not too worried. TRUST takes her time and is very thorough in her hacking. This will more than likely cost me close to a couple of grand which I will gladly pay and then add to the bill I'll present to Jennifer Brooks-Warren when the case is finished. I don't pad my expenses but I do expect my clients to understand that I work on promised pay and that I want them to be fair. Most of the time, I've had no problems with any bills I've presented to my clients. There was only one time when the client, a not-so-legit businessman with a cheating wife, nit-picked every expense I encountered following his wife and her lover. He was pissed at *me* for actually providing proof that she was cheating! I was after him for months to pay me. The bill was only grudgingly paid off after Myrtle informed him that if he didn't pay within seven working days she would personally bring his bill to the DA's office and have them check up on his rather shady business practices.

It's eight o'clock when I pull off I 95 south in search of a restroom, more coffee, and something hot to eat. I calculate that, barring any unforeseen traffic delays, I should be in Rosslyn, Virginia by nine-thirty. After a quick trip to the ladies room where I change my hoodie for a soft crème-colored cashmere top, I fill my thermos with coffee and half and half, grab a toasted bagel, and head back to the car. Virginia and a woman named Moira Hollis await me. Hopefully this Moira can give me the info I need to find the mysterious hit man.

Moira Michelle Hollis awoke and listened to the sound of nothing. It was a pleasant sound for her. It meant that she was alone and in complete charge of her life. Running on her treadmill, which was placed in front of the large bedroom window with a lovely view of an expanse of manicured condo property lawn, she made the decision to go to her boutique earlier than usual. Truthfully she could do whatever she wanted to do in life...now.

The freedom she had felt for the last two years had made her a different woman. Getting up early to run on the treadmill was something she never would have thought of, or wanted to do, when *he* was alive. No, back in those horrible days when his anger controlled her every move all she wanted to do was lie in bed until she heard him slam the front door around ten in the morning to go to his firm. Him, her hated, horrible father. She was glad he was dead.

She never allowed herself to think about "the incident" during the day but sometimes at night she relived the reason for her freedom and thanked a God who hadn't known she existed until she took matters into her own hands. "God helps those who help themselves" was certainly proven to be true when she had hired a stranger to eliminate her father. Then and only then, had God noticed her. Moira had bought her freedom for twenty-five thousand dollars and it had been worth every lousy cent.

She took a light jacket from the closet and cheerfully went out to meet the day, one of the many free, happy ones ahead of her.

―――

Hollis Bath Boutique is in the middle of a nice little square filled with other specialty shops in the town of Rosslyn, Virginia. There's a park in the middle of the square with park benches and carefully-tended flower beds. The boutique looks pretty and upscale. Sitting on a park bench, drinking coffee, I have to say that I'm impressed by the look of the place. Ms. Hollis must be doing well.

It's two o'clock and there are a lot of people on the street for a weekday. It seems as if nobody has a job but then I look around at the square and smile to myself. It's an affluent area, which means that the usual grind I see in New York City with workers rushing all over the place doesn't apply here. More money means a more leisurely attitude toward life and work.

The address for the Hollis condo is 842-12 Barron Court. It wasn't all that hard to find once I went into a real estate office in Rosslyn and made inquiries about wanting to look over the Barron Court property before committing to buying a condo.

"I'd like to just drive around myself," I told the overeager salesperson. "Trust me, if I like it I'll be back here today."

With my insistence on checking out the property and the area by myself, the salesperson directed me to the road that led directly from the town proper to the Barron Court condos. My luck held at the condo rental office. When the rental agent went to get me a map of the area, I leafed through the property manifest left on the main desk and found Moira's condo address: Hollis, M., 842-12 Barron Court South. Simple.

I don't want to approach Moira Hollis in the shop she owns. That's certainly not the place to ask very secretive questions about her hiring a hit man to kill her father or how she went about doing it. No. I'll wait until closing time, which the sign says is six pm. When she leaves I'll follow her back to number 842-12 Barron Court, allow her time to get inside her condo and then ring her bell. Whether she lets me in or not is another story; maybe I can get away with saying I'm a sorority sister from a different year.

I get up, toss my coffee cup in a trash can and make the most of a pretty spring day by walking along the square. There's a charming Federal-style bed and breakfast near a pond at the end of the square and I go in hoping that there's a room available. There is; a sunny room with expensive lace curtains framing double windows is available and I plunk down the one seventy-five charge, which includes a hot breakfast, for one night. I wash my face, refresh my make up, and change my sneakers for shoes. Then I go outside to wait for Ms. Hollis to appear.

Moira Hollis closes her boutique at six o'clock on the dot and leaves the building around six-thirty but she doesn't go home. Instead she walks to a local wine and tapas bar on the opposite side of the square. I follow discreetly, glad that I changed my top to something classier at the rest stop. I'm wearing designer jeans and so, it seems, are most of the women sitting at the outside tables. Fitting in is always good. No need to look as if I'm not from around here.

I study Moira; she's exactly as Jennifer Brooks-Warren described her: very thin with short black hair, and about five three in height. Her outfit, consisting of a black sweater and grey slacks, looks well tailored; and she's wearing designer wire-rimmed glasses. Her handbag is a discreet red Hermés Kelly bag, which Melissa once told me costs upward of $35,000. Moira, it seems, likes nice things.

Walking into the bar I hear her greet several patrons already there, as well as the young man behind the bar. "Hey, Moira. Joey is just setting up your table. The usual?" The bartender greets her in a way that lets me know she's a regular.

"Yes, please," Moira Hollis smiles at the man and walks toward a server beckoning her to a small table.

Scanning the room I see that it's one long, curved bar with backless stools and that at the end of the bar there are six raised tables with high-backed chairs. Moira Hollis is seated alone at one of the tables. There's a couple at another table but they are just paying their bill. I lean on the bar allowing my cleavage to show and smile at the bartender. He comes over quickly.

"Help you, miss?"

"Yes, I'd like a Mondavi merlot with one ice cube. And please fill the glass to the top."

"Ah-ha, a lady who knows what she wants. Coming right up."

I smile and lean closer over the bar. My "girls" are being rather lewdly eyed by another customer and I shoot him a death glance. He lowers his eyes. I know how to take care of myself.

Talking to the bartender I ask, "Can I get a table in the back? I need some privacy for a business call."

"Oh, yeah, sure thing, miss." He turns and calls to the server. "Hey, Joey! Come here a sec."

He hands me my drink as Joey walks over. "Set a table for this very nice lady."

I follow Joey toward the tables in the back and tell him which table I want. Of course it's next to Moira Hollis. Two businesswomen alone: a little polite conversation may be just the icebreaker I need.

Moira is checking text messages on her phone and I pretend to do the same all the while watching her and waiting for an opportunity to talk to her. She fiddles and frowns over one message, sighs and texts back. I see my opening.

"Damn!" I say just loudly enough to get her attention. "This stupid phone!" Moira looks over at me and I catch her eye. "Sorry. I didn't mean to disturb you."

"Oh, no, you didn't. These ridiculous phones." She smiles pleasantly. "Everyone says that technology is wonderful. Supposed to make our lives easier but it doesn't, really."

"I know! Mine just dropped a business call. Now when I try to re-connect, it won't even go through."

She nods and smiles. "My phone accidentally deleted a text message from one of my most important buyers and I couldn't get it back." She raises her almost empty glass. "Here's to technology!"

"Oh well," I sigh, "I think I'll just have another glass of wine and look at the menu. I'm starving." I pick up the menu and gesture to the server. "Another Mondavi merlot for me," I say.

Then nodding at Moira Hollis I add, "And another one of what she's having."

"Well, thank you. That's very nice of you." Moira smiles pleasantly the way we all do when a stranger is nice to us.

"My pleasure. I'm Cate Harlow."

"Moira Hollis. Are you from Virginia? Your accent says no."

"Guilty," I laugh. "New York City. Here on business," I say telling the truth and quickly change the subject before she asks what business. "What do you recommend from the menu?"

"I've ordered here so much I no longer need to look at the menu. Do you like prosciutto? Mozzarella?" I nod. "Then I suggest you try the tapas plate with prosciutto, mozzarella, olives, peppers, and crostini. I'm having some myself and another plate of stuffed mushrooms and shrimp. The dishes are tapas, you know, appetizers. Just right for a light meal."

"Sounds good, Moira," I say using her name to make it seem as if we are friends, "I think I'll follow your lead." I get up and ask shyly, "Is it all right if we share a table? Truthfully I hate to eat alone." I know I don't look threatening; that's to my advantage. She'll trust me.

"Of course. The company will be nice for a change."

Over two more glasses of wine and the tapas, we talk about nothing important. We're just two women having dinner and enjoying the pleasant night. I tell her that I'm from New York City and she tells me that she's visited twice but doesn't think she could live there. "It's too crowded and fast-paced for me."

"Well I guess I'm a city girl; I like quickness and even the crowds. But I grew up there so maybe that's why. Born and bred New Yorker. My parents too. I've never lived anywhere else. What about you? You live in this area all your life?"

Her face darkens just a bit and her jaw sets tightly. It's as if she's remembering something or someone unpleasant. My guess is that it's someone and that someone is the father she had murdered. Then she smiles politely and answers, "Washington, DC for a bit but usually around here."

"Always Rosslyn?"

Her face hardens again. "Falls Church, not far from Rosslyn."

"Guess your parents liked it here as much as mine did New York City."

"My parents are dead." She stops and looks out toward the bar. "Listen, let's order a bottle of that superb merlot you're drinking, my treat."

When the bottle of wine arrives encased in ice, I let Moira pour me a glass but I only sip at it. I need a clear head. When she isn't watching me I pour half of the glass into the ice bucket. I let her talk about nothing in particular then gradually steer the conversation in the direction I want.

"It's nice being able to sit and talk. I'm an only child so I generally spent a lot of time making friends. How about you, Moira? Any siblings?"

The wine has made her more conducive to talking about her life. She shrugs and says, "None of whom I care to speak." I've got to hand it to her; even with all the wine she has consumed, her grammar is prep school perfect. "Maybe you're lucky that you have no siblings, you ever think about that?"

"Oh, I guess. I was never really lonely. In fact I liked my solitude and being able to be number one with my parents."

Moira closes her eyes. "Yes, number one. Right."

I move the conversation around to other things. I want to gain her trust and then maybe zoom in to ask the hard question later on when we're away from here. The lady likes to drink and the alcohol makes her talkative. We discuss everything from the cars we like to makeup we prefer to men we've dated. After about an hour of this, I take a chance and tell her that I have to get going soon. "I have an early morning meeting tomorrow."

"Oh, what a shame. We're just getting to know each other. I guess I should go too. I have to deal with a supplier tomorrow."

When the bill comes I quickly grab it and hand the server my credit card. My dinner companion protests but I tell her truthfully enough that I'm charging it as a business expense; she can leave a nice tip, I say.

"This has been a pleasure, Cate. Since you're staying overnight allow me to reciprocate with a nice lunch tomorrow. All right? Meet me at the Hollis Bath Boutique around one thirty and we'll go to a restaurant nearby." She hands me a card similar to the one she gave to Jennifer Brooks-Warren two years ago, a card that had the number of the hit man. "We're slow at the shop until around four so you and I can have a nice long lunch and chat."

I tell her absolutely, I look forward to it, and agree to meet her at her shop. What she doesn't know is that there will be no lunch because I'll be heading back to New York early tomorrow morning. My business with her will be concluded tonight.

We walk out the door together and say good-bye and I head toward the B & B. Moira heads to her car. I watch her pull away and wait fifteen minutes before following her home. Now that she knows me she'll open her door readily.

In the parking area of Barron Court there are several spaces for people visiting the condo owners. The owners themselves park in garages underneath their respective condos. I check the garage under 842-12 Barron Court and see Moira's Mercedes nestled in the space under where she lives. There's a light on in what I assume is her living room. Taking a deep breath I climb the stairs and ring her bell.

The outside light is turned on and a minute later, Moira Hollis opens the door. She's still dressed in what she had on at the tapas bar but she's changed her heels for Ugg slippers.

"Cate?" She smiles a bit uncertainly. "Hi...I..."

I press forward just a bit so that she can't close the door. "Can I come in, Moira? I really need to talk with you."

She looks confused but opens the door wider and gestures me to come in the foyer. Once I'm inside she seems to shake off the confusion.

"Cate, I'm a little bewildered. How did you know where I live?"

She looks defensive; for all she knows I could be a criminal who chatted her up at the tapas bar with the intention of committing a crime. To put her at ease I lie smoothly and say, "You mentioned it during dinner tonight."

She shakes her head trying to remember if she did indeed tell me where she lives. "I did? Well, I guess I may have said something..." I'm in luck because the wine she consumed may have made her forget everything she said to me.

"Can we talk, Moira? This is really important."

"I guess so. I mean, I thought you had an early morning meeting tomorrow. What's this about?"

I ask her if we can sit down. Once we're on the couch, I pull out my PI license and tell her who I am and why I'm here. "Moira, I'm a private investigator from NYC. I came here to get information about a case."

"A private investigator?" I see a crack in her ladylike façade and her hand begins to play nervously with a bracelet on her wrist. "Are you telling me you're here to find some criminal?"

"No," I say calmly, "I'm here to see you. You're the person I came to find."

"Me? You came to find me? I have absolutely no idea what you could possibly want with me. I haven't been to New York in over ten years."

"I'm here because of something that happened two years ago in this area. I need a name from you."

"I know nothing of anything that happened two years ago that would involve a private investigator from New York."

"This is about your father." I hit a homerun with that one.

She visibly tenses and a mask comes down on her face. But she quickly covers and says, "Really, Cate, this is unbelievable. I have no idea what you are talking about; I think you should leave here." I notice that she doesn't say, "or I will call the police." She wants no police snooping around. That's a dead giveaway that she has something to hide.

"Moira, listen to me. You have nothing to fear from me. All I need is a name or at the very least some information."

"I don't know what you're talking about. I don't know what name or information you want."

She gets up and walks toward the door.

"Yes, you do. You hired someone to kill your father." She gasps when I say that and begins to protest, calling me a liar. I get up and move closer to her. "Truthfully, I don't give a damn if you did. As a PI I know I should; it's a murder rap after all, but that's not what I'm interested in right now. I need the name and information about the person you hired. A client of mine is in danger from this man. Someone has hired the same hit man you hired to kill your father, to kill my client. I need your help in trying to find him."

"Who sent you here?"

"No one sent me, Moira. I found you through a card, a business card you gave to my client. A card exactly like this one you gave to me this afternoon."

I see terror and recognition in her eyes as she stares at the card I'm holding.

"Two years ago in April you were at a bar called the K & K in Virginia, about 80 miles from Washington, DC. You were meeting a man there whom you had hired to get rid of your father."

"No, no, that's not true." She is backing away from me.

"Yes, it is true. He gave you proof that he had killed your father. He showed you a severed finger with a special ring on it. It was your father's ring. You got drunk that night and spoke to a young woman, a server at K & K; she was the one who was waitressing your table."

"Oh my God!" Moira Hollis starts shaking. "Get out, now!"

But I am relentless. "You felt sorry for this young woman at the bar, you thought she was having problems with some man and you gave her a phone number to call. You referred to the hit man as an 'eliminator.' You said that if she ever wanted to get rid of someone all she had to do was call the number on your card. You scratched your business name off the front of the card but I was still able to make out the letters. After that it was a simple task to check the phone directories online and make some calls to be able to locate you."

"No!" Moira suddenly falls on her knees, turns to the side and vomits on what looks to be an expensive oriental carpet. Her whole body is shaking. I walk over to her and hand her the travel pack of tissues from my jacket pocket. "How do you know all this? How can you possibly know any of what happened that night?"

"Moira, let's sit down again." As I say this I gently help her up from the carpet. She doesn't resist as I walk her over to the couch and help her sit down. "I promise you that I'm not here to get you arrested. I don't know why you did what you did but that's not my concern. I want to know how you got the name of the man you hired and if you can help me find him." I briefly explain the story of Jennifer Brooks-Warren as Moira stares at me in wide-eyed terror.

"Oh my God! That stupid child! He *will* kill her. No one will be able to stop him."

"I agree she was stupid but we all have done incredibly dumb things in our lives. Please Moira, you don't want to be responsible for someone else getting murdered. You don't want that on your conscience." As I talk I reach into my back pocket and press the bottom button of my cell phone to record.

She takes a shuddering breath and leans against the back of the couch. "I was so careful, so careful. Oh God! How did this happen? Please, you don't know what it was like, my father... oh God!"

I grab her shoulder and shake her just a little to get her to pay attention to me.

"Tell me about this eliminator. How did you find him?"

For the next twenty minutes Moira Hollis talks and relives her life leading up to her father's murder. She seems as if she's in a daze.

"He was a cruel man, my father. Really, his cruelty knew no bounds. Every aspect of my life was controlled by him. Tonight you asked about siblings. Yes, I have siblings, but I haven't seen them in years. My brother and sister were older than me by ten and twelve years. They both left home after college and never came back." She takes a shaky breath.

"All of us, you see, had to live at home while attending college. That was his rule." She cries into the tissue. "My brother and sister hated our father. I can't blame them for that but I do blame them for not taking me out of the prison created by him. You'd think that after either one of them had found another place to live and gotten a job, that they would come and get me. They didn't. I don't even know where they are to this day."

"What about your mother?"

"My mother drank to escape her surroundings and left when I was two years old. I wasn't a planned baby, you see. She wanted out of her marriage and because my father said he would destroy her in a divorce, she left him and me. I have no idea where she is, Europe maybe. I don't even know if she's alive." She sits up and coughs into the crumpled tissues I gave her. "People think that if you have money, life is good. I had money but my life was hell. From the time I was a child, my father ran my life. I was all alone with the monster who was my father; terrified of him. I became an obedient little girl who grew up to be an obedient woman."

"Why not just leave, Moira? Your brother and sister left. Why not you? What made you hire someone to get rid of your father?"

"I was afraid to leave for so many years, until..."

"Until what?"

She laughs mirthlessly and murmurs so low that I have to ask her to repeat what she said.

"Until... Anthony. I *did* try to leave...with him."

I ask her who Anthony is.

"He, Anthony, Anthony Cole, was my savior, he loved me, and my father got rid of him. I only met him four years ago. He worked for my father. We fell in love and Anthony knew what hell my life was. We decided to run away to Aruba and get married. I *had* to leave here and Anthony knew it. But my father found out and he had a...talk with Anthony. He offered him money to leave me but Anthony told him he didn't want his money, that he loved me and wanted to marry me. When my father found that he couldn't buy Anthony, he threatened him with all kinds of horrible things if he didn't leave. Anthony told him that he wasn't afraid of him. My sweet brave Anthony! He had no idea who he was dealing with! We were going to leave here and never, never come back! But, that didn't happen. All of a sudden Anthony disappeared and I *know* my father had something to do with it. I *know*, I truly believe that he had Anthony killed."

I watch tears stream down Moira's face. "And when I believed that he could kill the man I loved, I decided that I wanted my father dead at all costs. I wanted him to suffer before he died and I knew that there were people who could do that. I, I had heard stories about some of my father's criminal clients, you see. My father talked freely in front of me; I guess he thought I was either too stupid or too afraid to ever repeat anything I heard."

"Tell me about the hit man. How did you find him?"

"This man who calls himself the Eliminator was a god-send. My father was a lawyer for a great many nefarious men, real mob-type businessmen. I found out about this hit man through one of my father's associates, a man who used my father's legal services frequently. It was easy enough to get the hit man's number." A sad laugh escapes her and she puts her head in her hands.

"I went to see this client of my father's, this criminal with whom my father had done dirty business many times, and I begged him for help. He thought I was a sweet, innocent kid. To his credit, he was always very nice to me and I trusted him. He also was respectful toward women if you can believe that."

I nod. I have known men who had no problem committing violent crimes, even murder, but who were kind and gentle to women and children. It's a strange code of conduct; a lot of old mob men, wise guys, are like that. Women and children are untouchable in their code.

"First I begged him, *on my knees*, not to tell my father I had come to him. He promised me he wouldn't say a word then he asked how he could help me. I said that my best friend was suffering horrible abuse at the hands of her vicious husband. I could see that bothered him; he had no respect for men who beat women; his mother had been an abuse victim. I asked him if he had a person who could make her husband disappear. I elaborated the lie and said she was terrified that her husband was going to kill her when he came home from a business trip. Oh how I lied!" She hiccups from all the crying she's doing. "But oh did it work! He bought my lie, took a card from a desk drawer, and wrote down the number of someone he said was the best in the field, someone discreet and thorough. The rest, well, you already know. I called the number, made the transaction, and said I wanted proof of my father's death, that I wanted him to suffer, and I wanted the death covered up. It cost extra but I didn't care. I had to know the bastard was really dead and that it couldn't be traced back to me."

"Moira, there are no police reports of any dead body being found with a finger missing. I checked the police files from two years ago. How did you make that bit of information go away?"

She gets up and goes to a cabinet. Opening it she takes out what appears to be a newspaper clipping. Handing it to me she sits down again and watches me read it.

"'Damian Hollis, of Hollis and Fields Law Firm, died yesterday in what police are calling an accidental explosion outside of town. Mr. Hollis was inspecting a piece of property he was about to sell, the Whalen Gas Supply Warehouse, when the accident took place. The explosion, which occurred around eight thirty in the evening, was thought to have been the cause of a faulty gas line and a carelessly discarded cigarette. There were no reports of anyone else on the premises.'" It goes on about his life and testimonials from friends and colleagues but I've read enough.

Moira Hollis sits up straight and stares at me. This woman, dominated by a cruel father, deserted by her mother and siblings, and by all accounts not exactly a woman who fit the archetype of a murderer, had figured out how to finally leave her father's suffocating presence.

Not only did the eliminator murder her father and cut off his finger as proof of the murder, he put the body in a warehouse and blew it up so it was never found minus a finger. He's good, of that I can be sure. Jennifer Brooks-Warren is in more danger than she knows.

"Moira, listen to me. Try to focus here. I need to find this man, this hired killer. Perhaps you can call your father's associate, the one who gave you his number. Maybe he knows how to get in touch with him again."

Moira Hollis begins to laugh and the laughing turns into sheer hysterics. "You are *not* serious! What can I say to him? I have *another* friend who is being abused? Oh, dear, you are so funny."

I wait out her laughter and try again.

"I need this hit man's whereabouts. He's going to eliminate my client. You don't want that murder on your conscience."

When she doesn't answer me I decide the time has come for some tough negotiation. I stand up and take my gun out of my shoulder bag. "Sit up, Moira," I say, pointing the gun at her. Keeping my hand steady, I grab my cell phone from my back pocket. I key in a number and pretend to wait before pushing the call key. "Listen carefully to me Moira because I will not repeat myself. Unless you agree to cooperate with me, I'm calling the Virginia State Police and telling them that I'm a private investigator from New York City with some information concerning a murder that occurred around here two years ago."

"No! Please."

"Then get me the information I need."

"I, I don't know if he'll give it to me. I don't know!"

"Moira, you have exactly ten minutes to come up with a reason you need to get in touch with this eliminator. After that you have five minutes to get your father's associate on the phone and get him to tell you how to reach him."

Telling me she's going to be sick, Moira rushes out of the living room into a bathroom with me following, gun held level. I afford her no privacy but stand in the doorway while she vomits up her dinner and the booze. I can't risk her locking herself in the bathroom or going out the window to escape me. While I wait, I grab a face cloth from the sink counter and wet it with cold water. When she's finished I hand it to her.

"Come on Moira. You'll be fine. Just take deep breaths." I say this gently; I need her to see me as a confidante who is concerned for her. She takes a few minutes before she stands up. "Let's go sit down. Just sit down and breathe slowly, okay?" I say as I lead her back to where we were.

Once we're in the living room I put my gun away. Truthfully if she tries anything I can handle her. Right now I need her to cooperate so I pick up her phone and place it next to where she is sitting. "Call him."

"What should I say? I haven't spoken to him since my father's will was read."

This is going to be difficult. I may have to change tactics. She's in no condition to think clearly during a phone call; the wine coupled with the fear of being found out have made her a shaking mess. I assess the situation. It's possible she doesn't have to call anyone at all.

"All right. Maybe there's another way."

"There has to be another way! I can't do this!" She begins crying again.

"When you went to his office, how did he give you the number? Was it on his cell phone, in a file cabinet, or safe? Think, Moira."

I see her sit up straight. She's relieved that she might not have to call him after all. "It was in a drawer, a locked drawer in his desk."

"What is the name of this criminal businessman and where is his office?"

Moira looks at me with wide, scared eyes. "You should be afraid of him, Cate. He's a dangerous man involved in crimes you don't want to know about. Don't go see him."

"I have no intention of going to see him. I want the information he gave you. You have a choice: Either you call him right now or you tell me his name and where his office is located. I can break into his office and get what I need without you being directly involved. Understand?"

Moira Hollis looks at me as if I am crazy but slowly nods her head and tells me the criminal associate's name is Peter Karis. "His office is on Mead Avenue, 4860 Mead, third floor. It's an old building but I'm pretty sure that there's security there and probably an alarm system too."

"Do you remember which drawer it was in his desk?"

"I—I don't remember. I think maybe on the right side but I can't be sure."

I check my watch; it's almost nine o'clock.

"Are you, are you...going to call the police about what I...did? Am I going to be arrested tonight?"

Her fear is palpable and her hands are shaking. I see a liquor cabinet near the dining area and walk over to it. She needs a drink right now. Grabbing a bottle of cognac and a glass from the cabinet I walk back to Moira, set the glass in her hand and pour about a half inch into the tumbler. "Drink this."

She sips it and watches me.

"Are you ready to deal here, Moira?"

"What do you mean?" She coughs and cognac dribbles from her mouth.

Handing her the packet of tissues again, I squat down in front of her so that we're eye to eye. "This is what I mean, Moira. I won't report your father's murder to the police or your part in it." She sighs and begins to cry. "But, in return for *my* silence, you have to understand that you will completely forget that you met me or that I am going to break into an office tonight to retrieve crucial information for my case. That's my deal, take it or leave it."

"I promise I won't say anything, anything!"

"Your promise is no good to me. I don't go by promises, I go by consequences. All you have to know is that if you don't keep your part of the deal, the consequence will be the police knocking on your door tomorrow asking questions about your father's murder and questioning your part in what happened two years ago. You also need to know that if anything happens to me, my colleagues in NYC will be paying a visit to the police down here. It seems that, through your father, you know some unsavory characters who could possibly harm me and I've taken steps to protect myself."

She shakes her head in protest. "No, no I would never think to..." I hold up my hand to stop her.

"To let you completely understand how serious I am, I've recorded everything you've said on my cell phone. It's already been sent to one of my most trusted people. Technology really *is* wonderful."

"I don't want to harm anyone and I don't want that innocent woman, the one you mentioned, I don't want her death on my conscience. I will forget that you even came here if that is what you want." I stand up to pour her another drink. As I'm turning away, she says my name very quietly.

"Cate?"

I face her again. "Yes?"

"Please, I have to know something. I am very grateful that you are not bringing the police in on this matter but...why would you *not* tell the police about what I did? After all, you said you're a private investigator. Aren't you required by law to report a crime?"

I hesitate before I answer. She's right; legally I am bound to report a crime or criminal activity. But there are times when I've skirted that requirement. My decision always depends a lot on facts. In this case I have to determine if there is a definite assurance that Moira was involved in the crime and if she can be linked to it without reasonable doubt. There's only one person who could finger her as the woman who hired a killer and that person is the killer himself; money changed hands. As for Jennifer testifying as to what she heard, any good lawyer could argue that what was said in the bar to a young scared waitress was hearsay; the ramblings of an intoxicated woman. Even what Jennifer Brooks-Warren says she saw and heard in the alley behind the bar could be torn apart by a cunning lawyer. The law deals in facts, not suppositions.

Then too, I believed Moira when she told me about what a bastard her father was. I will check up on that and the disappearance of Anthony Cole for my own satisfaction, but I think Moira was telling me the truth as only a desperate person can.

"Maybe it's not in anyone's best interest, yours or mine, to notify the police if you cooperate with me," I finally say. "Goodbye, Moira. It's unlikely we'll see each other again." And with that I walk to the door and let myself out.

CHAPTER 7

BREAKING AND ENTERING is a skill every private investigator needs to have. I was taught by an expert, a break-and-enter professional I had used several times as a source for information on a case. She was, and more than likely still is, the absolute best. She could get into anything that was locked and she passed her skills on to me.

The building on Mead Avenue where Peter Karis has an office is gracefully old. It has aged well. This is the same as most of the architecture I have briefly seen in this area. It is not falling apart old as some historic buildings in New York City are. These buildings have a fine elegant patina about them. Besides the beauty of their age there's another plus; the locks are old as well.

Ask most people what kind of locks they think are good for doors and they'll probably say pad locks or deadbolts. They're pretty much on target with that answer. But there are new high-tech locks that can stall even professional burglars. Newer locks on high-rise buildings have locking devices that are computer-keyed with silent alarms built into the mechanism.

The outside lock of this building is a Federal style fancy one that looks complex but it's not. It's simply ornate, not complicated. A standard small Philips screwdriver in the right hands will open it within three minutes. It takes me five minutes to get in. Surprisingly there's no guard in the old building but there could be a silent system that connects to the police.

Once inside I crouch behind the door and wait. If there *is* a silent alarm a police car will drive up and I'll run. Sometimes there will be an unmarked car; I can spot one of those easily thanks to having been married to a police detective. But after waiting a breathless ten minutes I hear and see nothing that indicates security or police. I'm in and I'm unobserved. Checking the registry in the lobby for Peter Karis is next, after that I head to the stairwell.

I jog up the stairs to the third floor silently thanking God that the tennis I play has made my legs strong. Third floor landing and I'm only slightly winded. Room 303 bears the lettering, *Peter Karis, Land Surveyor*.

The lock on the door of room 303 is new and a bit more difficult but I see that the door itself is not fitted well to the frame. The screwdriver won't work on the lock but it just might help me push the locking mechanism open through the frame. It's a dead-latch, far simpler than a dead-bolt. I wiggle my screwdriver slowly through the small slit between the doorframe and the lock. Nothing. The lock mechanism is dirty and stuck. It needs some type of lubrication.

I look around for a bathroom and see a men's room down the hall. Sprinting down the hall I observe that there are only two other offices near the one occupied by Karis and I listen for sounds of movement. It seems I am alone in the building.

Inside the bathroom I find a soap dispenser. I need to put the liquid soap in something but there are no paper towels, only a hand dryer. Going into one of the stalls, I grab a roll of bathroom tissue and use my penknife to cut away the paper and take out the cardboard cylinder. Then I bend one end of it to make a holder that won't leak and fill part of the tube with liquid soap. Improvisation is a necessity. You work with what you have when you're an investigator.

Back at the door of *Peter Karis, Land Surveyor*, I dip the

screwdriver in the soap and try sliding it back between the doorframe and the lock mechanism. I use my knife to scrape away the dirt inside the jam. Fifteen sweaty minutes go by and the work is tedious. Pushing the screwdriver firmly against the lock I finally hear a slight click and I push the curved handle open. I am inside.

It is dark but the curtains are thin and the light from the street below illuminates the room enough for me to see what's there. Bookcases, a computer station, a coat tree, and a big mahogany desk. It looks as if it may be an antique. I walk over and sit at the desk, trying the middle drawer first. It opens as do the two on my left and the bottom one on my right. The top right drawer, however, doesn't budge. That one is locked.

I examine the lock, small, brass and most likely fitted with a tiny cylinder inside. My penknife is perfect as a key and after a few tries, I open the drawer. Inside is a pack of eight index cards held together with a rubber band. There are phone numbers and notations on them but no names. I shuffle through them, then lay them out on the desk and take a picture of them with my phone camera before returning them to the drawer and locking it with my knife.

Voices and a light showing under the doorway let me know I'm not alone in the building anymore. Looking through the slit in the poorly fitting doorframe I see a heavyset man in some type of a uniform coming down the hall. My watch tells me it's ten forty. I'm guessing he's the security guard for the building. With him is another man with Beats headphones draped around his neck and carrying what looks like a toolbox. I hold my breath as they pass room 303 going toward the stairwell.

"Listen, I had to come and disconnect the alarm, for Christ's sake. It went off around three-thirty this afternoon and the people who rent the offices here were screaming at me to do something. Nothing I could do would stop it so I turned the damn thing off. I called the alarm company but they said you were on another job. Thanks for coming. The sensors on the computer setup say the problem is in the box on this floor. We got to have that alarm set before I can leave again. It's our bowling night and my wife is pissed as hell that I'm not down at the lanes."

The man with the toolbox mutters something that I can't make out and I hear tools clinking on the floor. I look around for an escape exit but the only one besides the door is the window. Suddenly the lights flash on in the hall and in the office. I dive under the desk and pull the desk chair as close as I can to block me from anyone looking in. The lights flash off and on several times and then it's dark again.

"I found the problem here, Mac," says a voice I assume is from the guy with the tools. "You got a nest of ants. Got to spray them out then I can readjust the alarm. Take about an hour or so. Tell you what; I'll pop the system up to a less sensitive setting."

"Yeah, that's good for me. Makes my job easier," says the guard.

What he said is not good for me. I want to get out of here as soon as I can. If the lights stay off I can possibly make my exit through the window. I hesitate in case the lights flash on again then decide to take a risk and check the outside. As quietly as I can, I walk to the window and look out at the drop. The building is built right next to the walkway. There's nothing outside the window that would ease my exit; no awning, no fancy grillwork to hang on to. I would land, feet first hopefully, on nothing but a cement sidewalk. That's not an option.

I have to leave the same way I came in. While I'm wondering how I can possibly accomplish this I hear footsteps coming in my direction and quickly slide to the side of the door.

The footsteps go past room 303 and stop a ways down the hall. The big guy is going to the men's room. Good, now there's only one person I have to deal with.

Will once told me that it takes a man three minutes to unzip his pants, pee, and then zip up again. Another three minutes is spent to wash and dry his hands. That's a total of six minutes. I'm hoping the security man has good hygiene. Either way I have to take a chance. Once the alarm is fixed, I'll be stuck here.

Checking my watch, I carefully ease the door open and see that the repair man has his back to me and his headphones on. I close the door without a sound and walk as if I'm on eggshells to the stairwell. The bathroom door slams open just as I'm halfway down to the second floor. I glance at my watch. Only four minutes have gone by. It seems as if Mr. Security Guard doesn't wash his hands.

Back at the Bed and Breakfast I sleep as if I am drugged. The adrenaline rush I experienced the night before crashed as soon as I stepped into a nice hot tub. Making it to my bed wrapped in a fluffy white towel I collapsed and slept the sleep of exhaustion.

At 8:15 the next morning, there's a firm knock on my door. "Hello? Cate? You asked me to wake you for breakfast. I'll begin serving in a half hour."

Amused at the friendly use of my first name I call out my polite thank-you and add that I'll be ready to come down in about fifteen minutes. Then I swing my legs out of the incredibly soft bed and do a few ballet barre stretches before heading to the shower.

I arrive downstairs with my overnight bag and go into the large dining room. Two other people are present and we nod politely at each other. There's a side table set up with covered trays of hot food, a coffee urn, and, I am happy to see, a small pitcher of half and half. The owner of the B&B walks over to me and hands me an envelope. "This was dropped off earlier for you."

I thank her and open it. It's from Moira Hollis wishing me a safe trip home and saying that, despite everything, she did enjoy meeting me. *"Thank you for your discretion, Cate. I hope all goes well for your client. Moira."* I have to admit it, the lady has class. Then I head to the side table to get a cup of coffee and a breakfast of a bacon omelette, rye toast, and fresh fruit. I am starving from last night's ordeal.

Ten-thirty finds me back on the interstate armed with the information that may help me find the eliminator. I pass Moira's boutique on my way out of town. There's an "Open" sign on the door and I see Moira and her assistant, obviously the talkative one from my phone call two days ago, working inside. My grandmother, my Nonna Rita, would have said that Moira Hollis is a lost soul and I guess that term might apply here. She is a woman who has tried to forget her unhappy past and make a new, better life for herself. I wish her well.

I know Moira can't see me but I lift my hand in a wave anyway and continue on my way. I am anxious to get home.

CHAPTER 8

THE INFORMATION FROM the office of Peter Karis is in my bag as I run up the stairs of *Catherine Harlow, Private Investigations.* It's almost ten in the morning but the office is closed and dark. *Where's Myrtle?* I think as I unlock the door. I can only hope that my usually on-time Myrtle is off getting some Timothy's coffee and some bagels for the office.

The message alarm on my phone pings just as I'm dumping everything on my desk. TRUST has left me some info about the Eliminator.

Hey Harlow- last known appearance Duchovny last month around the 14th in Atlanta Georgia, √ police files, big shot male was offed there, looks like Duchovny's work. Later - TRUST

Atlanta, Georgia; let's check and see what criminal activity happened in Atlanta last month. I call Will at the same time I turn on my computer and begin a search of crimes in Atlanta during the last four weeks.

"You're back," says Will, "How was the trip?"

"Fruitful and tiring. What's new?"

"Not much. Want to meet for lunch? I can get away around two."

"Sure, that would be good. Enzo's?"

"Yeah, call ahead though. I could use a good dish of gnocchi with Bolognese sauce today. But baby-girl, as much as I'd like to think you called because you miss me and you're horny, I know you too well. What do you need?"

I laugh. He does know me. "Well, can you find out some information for me about a murder that occurred last month in Atlanta?"

"Atlanta? A little outside of your purview isn't it?"

"Yes, but it can directly relate to my current case. Will you do it? Lunch will be on me."

"Really?" I hear Will give a sensual laugh. "That would be delicious." Always thinking with his libido.

"Funny, ha-ha. But I will *pay* for lunch if you can check police files about any murders in Atlanta last month. Deal?"

"Deal. But I'd rather have lunch *on* you, babe." He laughs again. "See you at two."

Myrtle comes in just as I'm hanging up the phone. She is as well-dressed and groomed as ever but in some way she looks awful.

"How was Virginia?" she says, taking a container of coffee and a bagel out of a Timothy's Gourmet Coffees bag and placing both on my desk. Then she goes to plug in the electric pot to make her tea.

"I think I got what I needed. We'll see. I have to go through some phone numbers and all later." I open my coffee container and inhale. Heaven in a cup. "What's new here?"

"The check from the limo company arrived, a nice amount for a night's work. By the way, the limo company owner said that one of the drivers you busted, for want of a better word, said you *looked* like a hooker. I think he meant it as a compliment."

"Great."

Myrtle raises an eyebrow then continues. "You have two potential new cases. The clients' numbers are on your desk pad. First one is a Tiger Mom worried over her son's whereabouts; wants him, Robbie is his name, followed this weekend. She thinks he's meeting, as she so delicately stated, some 'unrefined girl' and said that she, the mother, is way too young to become a grandmother. She found a text message on his phone from this girl. Money here, Cate, the young man in question goes to a prominent school, is a high-ranking scholar, and Tiger Mom doesn't want anything to mess up his already-planned academic life. She mailed over a rather large retainer check for your services."

"Ah, the protective mother tiger! Okay, sounds easy. What's the second case?"

Myrtle pauses to add hot water to her tea bag. "Second case is a man who wants a background check on a several new employees; just routine."

"Anything else?"

"Your friend Bo stopped me outside yesterday and said he misses you, which I took to mean he misses the twenty dollar bill you forgot to give him before you left. I gave him two tens out of petty cash."

"Thanks Myrtle. That all?"

She takes a sip of her tea, "All? Hmmmmm. Let's see. They're waxing the stairs here over the weekend so if you come in to the office on Saturday, be careful not to fall. And, oh yes, I found a bottle of Cialis in Harry's underwear drawer."

※

"Would you ever take Cialis?" I ask Will over a hot lunch at Enzo's trattoria.

"Excuse me?" He almost chokes on his food.

"I said, would you ever consider taking Cialis if you needed some help in getting and maintaining an erection."

"Jesus, Cate! I didn't notice anything wrong in our recent encounters. Why this unexpected, and kind of inappropriate, dining conversation?"

"Myrtle found a bottle of Cialis in Harry's underwear drawer. So answer the question, would you consider taking it if it was ever needed?"

Will looks at me for a few minutes while he spoons grated parmigiana cheese onto his gnocchi then surprises me with his answer. "Yes, I would take it if the time comes and I can't get there on my own. Sure I would. Hey, listen, I don't care what age a guy is, no one wants to give up one of the greatest natural experiences we humans have, even if we have to use some unnatural means to have it. So Harry is still interested in Myrtle and wants a sex life? Good for him. I say go for it and enjoy every minute of it. Tell that to Myrtle. I'm betting she can be a wild one." He winks at me and I smile at the thought of a hot mama wild Myrtle.

"Well she didn't say any more about it and I was so surprised that she even mentioned it to me, you know how very proper she is, that I didn't know what to say to her. I just kind of let it slide. She didn't mention it again. Do you think I should, no pun intended here, bring it up again?"

Will concentrates on his gnocchi. The man loves his food and doesn't want anything to interfere with the pleasure of eating. Finally he says to drop it and not mention it. "If she wants to talk about it she'll initiate the conversation." He takes a long drink of water. "Anyway, my sweet Cate, let's get off the whole subject of Harry's investment in his and Myrtle's sex life and tell me what you need from me."

"There was a murder in Atlanta, Georgia that might be traceable to my case," I say. "I need you to check through Atlanta police files for murders committed there last month, most specifically around the fourteenth." I push my plate away and signal the waiter for two cups of cappuccino. "The search engines I can use don't offer a whole lot of information and, as an NYPD detective, you are able to get me more specific details."

"Any particular type of murder victim? Male, female, prominent?"

"Most definitely prominent male but also probably not well-known to the public. Maybe some business exec or power-broker."

Will takes in the everyday hustle of the passers-by on the street in front of him while he sits and relaxes with his cappuccino. "Okay. Shouldn't take long. I'll put one of the techs on it."

"How's the studying for the Bar going?" I ask and see him visibly sigh.

"Yeah, good, not too bad. Why, you want to help me hit the books?" His tone is a bit sarcastic but I let it go. The studying is hard for Will because he's not all that committed to the idea that once he passes the Bar, he'll have to make the decision to leave the detective job he loves.

"Sure," I smile sweetly, "Hit the books and then hit the sheets."

He laughs and relaxes. "Now you're talking! You free tonight?"

I assure him that I will be home before seven, he promises me he'll get me the info I want later today, and that he'll be at my brownstone by seven-thirty. Then we sit back and just watch the familiar city scenes taking place in front of us.

On my way back to the office I get a call from the security company's head man. "Cate Harlow," I answer, making my way between people on the busy street.

"Cate? This is Adrian at Sec.Co calling with an update on the Brooks-Warren surveillance. As far as we can tell, there's no unwanted activity; no one's tried to contact her, no suspicious people around her building and such. The only person who came there a few times is a business associate of Edward. Got Natalie shadowing her, going places where my men can't go, like a women's restroom. She sees nothing out of the ordinary. Tanya, one of my best field agents is similar in height and build to Ms. Brooks-Warren. We put her in a long haired wig and had her borrow one of Brooks-Warren's coats. Dressed like her she went alone out for a walk a few times. This agent is sharp and on-target, says she wasn't followed. This hit man? Must be one of the best. We're seeing nothing on our end."

I thank him and tell him to keep surveillance in place for now.

"Got it, will do, Cate."

I walk back to my office where the phone numbers from Peter Karis's office are waiting for me.

CHAPTER 9

FIND THE RIGHT number and you'll find who you're looking for...if you're lucky. The numbers from Karis's desk drawer are displayed on my own desk and I'm keying them into my laptop. They appear to be from the Washington, D.C-Virginia-Maryland area but that's not a certainty. Phone numbers, geography, and area codes no longer necessarily go together. While moving once meant new area codes, people now take their area codes with them courtesy of mobile phones, sort of like little memories of where they've been. There are people living in NYC who once lived in LA and still have their Los Angeles area code of 323 for their phones.

The phone numbers came with notations that seem cryptic; they look like gibberish but I know it's some type of a messaging system. It looks familiar. I know it from somewhere. It's a linguistic code.

I keep looking at the random letters in the notations and mentally going through the many courses in linguistics I took in college. My memory clicks in when I remember a course called *Coding Shifts and Substitution Ciphers*. Despite the rather dry and clinical title, taking the course was actually fun. There was the Acrostic Message Code where the first letter of each word in a series of sentences spells out a message. For instance if you wrote, "**H**ello! **E**verything is going fine. **L**ots of things to do! **P**lease remember to feed my fish," the first letters of the words used would spell **H-E-L-P**.

What I am looking at now appears to be a code called The Caesar Shift. Julius Caesar, master general and statesman, is known to have created it. It is a code that is simple to use and understand, making it one of the fundamental code systems still studied today as the basis for more complex ones. In its time the code was sophisticated and very difficult for Caesar's enemies to crack. Caesar was able to send messages to his generals without any problems.

In the Caesar Shift, you shift the entire alphabet a certain number of places, usually three, in one direction. In other words, a shift of three spaces forward would replace the first letter of the alphabet, A, with D, the second letter, B, with E, etc. For example, if I used the basic Caesar Shift of three letters forward to spell my name Cate Harlow, it would look like this: FEWI KEUORZ. It seems that Mr. Karis was either a student of Roman history or someone had given him the basics for using the code.

There are eight numbers all followed by a string of letters. Next to each phone number I write the letters. 301-555-9243 JLO EURFN followed by the word "main." That's a phone number for a person named Gil Brock and I'm assuming some type of mob maintenance. 301-555-6021 ORXLV NLULQ followed by "dep." is a number for Louis Kirin. I'm assuming that dep. may be an abbreviation for deposit. Maybe a bank manager? I find that I am using the Caesar Shift easily; it is all coming back to me. There's even a number for Moira's father, 301-555-6623 GDOLDQ KROOLV, Damian Hollis. Next to his code is "lw." for lawyer.

Finally, on the sixth number, 443-555-0871, I hit pay dirt: PEUF FURIW aka Marc Croft. The word next to his jumbled letters is the ominous abbreviation "elim." which I'm positive is short for eliminator. There's also an asterisk with the number 5 next to it. I key in the number for Marc Croft and after two rings an automated voice informs me that I have dialed incorrectly and to please check the number and person I want to reach. It's a burner phone. Looking at the number next to the asterisk, I wonder if 5 might mean that this number was the most recent one in a series used by Marc Croft. In the business my eliminator is in, he would have to keep changing phone numbers very frequently. Two days ago when I was in Karis's office this number was probably viable; now it's most likely been discarded. The eliminator seems to be untraceable, at least through phone numbers. He *is* a ghost.

"Got some info on an Atlanta murder that might fit your case. Name and number of captain you can call at the police department there."

Will has just come through my front door carrying a small leather case with his nice compact notebook computer. It's roughly the size of a five by seven picture frame, has all the nifty bells and whistles you can want, and was a gift from his mother, Francesca who is eager for her son to become a lawyer. "And why do you leave your front door unlocked?"

I turn from popping some chicken parm that I picked up at Enzo's on my way home in the oven. "I just unlocked the door two minutes ago. You *said* you'd be here by seven-thirty."

I'm still dressed in blue tennis shorts and a sleeveless top from my late afternoon match with Ani. My hair is piled on top of my head and I feel overheated. Maybe playing tennis in the late afternoon after my hectic day wasn't such a good idea.

Will comes over to me and kisses my ear then turns me around to face him. "What if I was late? Any whack job could have walked in, baby. Just be careful, okay?"

I point to my gun lying in its place in a ceramic tray on the counter. Will just sighs, repeats his statement about being careful, then pulls me tightly against him. His hands begin a gentle massage up and down my body as his tongue licks my lips. As he's sliding his hands down the back of my shorts he says, "Turn off the oven. Let's have dessert first."

Will stays overnight at my brownstone. I tried, I really did try, to quiz him on crucial questions for the Bar exam but it was a losing game. He had other, as he said, *urgent matters* that needed his attention. So much for a study date. We didn't hit the books but we sure hit the sheets and pretty much never left them. Twelve o'clock midnight found us eating cold, but very delicious, leftover chicken parm in bed.

The next morning I'm busy at my computer when I hear the bedroom door open. Good, Will's up. I need to ask him about that info from Atlanta. He walks totally nude over to where I am and massages my neck.

"Why'd you get dressed, baby? It's not even seven yet. Come back to bed, okay?"

As much as I would love to have a repeat performance of last night, I know that I can't take the time. "No, I need to get to my office early. But first I need that info you told me you had pertaining to my case."

"Sure, no problem. Come take a shower with me, then…we'll …talk."

"I already had a shower around four this morning. I woke up feeling achy from playing tennis yesterday afternoon with Ani. I needed a hot shower. Besides, to take another one I'd have to get undressed."

He grabs my hand, "That's the whole point, Cate."

"No, seriously, Will! Go shower on your own; you're a big boy. I'll make more coffee, and then we *will* talk. I need that info."

"I'll be out of town later today for that conference in Connecticut. I'll be gone for three days. You're missing a great chance to get back into bed with me," he teases.

"If I miss you, then getting together when you return will be even sweeter. Here," I say grabbing his hand. "I'll even give you the key to the brownstone so you can let yourself in if I'm not here."

Big sigh, a kiss on the back of my neck, and he's off to the shower. I watch him walk away, thinking what a fantastic body my man has and that it's all mine.

***

The captain's name is Billy Gene Ramsay. Every sentence he utters seems to end with "Ya know what I mean?" His southern drawl reminds me of every movie I have ever seen where a police story was based in the south and one of the main characters was a southern sheriff. He keeps calling me "ma'am," which is a little disconcerting for this northeast urban girl but I find it very charming nonetheless.

"Yes, ma'am, we have had a possible murder of a prominent male which occurred in our city on the fourteenth. I say *possible* because it can still be described as an accident. I don't think so myself, an accident, nope, no way. Got the cop feelin' that this was some kinda hit, ya know what I mean?"

I do; my gut instinct has never failed me. I go by what I feel and it always pans out. I ask him about the possible murder.

"Well, see, it went like this. A businessman name of J.M. Martell didn't come home on the night of the fourteenth. When he hadn't come home after April fifteenth, his wife reported to my office that she was real worried about him. She was a person of interest at the beginning but we ditched that almost right away. She was damned, beggin' your pardon ma'am, truly upset when she found out what had happened.

"But see, here's the thing, I think she *knew* what had happened or had an inkling of it, ya know what I mean? I got the feeling she was afraid for her own self if she said anything about what she did know."

"What exactly *did* happen, Captain Ramsay?" I ask, anxious to avoid a longwinded description of the possible murder.

"I was gettin' to that, ma'am," he says patiently. "Now just wait on the details, okay? We had gotten a report that there had been a car explosion so me and my men went to check it out. Well, it seems that the car blast had a lot to do with why Mr. Martell didn't come home. Martell was accidentally blown up in that explosion, his own car, or so everyone but me seems to think.

"Everything about it seems suspicious. Excuse me, ma'am, hold on for a minute." I hear him talking to someone in the background.

"Sorry 'bout that, ma'am. Busy office here. Anyway, about Martell? Strange that he was even in his car; seems he *didn't like* driving his car to work and he rarely did drive it there. He usually took the open air tram, the trolley car, to and from his office. He never drove except on the weekends. Wife said he liked takin' the tram during the weekdays 'cause it gave him a chance to close his eyes and relax, before and after work. But on the day in question, the day he got blown up? Well, supposedly he texted his housekeeper to bring the car on along into town and park it in the garage next to his office.

"Now my question is *why* would a man who didn't like drivin' his own car weekdays suddenly text his housekeeper late on a Tuesday afternoon to bring the car to him. Text also said that there was a twenty dollar bill taped to the driver-side visor for her cab fare back home. Don't make sense, ma'am. And the thing is, anybody could've sent that text from Martell's phone, just like anybody could've stuck that twenty dollar bill up there on the visor, ya know what I mean? His car was always parked down a long driveway, a fair distance from the house."

"How did the explosion happen?" I'm thinking about how Moira's father died. A carelessly tossed, read that as a *deliberately tossed*, cigarette near a natural gas leak.

"Well now, our CSIs said that it looks like a leak from his gas tank was what made it blow; some spark from the engine lit the liquid gasoline up, they guess. But, I don't know. If this *is* a murder, though, I got to say, it's a very professional one. Body was burned beyond recognition so's there not a lot of evidence. No hack amateur, ya know what I mean?"

I do know exactly what he means and I ask, "Did Martell have any known enemies?"

"Well now, no. Wasn't the friendliest man, no good ole boy,

if ya know what I mean. Did belong to the Rotary from what I learned, member in good standin' and all. Yes, he was a prominent figure in our community; he ran a brokerage business, did pretty well. I'm guessin' he had his share of people who didn't care a whole lot for him and all, but real wanna-kill-him-enemies? No, didn't find anyone who hated him enough to actually *kill* him."

"You still think the wife knows more than she's saying? Are you talking to her about what she might know?"

"No, ma'am, we're not still talkin' to her. She's like a wounded scared little squirrel; can't get nothin' more out of her. But, I got to say that yes, I do, I do believe she knows a whole lot more than she's told us. Trouble is, can't get blood outta a stone, ya know what I mean? But, truth now? I think someone has her scared enough that she won't be sayin' much to any one of *us*, ever. And anyways, after we cleared her as a person of interest, she was admitted to a local hospital. Doctor says she's sufferin' from stress-induced trauma. She ain't *going* nowhere but that dog won't hunt again, if ya know what I mean by that statement."

"I can pretty much figure that out, Captain. So, no leads?"

"No, ma'am, not at this time. Case is open; gonna remain open." He pauses, "Well now, that's about all I know. We're gettin' pretty busy here. Anything else I can help you with, ma'am?"

I tell him no, he's already helped a lot and he promises me that he'll call me if he catches a break in the case.

"Bye now, ma'am. You take care. You ever down this way, come and say hello, hear?"

"I will. Same goes for you, if you ever find yourself in New York City that is. Good-bye, Captain Ramsay.

After I hang up I go to turn off the air conditioner that Myrtle has left on. I've been sneezing all morning and Myrtle thinks it's because of the pollen coming in the open windows so she turns on the air.

But I hate air-conditioned air. The cold blast has me feeling chilled and my head hurts. Grabbing a bottle of an over-the-counter pain reliever from my desk drawer, I swallow two of the pills washing them down with an entire bottle of water. It's going to be a long day; I need to cross-check the Atlanta hit with similar ones that may have occurred in that area.

CHAPTER 10

AT ELEVEN THIRTY that night I awaken with a massive headache, a fever and horrible chills. I feel like crap. I swing my legs over the side of the bed but when I try to stand I sway and fall back down. I'm shivering badly and I grab as much of the blanket around me as possible.

I worked until nine at night and had wanted to work even later but my eyes were getting blurry and my head began to throb again so I came home and fell into bed exhausted. The small amount of sleep I got has only made me feel worse.

There's an urgent care doctors office about ten minutes away and I know I should get myself down there but my body is shaking so much that the thought of standing up again is out of the question. For some reason tears fill my eyes. I'm alone and sick. Will is out of town attending that conference he mentioned this morning. Melissa doesn't usually answer her phone if she's with a client and I know Myrtle is at a bridal shower. If I call her she'll worry and I don't want that. I call Giles on his cell. After three rings I hear, "Dr. Barrett." Then, because he must have looked at his caller ID, "Catherine? Is everything all right?" The sweet concern in his voice makes me start crying.

"Giles," my voice breaks, "I'm so sick. I can't stand up. I'm hot as hell and my body is shaking with chills." I didn't mean to blurt that out but it's all I can do to talk on the phone.

"I'll be right over, Catherine. And you're in luck. I've just finished having dinner with another doctor, an internist. We'll be there in about fifteen minutes. Stay in bed until we arrive."

The internist's name is Felicia; she's pretty and she's kind. She is also wearing a very sexy low-cut chiffon dress made for dinners at fancy restaurants. After taking my temperature and asking me questions about my symptoms she calls a prescription in to an all-night pharmacy that delivers and tells them to hurry. "I'm ordering you some Augmentum, you've got quite a bug there, but after taking two of them, you should start to feel better by late tomorrow morning. Try to get some sleep tonight." Turning to Giles she says, "I'll wait outside in the other room for the pharmacy delivery."

I watch her sway through the bedroom door in her float-y cranberry-colored dress and take a good look at Giles. He looks dramatically handsome in a black striped suit with a light maroon shirt and tie. Obviously he was on a date. I feel compelled to offer an apology.

"Sorry to ruin your date. She's very nice, Giles."

"I think she is. I met Felicia at a medical conference. Her office is on Queens Boulevard in Forest Hills; she's a very good internist. And you *didn't* ruin anything. We went to the theatre and then a late dinner."

"Does she know our past history?"

"Does she need to know?"

"No, I guess not. I'm glad to see that you're moving on."

He sits on the side of the bed and kisses my head. "It's only a second date, Catherine. I need to go out too."

"Right. I know and I'm glad for you, that you're, you know, that you're...moving on."

"Cate!" He smiles and cuddles me in his arms. "I said it was a date, I didn't say that I was bedding her."

"You don't owe me any explanation, Giles."

Still holding me he says, "And I'm not giving you any." He gets up. "Now do as the nice doctor ordered, take the meds she prescribed, get some sleep, let them work tonight, and call me in the morning." He grins when he says that last part.

I hear my doorbell ring and voices in the foyer. After a short while Felicia comes back into my bedroom carrying a small bottle of antibiotics and a bottle of water. "Here they are. I took the liberty of getting you a bottle of water from your refrigerator." She opens the bottle and hands me two pills and the water bottle. "Take these now and you can read the label for the daily dosage tomorrow morning. Try to get some sleep."

After guzzling the water to wash down the huge pills, I tell Felicia that there's money on the dresser. She just shakes her head and smiles. "No problem. Just a few dollars."

Giles come back to my bed and bends to kiss me good-night. "I'll call you tomorrow. Felicia has early rounds in the morning so we'll be leaving now. Call me if you need me."

"Good-night. Feel better," smiles Felicia, patting my shoulder.

After giving me a sweet kiss and hug, Giles leads the pretty Felicia out of my bedroom and out the front door.

Damn it, I know I shouldn't be jealous; hell, I *am* the one who started sleeping with my ex while Giles and I were still technically together! Giles never asked me why Will was back in my life again but I think he knew. Both Giles and I had gotten so involved in our respective jobs that we hadn't really seen one another for a couple of weeks but hadn't officially gone our separate ways. Then one night Giles unexpectedly rang my bell to ask me if I wanted to go to dinner and was met at the door by a towel-clad, bare-chested Will. Awkward for me you can bet. Even Will was visibly uncomfortable and felt compelled to tell Giles he thought the person ringing my bell was a delivery man from the Thai place nearby. He then asked Giles to stay and have something to eat with us. Giles declined Will's offer and was very gentlemanly about the whole embarrassing situation.

I shouldn't be jealous of *him* dating again, but I am. What's wrong with me? When I was with Giles, I dreamed about and lusted after Will. Now I'm with Will I have a craving for Giles. Maybe it's the fever, maybe I just needed a little TLC; more likely I'm just acting like a jealous bitch. I don't like the bitch idea and put my ideas about Giles down to my feverish state. Snuggling down into the blankets, I fall into a sleep that has Will, Giles, Felicia, and me playing a tennis match. In my dream Felicia is still dressed in her lovely cranberry-colored dress, this time with matching sneakers, and telling me to please take the medicine like a good girl. Then she stops playing and smiles at me.

"And please don't worry about Giles. I promise I'll take good care of him."

Seagulls and the sound of waves awaken me. I must be on a beach, the waves sound close. Nice, so nice. I love my city but there's a part of me that longs to live in Hawa'ii or even the classy west coast of Florida. Waves, warm sun, seagulls, and Will; a perfect combination.

The gulls are getting noisier and I open my bleary eyes to sunlight coming through my draperies. It takes me a few seconds to remember that the gulls and waves are the new ringtone I put on my cell phone.

"Hello," I sound horrible, scratchy throat and stuffed nose. "This is Cate Harlow."

"Cate, this is Edward Penn, Jennifer's fiancé. I'm sorry to call this early but you did say that we could call at any time if we heard from that...hit man."

I glance at the time on my phone. It's six-ten. I struggle into a sitting position and finish the bottled water left on my nightstand to clear my throat.

"You've heard from him? Phone call?"

"No, Jennifer received a note from him. It was left at the front desk of our high-rise last night. The manager gave it to me when I went down to get the paper. I'm an early riser, you understand. Comes from years of following the overseas stock markets."

"Where is Jennifer now?"

I am awake and trying to get out of bed. The room spins a bit as I put my feet on the floor but I stand up without too much trouble.

"She's in the bedroom getting dressed. We want to talk to the police."

"Mr. Penn, Edward, I can be at your place in a half an hour. Keep Jennifer inside and away from windows. Let me talk to her first before you call the police."

"All right, Cate. I'll do as you suggest but please do hurry. Jennifer is terrified and so am I. Please hurry."

I'm walking to the kitchen and holding the phone next to my ear. "I'll be there in thirty minutes, Edward, just hang tight."

I shake out the dry cat food my two lovable kitties get in the morning and change the water in their bowl. Then I go to take a quick shower sending up a prayer that I'll have time to stop for a Timothy's coffee on the way to Jennifer's.

CHAPTER 11

OUTSIDE THE LOBBY of the genteel, slightly age-shabby high-rise where Edward lived alone and where he and Jennifer now reside together, I pop one of the antibiotics prescribed by the lovely Dr. Felicia and take a huge gulp of Timothy's hazelnut coffee made cool by the large amount of créme I put in it. I feel horrible and I walk a bit wobbly from the parking garage to the shining glass doors of the building. The building itself borders the 19th precinct, Will's police domain. I know this area well.

The doorman gives me a look that says he thinks that I'm nursing a hangover, certainly don't belong in the building, and is reluctant to let me in. I can't worry about what he thinks so in my most proper voice I say, "I'm *expected* by Mr. Edward Penn and his fiancée Ms. Jennifer Brooks-Warren. Please be so kind as to buzz their condo and inform them that Cate Harlow is here." Myrtle would be so proud of me.

Still looking at me askance, he does what I ask. From the conversation on his end I gather that he is obviously being told to send me up immediately, because as soon as he replaces the receiver near the door, he admits me without another word.

My feverish swollen eyes are hidden by my sunglasses and my hair is in a droopy ponytail because I didn't have time to wash it. I know I look like hell but I want to see what the note says and if there's a possible clue to gain from it.

The private elevator lets me out in the foyer of Jennifer's apartment. I've always wondered what it would be like to have my own private elevator zip me straight up to my own place. It feels so elegant.

As soon as I step forward I see Edward coming to greet me. "Thank God you're here," he says with concern. "Jennifer is thoroughly frightened and I don't know what to do. Her doctor has prescribed something to calm her but they make her drowsy and she refuses to take anything until she speaks with you. May I offer you something?"

As answer to his offer I hold up my large container of coffee and, without any preamble, ask for the note that has gotten Jennifer so upset. I am not in the mood for social pleasantries just now. I feel horrible and just want to do the job I was hired to do. Edward slips his hand into his elegantly tailored pants pocket and gives me the folded note.

"Has anyone but you and Jennifer touched this paper? The building manager maybe?"

"No, the note itself was in this sealed envelope. Here." He put his hand in his other pocket and produces a plain white envelope with Jennifer's full name printed on it. "I assume other people touched the envelope but not the note itself. I gave it to Jennifer and we opened it together."

I open the note and read it. Anyone knowing Jennifer's situation would know what the words imply and it is chilling.

Have you made arrangements yet?

Simply printed with thin black marker. It's a sinister message. I can understand why Jennifer and Edward are so upset. The Eliminator is asking Jennifer in a subtle way if she's made any arrangements for her funeral. The police do need to be notified but this note and the one she showed me in her office, the one that came with flowers and read, *"Can't wait until your birthday. Twenty-five is special"* are not necessarily threatening. Any savvy police detective, including the astute Will Benigni, would tell you the notes *seem* as if they came from someone who is eager to come to a birthday party and who wants to know if everything for the party has been arranged. It's a delicate situation, they'd say, when the threats are not overt enough to warrant police protection.

Jennifer comes out of the bathroom holding a cold cloth to her head. She looks at me and offers a small smile. She is a stunning woman and even in a crisis, still manages to look beautiful. Edward takes her hand and leads her to a chair.

"How are you holding up Jennifer?" I ask walking over to her and sitting opposite.

She gives me that small smile again and says, "Not so good, Cate. Thanks for coming so early."

"Not a problem, Jennifer. Let's see what I can find out." I turn to Edward. "Did anyone see who delivered this note? The building manager or the doorman?"

"No, I, no, I don't know. I didn't ask."

"Okay, I'll ask the building manager before I leave. Is he still here?"

"Yes, he is on duty until twelve."

"His name?"

"Paul Demaret. Shall I call him?"

"Yes, but tell him that I'll see him on my way out, preferably in his office. Also tell him that I'd like to speak with the doorman after I talk to him."

"Of course. I'll do that now and I'll make a call to the police as well." He looks at me and Jennifer. "I'll use the bedroom phone so you can talk to Jennifer without disturbance." Edward Penn kisses his fiancée gently and leaves us alone.

"You know what the message means, don't you, Cate? He's asking me if I have my affairs in order before I die, before he murders me."

I nod absently. "I won't lie to you, Jennifer; the message is pretty clear to you, Edward, and me. We can bring this to the attention of the police and ask for their help but without an outright threat there's not a lot to go on. Remember, cops deal in facts, so it isn't that they won't necessarily take it seriously but the fact of the matter is that there is no threat, written or otherwise. "And, Jennifer, the arrangement for the hit was made by you two years ago; they'll assume that this man has taken your money and forgotten about doing the job. You have to remember that the police will be very leery of the fact that you ordered the hit on yourself. They'll send a car to patrol this area but without a solid threat it isn't a real priority."

"So my time is almost over." She says this without emotion, just quiet resignation.

I get up, walk over to her chair, and kneel down in front of her. "No, listen to me, Jennifer. I have the best security team in New York City keeping tabs on everything that goes on here. After I'm done talking with the manager and the doorman, I'm going to call Sec.Co to double the security detail. Believe me, Jennifer, I'll find this man and I'll do everything in my power to stop him from...harming you." I hesitate over the word "harming" and she knows it. "Killing" is the word that hangs unspoken in the air between us. I close my eyes and ask her with as much confidence as I can muster, "Can you trust me to do that?"

"Yes. I have to trust you, don't I? What other choice do I have? If I leave here, he'll find me again the same as he found me after I changed my appearance. He will find me, of that fact I am certain. You believe that too, don't you?"

She looks at me for confirmation when she says that and I just nod my head yes. He'll find her. "Leaving won't really benefit you and it won't stop him, Jennifer. Staying here and letting me find him is the best thing to do right now."

Edward comes back to the living room; we talk about having the police come to their condo but Edward tells me that he'd rather meet them in the lobby so as not to upset Jennifer any further."I can handle this, Jennifer," he says gently taking her into his arms.

As I leave I whisper to Edward that after they talk to the police, he should give Jennifer one tranquilizer just to help her relax. With that done I leave the condo and head down to talk to the manager and doorman. I'll call the security team on my way to my office. The manager and the doorman know nothing of how the envelope with Jennifer's name on it arrived at the front desk. I ask if someone hand-delivered it because there's no stamp on it but neither man remembers anyone, male or female, coming in to deliver the note.

The doorman is amazed that the woman he thought was not fit to enter the building is a private investigator and treats me with a new respect. The manager shows me the security cameras. It's very clear that there's no one entering the building except the condo owners. A couple of packages are seen being delivered but the doorman swears he knows the delivery service drivers and I have no cause to doubt him. The only other person who showed up late yesterday is the mail carrier, a short, muscled woman in her fifties.

"Where was the envelope when you found it?" I ask the manager.

"Oh I didn't *find* it. We offer a service here; tenants can either opt to have their mail brought up to their apartments or ask that we keep the mail for them in personal mail cubicles behind the front desk and they'll pick it up sometime during the day." He gestures behind the desk to a small grouping of varnished wooden boxes affixed to the wall, many of them containing mail.

"Mr. Penn, Ms. Brooks-Warren's fiancé, had asked that both their mail be kept in a cubicle. They usually pick it up in the late afternoon but neither one of them came down last night to pick up the mail. When Mr. Penn came down early this morning for the paper. I handed him the mail from yesterday."

"A lot of mail?"

"Just the usual. I guess some bills and of course a circular. In fact, now that I think about it, the letter must have fallen out of the circular when Mr. Penn dropped the mail. I remember that he had to bend down to retrieve everything. He held that particular envelope up to the light after he had picked the mail up. I could see it clearly, a plain white envelope with Ms. Brooks-Warren's name on it. Of course I would have picked the mail up for him but I was..."

"A circular from what store?" I interrupt him abruptly.

He looks at me a bit distastefully for the interruption and thinks for a moment. "Oh not from any *particular* store. It's those advertisements from many stores. You know; the stores offer coupons and the circulars are delivered to everyone. You must get some in your own mail. I know I do. My wife likes a few of the coupons; says we save a lot of money by using them."

I do remember getting coupon circulars in my mail. Usually I just recycle them on Thursdays when the trucks come around for paper and plastic. The Eliminator must have known where the circulars came from, when they would be sent out to be delivered to this block, and was able to put an envelope inside the one with Jennifer's name on it. Nice work and almost untraceable.

"And the mail carrier," I ask the doorman. "Trustworthy?"

"Carmen? Been delivering mail here for the past eight years. Yeah, I would trust her with my life. Very professional and *always* on time. You can set your watch by that lady."

I thank them both for their time and make a note to come back around 5:30 when Carmen delivers the mail. On the way to my car I call Adrian at Sec.Co. but they've seen nothing out of the ordinary.

"No strangers hanging around, only regular tenants entering the building. Not even many visitors. It's an old building, Cate, for older people, not a lot of activity there. I don't know why your very attractive client wants to live there. Sort of boring if you ask me."

"Maybe she likes the quiet, who knows? Anyway thanks Adrian. Double the detail and call me if anything comes up."

"We will."

I drive back to my office hoping that I can take a nap on the sofa there and then get some work done on this case.

⁂

Having reached my office around 8:00 am, I am able to sleep for almost ninety minutes before I hear a key turning in the double locks of the antique oak door that proclaims, *Catherine Harlow, Private Investigations* on a shiny brass plaque. Myrtle walks in with her usual bustle carrying a bag from Timothy's. I smell coffee and bagels.

She walks over to me and gently shakes my shoulder. Taking in my disheveled appearance she purses her lips and says, "Don't tell me you slept here all night, Catherine. You look horrible. Here, have some coffee and a nice bagel, then please go home to take a shower and get freshened up. I'm more than capable of holding down the fort when you're not here."

I grab the coffee and bagel. The bagel is thick with butter and cream cheese just the way I like it and I am so grateful to have it. I feel queasy from having taken the antibiotics on an empty stomach. I eat and drink like a starving woman for a few minutes while Myrtle tidies up my desk, throwing away my used coffee container from this morning and empty bag of chips from last night.

The food and coffee make me feel a little better and I get up to stretch. Myrtle is feeding the turtledoves outside on the fire escape. I go over to give her a hug. "Thanks Myrtle."

"Did you pull an all-nighter, honey?" she says turning toward me. "That's not exactly healthy." She sighs deeply as she says this.

Her voice is so maternal and concerned that, as awful as I feel physically, I have a hard time not bursting into tears. I decide to not tell her about being sick, having Giles come over, and my jealous bitch feelings. She'll only worry about me and I don't want to add to whatever problems seem to be on her mind right now.

"Yes, I know and maybe going home to shower and change will be a good idea. I'll be back later, okay? By the way, how was the bridal shower?"

"Very lovely. I felt sorry for the bride-to-be though."

"Really? Why?" I ask grabbing my bag and sunglasses.

Myrtle gives me the top-of-the-glasses stern teacher look as if I should know what she means. "She'll be promising 'for better or for worse', won't she?"

"Part of the wedding vows, Myrtle."

"Yes, well, unfortunately you never can predict when the 'for worse' will happen in a marriage, now can you?"

And on that disconcerting note, I go out the door of *Catherine Harlow, Private Investigations*.

CHAPTER 12

AFTER ANOTHER AUGMENTUM antibiotic followed by a hot shower and a shampoo, I feel considerably better. Sleep though is a priority so I call Myrtle and do what I usually do when I don't want her to know what I'm doing; I lie. I tell her that I have to be out of the office on a case and that I'll be in around four o'clock.

"Anything that needs my immediate attention?" I ask guzzling a large glass of orange juice and seltzer.

"No, we're fine. Just received an update from that woman, the one who wants you to follow her baby-boy to make sure he's not being corrupted by the wrong kind of girl. That's tonight by the way. Says he *said* he was going to meet a friend at seven thirty concerning an art project on the Renaissance at the Metropolitan Museum over by Eighty-First Street and Fifth Avenue."

"Okay, tell her that I'll follow her son to see if he's being naughty. See you later this afternoon."

It's a quarter to eleven. I set my cell phone alarm for three o'clock and, bundled in a large, soft throw, go to lie down on the couch. A couple of hours of sleep and I'll be fine.

Just as I'm dozing off my phone rings but I let the answering machine pick up. When I hear the voice I'm glad I did.

"Catherine, this is Giles. Just wanted to see how you're

feeling. I can only hope the fact that you haven't answered the phone means that you're sleeping as you should be. Feel better and call me later."

"Oh sleep! it is a gentle thing,
Beloved from pole to pole!
To Mary Queen the praise be given!
She sent the gentle sleep from Heaven,
That slid into my soul."

So wrote Samuel Taylor Coleridge, and the "gentle sleep" he mentions has done me a lot of good. Of course the antibiotics have helped tremendously. Felicia was right; I do feel better. Glancing at my watch I see that my morning has turned into afternoon and I have to go shower and wash my greasy hair.

Since I feel better I decide to dress in a little more sophisticated manner. A light blue silky top paired with navy pants suit me well. A pair of navy sneakers with pink laces completes my outfit. I'll be in a high-rent district later tonight and I don't want to stand out. Melissa, who has her own high-priced pied-á-terre, told me that the trend for women who live on Fifth Avenue is to wear expensive designer sneakers after five o'clock. They dress elegantly and have their sneakers match their outfits. Comfort and class.

My first stop after my office will be outside Jennifer and Edward's building to speak with the *"Always on time, you can set your watch by her"* Carmen the mail carrier. First I have to check with Myrtle for any new business or messages. I also need to take a picture with my phone of the boy I'll be surveilling later tonight.

"Well *you* look nice, shiny hair and all," exclaims Myrtle with raised eyebrows when I come in the door. "Hot date later tonight? I thought Detective Begnini was out of town until Friday."

"He is and I don't have a date at all unless you count spying on teenage lovers as a sort of pseudo-date. I'll be on Fifth Avenue and Eighty-First Street doing my spying and want to blend in with the museum crowd."

"Oh, that's right; I forgot about that." Now that's odd because Myrtle forgets nothing. "Well, you do look very pretty, Catherine," she says looking annoyed with herself. What's up with her and Harry? I have to check it out on my own since she doesn't appear to want to discuss any personal problems with me.

"Messages?" I ask.

"Just one from Jennifer Brooks-Warren. She says to thank you and tell you that Edward told her the police were very polite but that you were right about them dealing in hard facts. Unless an actual crime has been committed, it seems their hands are tied. Edward did tell her that the only thing they can promise is to have a patrol car passing by the condo more frequently. She said she'll speak with you tomorrow."

"Okay, thanks." I take everything I need and head off to speak with a mail carrier.

Just as the doorman said, a woman pushing a wheeled mail cart arrives at precisely five-thirty. She and the doorman exchange a few pleasantries as she looks in her cart for the tenants' mail. I step out from the shade of the building and approach her.

"Carmen? I'd like to speak with you if you have a minute." I hold my PI license up for her to see. She looks startled for a moment but it passes quickly.

"I cannot stop," she says politely but with a distinct Hispanic accent. "I'm working and I make sure that the mail is delivered on time and that my route is completed on time also. You can see me back at the post office tomorrow morning. Here is the address." She pulls a card from her shirt pocket and hands it to me.

"No, Carmen. What I have to ask will only take a few minutes of your time."

She pushes her cart of mail to a stop outside the glass doors of Jennifer's building and looks at me again. It's possible that she's here illegally or has someone living with her who is. I put her possible fears to rest.

"Carmen, I'm a private investigator working a case for someone in this building. I'm not from Immigration if that's what you fear."

Carmen pulls herself up to her full height which is just about five-feet tall. Glaring at me she says clearly, "Immigration? I am a full citizen of this wonderful country. I am a naturalized United States citizen. I have nothing to fear from agents of immigration."

I feel uncomfortable for having assumed that she is an illegal. "I'm sorry; it was wrong of me to imply that you are an illegal. It's just that you seemed so hesitant to speak to me that I just wrongly assumed that immigration was the reason."

She relaxes and even offers me a smile. "No, miss. It is not immigration I worry about; it is making sure that I finish on time to be able to pick up my hija, my daughter from the music program she attends from three to six thirty every day after school. She is just twelve. I do not want her to walk home alone. I must finish my route by six o'clock, no later. Please understand; I worry about my girl."

Oh shades of Mom and Dad! They made sure that I was always picked up from school, from tennis practices and matches—from just about any activity I was in so that I didn't have to walk home alone. They relied on themselves, my grandmother, Nonna Rita, and parents of friends. I was well protected from the "real" world even though there were certainly times I resented it.

I assure Carmen that I do understand and tell her about my own parents always being there to make sure I got home safely. Then I tell her I have only two questions. "You can continue working while I ask them." She nods assent and continues her work pushing the cart inside the foyer, taking the mail for the building out in a bundle and bringing it to the manager's desk where she greets him politely and quickly. We go outside and she begins to push her cart to the next building while I trail along.

"Did you see anyone down by the mail office who wasn't supposed to be there this week? A stranger kind of lurking around the mail bins?"

She thinks carefully before she answers then shakes her head. "No, not on my shift, I didn't."

"Anyone come near your mail cart while you're on your route? Could something have been slipped inside a circular?"

"Oh no, I always take my cart inside the buildings, never leave it alone. There are credit card bills, bank statements; I can't have anyone stealing these important papers. Also, miss, there is no one who walks near enough my cart to be able to slip something inside it. I would know."

I thank her for her time and turn to go. "I hope your daughter knows what a good mom she has, Carmen."

She smiles at me. "Yes, I think she does."

Walking back to my car I think about the elusive hit man and where he might be at this moment.

CHAPTER 13

HAVING TREATED MYSELF to a late lunch of hot chicken soup thick with spicy pieces of chicken and celery at a local Indian restaurant, I drive over to my friend Melissa's place near where I will be doing my stake-out later today. The only space I can find is two blocks away. Once parked I call Melissa's number. After five rings she answers.

"Hello, this is Melissa." Her voice is smoky and sounds like soft crystal chimes.

"Hi Melissa. Are you busy? I'm right near your place and if you'd like some company, I'm available."

"Of course, Cate. It'll be good to see you. Come on over. I'll buzz you in."

I pop another antibiotic and walk the two blocks to Melissa's pied-a-terre. I haven't seen Melissa since the night she helped turn me into a 'lady of the evening'. The walking does me good; I'm tired but feel better than I did last night. What a difference a little sleep and the right medication can do!

Melissa buzzes me in to her brownstone and I climb the stairs to her second floor where she greets me. Dressed in a silky flowing caftan she looks as perfect as always and offers me some mint tea she is making.

"Are you going out tonight, Cate? That blue looks lovely on you," she says surveying my outfit approvingly.

"Stake-out," I respond. "I'll be tracking Romeo and his Juliet tonight around seven o'clock." I explain about my client and her concern that her son might be with the wrong type of girl.

"Poor boy!" Her laugh is like bells tinkling. "Well, who knows, maybe his mother is right to want to protect him. A wrong move could mess up his life."

We talk about what classes Melissa is taking for the upcoming summer semester, basic info on my hit man case, and Will. I hesitate, then tell her about Giles and Felicia and the jealous bitch living inside me. She smiles and tells me that's normal and not to hate myself for simply being human. "You're probably better off with Will, for now at least, but there *is* something about Dr. Giles Barrett...Don't over think it, though."

Finally I tell her about my concerns for Myrtle and she listens sympathetically, offering some simple advice to let Myrtle talk to me only when she's ready and wants to talk.

"Don't ask her too many questions, Cate. Let her be the one to initiate any talking. Obviously she is worried about something concerning her and Harry but let it go for now."

I sigh. "You're right on all counts. So...what's going on in your life, Melissa? Any new events to attend?" She goes to openings of art galleries, museum galas, and all the glamorous events most people can only dream about. I live vicariously through her social life.

"Well, there is the Met's gala next week. I haven't decided what I want to wear to it. If I can't find something in my closet I'll just have to go shopping again."

I smile and dream. Every year the Costume Institute Gala throws an event known as the Met Ball or Met Gala. It is a yearly red carpet evening hosted by Vogue magazine that celebrates the annual opening of the Metropolitan Museum's fashion exhibit at the Costume Institute. Two years ago Will and I were Melissa's guests and I still remember how very handsome and hot Will looked in his tux. I didn't look too badly myself in a low-cut jade-colored evening gown that cost me way too much and now hangs in a special garment bag in the back of my closet begging to be worn again.

"Come and help me look in my closet." Melissa gets up and leads the way to the walk-in closet off of her bedroom.

I could happily live in this closet. It is as beautifully appointed as an exclusive dress designer's shop with comfortable cushy chairs and pristine light oak floors. There are expensive plush throw rugs by the chairs. The back wall is nothing but an array of shoes stacked floor to ceiling according to color and event or activity. Beautiful outfits hang on rods inserted into another wall and shelves and drawers on the third wall hold everything from sweaters to lingerie. This is a real woman cave. For an hour Melissa does a mini fashion show. She looks great in everything she puts on but in the end she decides that a shopping trip is in order.

My watch says it's almost seven o'clock and I tell Melissa to let me know when she's going shopping. Looking at her shelves of intimate apparel, I feel a need to buy expensive silky lingerie for myself. It's my one weakness.

As she walks me to the door I ask her about her friend's memorial service. I see her eyes mist over before she speaks.

"It was a good one which honored his life and achievements. He is, was, a very decent, kind, and generous man. He should be remembered for that. I miss him."

"I'm sorry for your loss."

She hugs me and says, "So am I. Sorrier than anyone knows."

I head over toward Eighty-First and Fifth to begin my surveillance of two kids in puppy love.

᪽

It's seven forty and I'm into my second hot pretzel with mustard when I see three teens headed toward Central Park. Two teenage boys and an older girl who is maybe eighteen or nineteen years old or so, come down the steps of the Metropolitan Museum of Art. Pulling out the picture of the boy whose mom has hired me I determine that one of the boys is her son. Seems as if the fifteen-year-old Robbie prefers older women. They pass close by me talking and laughing as they make their way to the East Drive of the park. I follow at a discreet distance keeping them in my sight and dumping the half-eaten pretzel in a trash can.

The trio walks deeper into the park. I'm not fond of being alone in Central Park at night and I put my hand on the gun in my pocket just to know it's there. Obviously the teens don't feel the same way; maybe it's their youth. People tend to feel immortal when they're still teenagers.

After walking quite some distance from the entrance they finally find a spot hidden by thick bushes and trees and sit down on the grass. It's isolated and no one else is around. I can faintly hear their music from where I stand. My phone camera is set and ready. I feel like such a scuzzy creep for spying on these kids. All the three of them are doing is listening to music and talking. Nonetheless I aim my camera trying to get a good distance shot.

The sound of something nearby startles me and I turn around to see a possum hurrying into the brush behind me. When I look back I notice that there are only two teens now and they're lying on the grass in an embrace. The other boy must have left the lovers so they could be alone. Great. I guess Tiger-mom was right. Her baby boy is getting it on hot and heavy with this girl.

Okay, sorry, this can't be helped, kids, I think. Mom's paying me and I need the money. God knows I'm not independently wealthy. I sneak around to one of the bushes to get near enough to get a few good shots.

The two are really going at it so passionately that they don't even notice when I am in a position to snap my camera. I focus my lens to shoot. A picture or two of Romeo and Juliet given to Mom and I'll let her handle it. But instead of Romeo and Juliet, I come upon Romeo and Romeo. Tiger-mom's son and another boy. The person who left was the girl!

"You fucking pervert!" The voice is female.

My phone is knocked from my hand and someone punches me hard in my mouth. I taste blood. The second punch is to my chest but as stunned as I am, I still manage to grab the person's wrists, kick her hard in the shin, and wrestle my assailant to the ground.

"Let go of me you bitch! You weirdo bitch!" She tries to bite my hand but I kneel on her with all my weight. She stops struggling but not yelling. "Robbie, Tony! This sicko is taking pictures of you!"

"Shut the hell up!" I say through gritted teeth, feeling a wave of exhaustion hit me. I may feel better than last night but fighting an attacker is taxing my physical reserves. I let go and she scrambles back away from me as I stand shakily. I lean against a tree facing her, my hands balled into fists, ready in case she attacks again.

The two boys who were on the grass come running over to us. I pull my PI license out of my pocket. They gawk at it and seem on the verge of running away.

"Wait! You Robbie Samuelson?" I ask the boy who is the face in the picture I have from his mother.

"Don't answer her!" shouts the girl. "She's a fucking pervert!"

I turn to the girl whose stare is full of venom. "You've got a filthy mouth, little girl. As I told you before, shut the hell up. And I'm no pervert, I'm a private investigator hired by a Mrs. Andrea Samuelson to follow her son." I face the two boys. "Are you Robbie?"

The boy I address looks scared and the other boy puts his face in his hands and curses.

"My mother hired an investigator to follow me? Oh my God! How long have you been following me? Does she know about Tony? How long has she suspected me? Does she know I'm gay? Did she tell you to get some type of evidence? Oh my God! This is so fucked."

I shake my head at the way the three of them use such a colorful word so casually. Not that I haven't used it myself on occasion but with most teens it seems to be a favorite word used as an adjective, adverb, and noun.

The boy called Tony, the one who had his head in his hands suddenly looks up and grabs Robbie's shoulder. "No way, Rob. We can go away somewhere, maybe Europe or some place. You know, some place where they can't send you back, where they don't, they don't..."

"Extradite," I offer and all three stare at me again. "Extradition is for criminals. You haven't committed a crime. You may be getting upset for nothing. Maybe you're judging your mother unfairly. There's nothing wrong with being gay and she may be more understanding than you think."

"No, you don't understand. My parents, they're both unbelievably homophobic. They'd rather see me dead than know I'm gay!" He shakes his head. "Oh, fuck! She'll call my dad and he'll send me away to that military school he always talks about. She'll have Tony brought up on charges."

They're confused at the moment and that gives me an edge. I decide to take charge of the situation and tell everyone to just stop talking and pay attention. They're kids, I'm the adult, and hopefully I can get them to listen to me by acting in a calm decisive manner.

"Look, Robbie, I haven't given *any* report to your Mom, not yet. This is the first time I've followed you. She called my office last week and retained my services. I was told you'd be going to study with a friend at the Met and I came here to do the job I was hired to do. Truthfully your mother thinks you're seeing a girl and she's afraid that you'll get her pregnant and ruin your academic career. She found a text message from some girl on your phone."

They all stare at me for a few minutes and then Robbie begins to laugh. "She thinks I'm fooling around with a *girl*? That message was from... holy shit! It was from Tony's sister *Laurel*. Oh shit, that is so...did you hear that, Tony? Your sister! God, my mother doesn't know..."

The girl, Laurel, steps closer to me and says, "So? What now?" Her brother and Robbie look at me questioningly. I bend to pick up my phone and put it in my pants pocket. I don't quite know what to say to her. Turning to the two boys I say, "You kids hungry? There's a coffee shop a block from here."

"What?!" says the girl in disbelief. "You're fucking joking, right? You *are* a sicko!"

I have had enough of her viciousness and before she can react I grab her shoulders. "Listen to me, you foul-mouthed little jerk. I'm trying to think a way through this situation. Robbie's mother will be waiting for a report from me. I have to give her something. You curse at me one more time and I swear I will smash you in the mouth so hard you will swallow your teeth. I'm sick and I'm tired and you had better believe me when I tell you that that's a volatile combination for me. I don't give a damn what I do to someone who annoys me when I feel this badly.

"This situation has almost nothing to do with either you or your brother Tony but I am willing to take all three of you someplace quiet to get something to eat and talk this over. You understand me or not? Just nod yes or no because I sure as hell do not want to hear you talk again."

She nods yes and I release my grip. I tell them to follow me to the coffee shop and to order something quick and easy. I feel like a teacher leading a group of kids on a field trip.

CHAPTER 14

ROBBIE SAMUELSON is a nice, intelligent boy. Once he calms down and understands that I'm not out to make trouble for him and that his relationship with Tony is none of my business, he is ready to discuss his, and my own, problem concerning his mother.

"She is always after me to get good grades, to play certain sports that will appeal to college recruiters, and to be the person she thinks I should be. Very upper-class, you know? My parents are divorced and I live with my mom but my dad is still pretty involved in my life. He travels a lot for his business but Mom keeps him informed of everything I do. They both have very specific, set-in-stone goals for me. Trust me when I tell you that if either one of them finds out about me and Tony my life will be over."

"How did you and Tony meet?"

"At school. Tony is a scholarship student at our school." He looks at me quizzically and then asks, "Do you know what that is?"

I nod. Every prep school in the city has a program where high-achieving kids who can't afford the tuition can attend based on an academic scholarship supplied by wealthy alumni. The scholarships are vital to excellent students whose parents can't pay the exorbitant fees charged by the prep schools.

"Anyway, no one knows that fact except the headmaster, not even the faculty or school board know. Tony only told me because he knows he can trust me." He smiles at Tony who smiles back shyly.

"Why does your mom think you're dating Laurel?"

"Oh that. Tony used Laurel's phone to text me because his phone got stolen last month. We're, Tony and I, saving up to buy him a new one. I can't let my mom know that though." He looks at me pleadingly. "Please don't put that in your report, please." I shake my head and assure him I won't.

Tony and his sister are silent during our conversation. I'm guessing Tony is quiet because he is upset by what could happen if Robbie's mother finds out about them. His sister Laurel doesn't say a word. I think that she is still afraid of my threats concerning my fist slamming into her expletive-filled mouth if I hear her talk again.

In the end, after consuming cheeseburgers, fries, and chocolate drinks, Robbie and I reach a decision. I have to give a report to his mother; that's how I get paid. And I will truthfully tell her that Robbie is not fooling around with any girl; there's no danger of him getting stuck being a baby-daddy or of Mrs. Samuelson entering premature grand-motherhood.

I can tell her quite honestly that Robbie was with a boy named Tony and that they were indeed at the Metropolitan Museum of Art tonight. She'll assume that they were working on Robbie's art project. I will say that Tony's older sister was helping them. I won't mention anything else because it is immaterial to what his mother requested of me. One rule that I follow scrupulously is don't give non-essential info to a client especially if that info can cause harm to innocent people. Robbie is guilty of nothing more than puppy love.

I take him and Tony aside and counsel them about safe sex if their relationship does progress that far. Their young faces turn a bit red. Both boys thank me for my discretion and I pay the bill and get up to leave.

"Good-bye boys; don't stay out too late. Remember that tomorrow's a school day." Myrtle would be proud of me. I turn to the girl, "Good-bye, Laurel, you're one hell of a sister and a protector."

"You're not so bad yourself," she says grudgingly.

I watch all three of them walk away up Eighty-First street before I head back toward my car. I am exhausted.

Having turned off both my home and cell phones, I sleep until ten o'clock the following morning and find nine messages on my phone. Three from Will, one from Giles, two from Myrtle, and one from Jennifer Brooks-Warren. There's also an e-mail from TRUST. I go put on the coffee and listen to my phone messages first.

Beep

Will: "Hey, baby, call me when you get this message. I am bored out of my mind at this conference and I miss my girl."

Beep

Giles: "Cate, just checking in to see how you're feeling. Called your office and Myrtle said you seemed fine. I think I may have inadvertently let her know that you were sick; she sounded surprised. Sorry about that. I'll call later."

Beep

Will: "Hey baby? You okay? I called Myrtle and she said you were on a stake-out so I'm guessing you got home really late. Call me. By the way, how sick were you and why didn't you call me? Myrtle sounds concerned."

Beep

Myrtle: "Catherine, are you all right? Why didn't you tell me you had a virus?"

Beep

Will: "Okay, now I'm worried. I'm imagining you passed out on the bathroom floor with a fever of 103. Call me, baby."

Beep

Myrtle: "Catherine, if I don't hear from you, I am coming over."

Beep

Giles: "Catherine, Will called me to find out how you are. Call him, *please*. I said you were fine but please call me too so I can be absolutely certain that you're not still sick."

Beep

Jennifer: "Cate? Just calling to thank you again."

My return calls, all but Myrtle's, can wait. I grab my coffee, fix it the way I like, and sit down to watch the traffic outside my brownstone. Grabbing my cell phone I hit speed dial for Myrtle's mobile.

"Catherine! Where are you?"

"I'm home, I'm fine, and I didn't tell you I was sick because I didn't want you worrying about me. You worry enough. I'll be in later. I slept until ten and I feel so much better."

There's a long pause. "Next time, call me and let *me* decide if I have to do extra worrying about you."

"Okay Myrtle, I promise. I'll be in after noon."

Feeling very loved by everyone's concern, I sigh happily and check my e-mail from TRUST.

Possibility Duchovny in ur area

Right on, TRUST. That he is.

CHAPTER 15

CARRYING A LARGE coffee, I hustle up the stairs to *Catherine Harlow, Private Investigations*. My calls to Will and Giles were assuring but brief. I told them I had a report to send out and that I'd call later. Giles was fine with that, just told me to finish all the medicine and to call "Dr. Felicia" if I still wasn't feeling well.

Will was concerned and pissed that I hadn't called him but let it go and said he'd be back in two days. "Promise me that you'll take good care of yourself, Cate. And for Christ's sake, don't let me have to call *Giles* to find out how *you* are."

On the way to my desk I pass Myrtle who is looking intently at her computer screen. Without looking up she says to the computer, "Ah yes, Catherine has finally returned, alive and hopefully well." I ignore the comment.

"Is there any yogurt left, Myrtle?"

"Plenty. I just went shopping yesterday. You know, yesterday? The day before today when I had to find out through a third party that you were at death's door." She keeps staring at her screen. I grab a pomegranate yogurt and a spoon.

"Oh for God's sake, I was *not* at death's door! I simply caught some type of virus. I'm better now. Jeez!" I sigh loudly. "Any calls?"

"Just Tiger Mom and a company selling bogus land in Central Park." Her eyes are glued to whatever it is that seems to fascinate her. Curious I walk over to take a look. What I see is a picture of woman's face swathed in bandages. What you can see of her eyes and lips are a swollen mess.

"Crime scene victim? Domestic violence? Hit-and-run?" I say, wondering where this has occurred.

"Face-lift," says Myrtle. "That picture there is right after the operation. According to the surgeon's website, she healed in six weeks. Probably looks like your client, Jennifer Brooks-Warren looks now. I wonder where Jennifer got her face done. I may call and ask her."

This statement is very strange coming from a woman like Myrtle who acts discreet and professional with my clients. She'd never think to call any one of them with a personal question.

"Why the sudden interest in cosmetic surgery? You never thought much about it before."

Still staring intently at the screen as she goes from one picture to another before saying, "Maybe it's time for me to reconsider. I've been thinking of getting a fresher look."

"Seriously? Come on, Myrtle!"

"Yes, Catherine, seriously. And," she turns from the screen and fixes me with a stern look, "I definitely don't want to discuss that either, understand?"

I nod yes and walk back to my desk. It doesn't seem as if it's going to be a fun day at the office.

My report to Robbie Samuelson's mother is detailed and to the point without giving out Robbie's personal information. Only one small lie was added about Tony's sister.

"Mrs. Samuelson: As you requested I did a complete surveillance of your son Robbie on Thursday night. I can report that he was studying and working on his art project at the Metropolitan Museum of Art with a male classmate. No romantic girl-boy interaction. The girl whose text was on Robbie's phone is his friend's older sister who is an art major. She was there helping both boys to complete their art project term papers. All three left the area around 9:30 p.m. Robbie caught the bus back home and his friend and his sister walked a few blocks to their home. All in all I found no reason for you to be concerned about any girlfriend. There was none.

Robbie was doing exactly what he had told you he would be doing and was exactly where he had said he would be."

I attach the report to an e-mail telling Mrs. Samuelson that a paper copy, along with my bill, will be sent to her later this week and hit send. Then I print out the report and my expenses and bring both papers to Myrtle.

"Lunch?" I ask casually as I place the report on her desk. The dead silence in my office has been going on all morning and I hate it.

"Sure, as long as it's a salad, honey." Myrtle gives me a half-hearted smile. "Watching my weight."

"Well, okay then, let's go out for lunch. Let's take a long walk and find some nice place we've never been and grab a late lunch. There are so many places that have great salads; this is New York City after all. We can take the afternoon off."

"Well…"

"Oh come on, Myrtle, I'm the boss and I say we *should* take the rest of the day off. Besides," I add, playing on her concern for my health, "I *need* to take a long break today. I'm still not feeling all that great. A walk and a good meal will do me well."

My ploy works. She looks at me and smiles with a little more warmth. "All right, Catherine. The weather is perfect for walking and I think we should look for a restaurant where you can have some good hot soup and a healthy sandwich. Let's go."

Lunch is long and pleasant. More hot and spicy chicken soup with lots of chicken pieces and a BLT on toasted rye make for a delicious meal. I pop my last Augmentum with a glass of seltzer under Myrtle's approving eye. I feel a helluva lot better and I have to seriously thank Dr. Felicia when I can. Maybe she's a good match for Giles. I mention as much to Myrtle and tell her about my bout of bitchiness. Her response is, as always, practical.

"There's nothing wrong with feeling jealous, cookie. You and he had a good thing going there for a while. There was a time when I truly thought that Dr. Giles Barrett might be the one for you. I had my misgivings because I always felt, and *still feel* that you and Detective Benigni belong together somehow. Still, Dr. Barrett seemed to make you happy and he is a steadying influence on you, even now." She looks away then back at me. "You're back with Detective Benigni, with Will, now and I hope you two can make a go of it and that it's not all sex with no real substance. "Of course," she continues with her schoolteacher voice, "sex is normal and healthy and you're a young woman. If Will satisfies you in that area, then good for you, enjoy it."

I'm a bit shocked; Myrtle has never mentioned my sex life before. "Sex *is* important, Myrtle. We can't discount that. I really don't know if Will and I can have more than that. It's complicated. Lots of relationships are, but many times the sex aspect of it is good." I look at her before continuing. I don't want to go too far but this seems an opportune moment to find out what's been bothering her and Harry. "I mean, sex is healthy at *any* age, right?"

"I guess."

"Yes, well, um, I didn't want to say anything but since you brought up the topic of sex, you did mention that Harry has gotten a bottle of Cialis. It seems as if he's happy with *that* part of the marriage and wants it to continue."

Myrtle closes her eyes and puts her hand on her forehead. "My dear Catherine, stop. I did find the bottle of Cialis in his drawer but I have to tell you that Harry and I haven't had any intimate relations for over two months. Obviously the Cialis either isn't working for my benefit or its effects are being enjoyed by Harry with *someone else*. And Catherine?" she gives me her schoolteacher look, the one that has silenced scores of eighth graders over the years.

"Yes?"

"*This* conversation has come to an end."

CHAPTER 16

MYRTLE PUTS A CALL through to me while I'm driving on the Long Island Parkway. The word driving is a joke; traffic is a bitch, as usual; the L.I.E. is a virtual parking lot.

"Catherine, I'm putting through a call from a woman named Moira. No last name but she says you'll want to speak to her. Moira? Hmmm. That name sounds very familiar to me. Should I know her? A client, maybe? Anyway, here she is." The line clicks over to the call.

The only Moira I know is Moira Hollis, the woman who used the services of the eliminator to 'off' her abusive father. Now why is she calling me? I assumed that she'd never want to have anything to do with me after my late-night visit to her condo and thinly veiled threats. I hit ok on the phone button of my steering wheel.

"Moira, this is interesting. I never expected to hear from you again."

A cool but uncertain voice answers me. "Yes, I'm very sure you didn't...*I* certainly never expected to call you but I have some information that you might want for that case you mentioned to me. I couldn't stop thinking about that poor woman, you know, the one whose life is in danger, and how frightened she must be. Whether what she wanted done was rational or not, she doesn't deserve to die for her stupidity." There's a pause then she says, "Are you recording this conversation? You are a PI and what I have to say, I don't want recorded."

I assure her that I'm not recording anything and that she can speak freely. "It's just me, Moira. Go ahead."

"All right. I am sorry but I had to know. I know you told me that I was to forget that we ever met but after you hear what I have to say I think you'll agree that calling you was the right thing to do." She pauses and I hear her take a shaky breath. "Cate, I think I saw that man, the Eliminator, yesterday evening. I debated calling you but, after a sleepless night, I knew that I had to let you know what I overheard."

"Overheard?" I'm all ears.

"Yes. I was at a cocktail party last night held at the home of an older couple I know, the Ramsteins. It was a charity event for a women's shelter and I always donate bath linens and other items from my shop to local charities. Peter Karis was there; his wife is co-chair of this charitable organization. We see each other rarely but sometimes it is unavoidable and I do run into him. He's always kind and friendly to me. Oh if he only knew what he unwittingly helped me to do!"

I don't need drama so I say tersely, "Yes, go on."

"Peter was talking to a group of people and then I saw him go over to a man who was standing alone by the bar. The man turned and looked around the room very casually and then he looked right at me. If he remembered me he didn't show any trace of it at all. He did not seem as if he knew me but I knew that he was the man who...took...care of...my father. It was him but he was different somehow. His hair was darker and a bit longer too. He was wearing sunglasses."

Dark hair to change his appearance, sunglasses of course. Goes with the territory.

"Did he approach you?"

"Oh no, he acted as if I was a complete stranger."

"Is this it? You called to tell me that you saw him there? My sources believe he was in New York City three days ago, Moira.

Are you sure it was the same man?"

"Yes, yes I am sure, absolutely certain. I saw his eyes. When he was talking to Peter he took his sunglasses off and turned in my direction. I saw his eyes, those cold, blue eyes. I'll never forget those eyes. It was definitely him!"

I'm skeptical but need more information. "Moira, just because you saw him last night in Virginia doesn't mean that he's still there. I have it on very good intel that he's been around doing what he does best. My sources tell me that his last known job was in Georgia last month. He could be anywhere now."

"I think he talked about your case, about having to finish a job in New York City."

"How do you know this bit of info?"

She takes a deep breath before continuing. "After I saw him there I was so unnerved that I wanted to get away, just get away from the house where the benefit was being held. But I couldn't leave without telling my hosts. I was scheduled to make a presentation of my gifts. I wanted to ask if one of them would do it for me. I was going to say that I felt unwell."

"And?"

"Well, I couldn't find either one in the living room or dining room so I went looking for them. I searched the house and was about to go outside by the pool. I felt dizzy so I sat down in the library. That's when I heard Peter's voice and the voice of that... other man. They were coming toward the library. I should have made my presence known but I didn't. I hid."

"They didn't know you were there? How's that possible? The Eliminator would have searched the room."

"Yes, he did. But he didn't know about the door hidden behind one of the bookcases. It is a secret door that leads to a panic room. No one knows about it. I only know about it because of my father. Isn't that strange? There had been a series of break-ins in the Ramsteins' neighborhood. My father was their lawyer. When they went to him for legal advice on another matter and mentioned the break-ins, he suggested they have a panic room built. This was quite a few years ago and panic rooms were a new type of security for those who could afford them. And my father, for all that he was a bastard to his family, was very good at keeping client-lawyer confidences. He told them not to let anyone, not even their friends or relatives know of its existence. I was working part-time as his secretary that summer and overheard the conversation. My father never thought of me as anyone who would break a confidence. But he swore me to secrecy when I went with him to see the panic room.

"The room is completely concealed if you don't know where to press the entrance button. After you enter the panic room the bookcase closes tightly and locks. Believe me there's no way anyone would suspect there's anything but a bookcase there."

"So you were able to hide before they came in?"

"Yes, when I knew they were going to enter the library I quickly got into the room and the bookcase closed behind me. I heard the Eliminator going around the room checking everything. I nearly screamed when I heard him pause near the bookcase. He seemed to be examining something there for so long. Then he said that it was clear and told Peter to close and lock the French doors of the library. When that was done they began talking."

"What did you hear?" I'm maneuvering slowly to the next lane as I listen to her.

She takes a deep breath and says shakily, "The Eliminator said, 'Do you need a memento?' and Peter laughed. 'Of course I do. Make it his left thumb. He's got a mole on it. I want to know the mission succeeded.' He told him 'It'll be done by the weekend. I have a job in New York City in a few weeks and this new contract is a very interesting and lucrative one, a nice double dip.'

"Peter laughed again and said something that sounded like, 'You certainly know how to work it.' Then someone knocked on the door of the library and I heard Mrs. Karis saying that the presentations were about to be made and that her husband had better hurry. I heard Peter and that man leave. I waited for about twenty minutes before I felt safe enough to come out."

There's a silence on both ends of the call. Finally I ask her if she knew what the Eliminator meant by double dip.

"I have no idea. But...doesn't that usually mean to get something twice?"

"Yes, it does but we don't know if what he said in reference to a job has the same meaning. Did you hear anything else before they left the room?"

"The Eliminator, oh I hate saying that word!"

I tell her it's just a word to describe him and what he does. "Go on, Moira."

"He said there was a nuisance factor involved in his job up north and he had to deal with it. I don't know what he meant, but that's what he said."

I think about what she's saying. A nuisance factor; that can mean he knows about the security detail or intends to make sure Edward Penn is out of the way. It can also mean that he knows Jennifer retained a private investigator.

"Cate? I did the right thing by calling you didn't I? That woman doesn't deserve to die."

Traffic is moving at a brisker pace and I merge with it toward the fast lane. "Yes, Moira, you did the right thing by calling me. I'm on high alert anyway and this lets me know that I have to be even more vigilant. Thanks."

"All right, well, then, good-bye."

"Good-bye Moira."

I go with the flow of traffic letting my convoluted mind think about the Eliminator, the possible meaning of the words "a nice double dip," and the courage it took for Moira Hollis to call me.

I sleep fairly well that night. The exhaustion from the viral bug and strong antibiotics has given way to restorative sleep and I awake feeling good enough to go hit some balls out at the courts. I hope my tennis ace, Ani, is there. That girl gives me a solid workout.

I make coffee, feed my cats, and check my e-mail and texts.

I'm surprised to see a text message from Dr. Felicia, the beautiful internist Giles brought to my brownstone when I was so sick. It's a very professional one simply asking how I'm doing and telling me to call the office if I'm still not well. It's probably from one of her office staff. Myrtle sends text messages and e-mails out to my clients all the time although she much prefers sending a real letter.

Still, the message is nice to receive and to know that I have a doctor to call if I need one. My own doctor, or more correctly former doctor, is eighty-seven years old, still sharp as a tack but he retired last year. I've been self-medicating with over the counter cold and flu meds when the need arises. A couple of shots of Grey Goose vodka in a tumbler of cranberry juice helps a lot too. Maybe it's time I got a new doctor.

Maybe.

I'm walking back to my office after lunch when my phone buzzes. It's Jennifer.

"Cate! Help me. I'm so scared I don't know what to do! Please, please, please, I can't do this anymore, I can't wait for him to kill me. Help me! Oh my God! Please!"

"Okay, Jennifer, calm down. Listen to me. I'm texting my security people outside your place right now." Unlike its owner, my new phone can multi-task. I key in info to Adrian and his team to up their surveillance. "Are you alone?"

"Yes, yes I am! Edward went out a half hour ago to pick up my prescription. He said he was feeling claustrophobic. I—I know what he means. Help me, Cate, I'm so frightened!"

"I *will* help you. I'm on my way. How did he get in touch with you this time?" I pull my keys out of my pocket as I race back to my car. Damn it! Today there were no spaces and I had to park three blocks away.

"He, oh God, he, he ordered a, a casket! For me! Oh my God! A *casket*!"

I run down the street dodging mothers with strollers and

tripping over a couple of drunks lying next to buildings. Trying to keep my voice calm I ask Jennifer how she knows about the casket.

"They called me! This funeral home called me and said the casket I ordered was ready and they would keep it in their showroom for when it was needed."

"Jennifer, what is the name of the funeral home? What was the name of the person who called?"

"I don't remember! Cate, I don't remember!"

"Was that call the last one that came in on your phone?"

"Yes. No one else has called here. No one..." Then I hear her scream.

"Jennifer! Jennifer, what is it? What's happening?" A few tense seconds pass before I hear her voice again.

"I'm sorry, I'm sorry! It's the security people buzzing from downstairs. The noise scared me. That security woman you introduced to me, she's here. Should I let her up?"

"Yes, absolutely. Buzz her up now. When she gets to your place put her on the phone. I'm coming right over but I can't predict traffic and I want to speak with her."

I get in my Edge and race as fast as is safe down the street. There are delivery trucks blocking the street and pedestrians texting on cell phones not looking where they're walking. Twice before I get off my street I'm forced to slam on the brakes. Shit!

"Cate?" A calm, strong voice comes on the Synch system in my car. "This is Natalie. The place is secure and Adrian placed three additional people outside. No one will get in the lobby without being thoroughly checked out. We're all good here."

"Thanks, Natalie. I'll be there as soon as I can. Try to get her to talk about the call, see what info you can get her to remember."

"I'll do that. See you soon."

CHAPTER 17

TO THE AVERAGE person, the condo building where Jennifer and Edward live doesn't look as if it's being protected by armed and trained personnel but I spot the security detail immediately. A man drinking coffee lounging on a bench near the building, a woman at the corner texting on a cell phone, another woman and a man seemingly deep in conversation across the street; these are the professional security people from Adrian's service. If I can spot them, so can the Eliminator. At the very least it will give him pause before he tries to enter the building. A woman inside the building tells me to take off my sunglasses as she checks my face against a photo of me she has on her phone; Adrian has it all covered.

When I arrive at her condo via the private elevator there's a man standing guard and he nods at me in acknowledgement. Jennifer is sitting on the couch drinking a mug of tea, the teabag string hanging limply over the mug's handle. Natalie is on her iPhone talking in hushed tones.

"Cate," is all Natalie says by way of greeting as she nods toward a bedroom where we can talk in private. Jennifer just looks at me and shakes her head.

"How is she?" I ask when we're alone with the door closed.

"Not good. I'll stay with her today and tonight we'll have others here. We're doing eight-hour shifts. Her fiancé still hasn't come back and now she's beginning to worry that this hit man has done something to him. We can't locate him; he left the pharmacy about fifteen minutes ago. He's not answering his cell. Adrian has two of our agents searching the area but so far, we got zip."

"All right. Keep the schedule for the shifts. I'll check in with Adrian later. Any other calls come in on her phone after we hung up?"

"No."

"Okay, that's good. I'm going to check Jennifer's phone for the last number that came in. Let's see who really called here and if it actually was a reputable funeral home."

The call Jennifer received came from Luca Memorial Services. Arriving at their downtown office I find that they are not a funeral home at all; they are, as the manager politely tells me, "providers of services for those deceased and their families." In other words, they *provide* the families of the deceased with just about anything needed in their time of grief and confusion. From specialized coffins to urns that double as clocks for your mantle to quick-freeze cryonics of the dearly departed, to making arrangements for burial at sea, and carrying out a loved one's wish to have his or her remains sprinkled over a certain ocean or shot into space, Luca Memorial does it all and at a hefty price. I never knew there was so much money to be made from the business of death. Unfortunately they have no idea who ordered the casket for Jennifer Brooks-Warren. The order and payment was by phone.

"The name on the credit card was assumed to be a relative of the woman," says the solemn-faced manager handing me the invoice and sale data for *the product*. We're standing in what Luca Memorial calls the showing room. "It's really quite a lovely, lovely model," he sighs as he gently caresses the casket he insisted on showing me. "The product is called the Perfect Ruby Rest 0557," he whispers to me with something bordering on awe. His ghoulish enthusiasm makes my skin crawl. As caskets go I guess it's the best money can buy, but it, and what it is used for, are what bothers me. You'd think that as a private investigator I would know that death and an occasional dead body are pretty much part of the job but it still creeps me out. I'm not good with the dead.

I take the info he gives me but when I run the MasterCard number through my iPhone I find that the card was a prepaid one, the same as the other card used for the flowers, and of course the name, address, and phone number are fake. I expected as much. Thanking the manager and giving him my PI card I say firmly, "If anyone else calls concerning this matter, let me know immediately. And please do not call Ms. Brooks-Warren again. This is a horribly vicious game someone wants to play."

"Someone is playing a cruel joke on the lady?" the solemn-faced ghoul asks me.

"Cruel doesn't begin to describe it."

In my car I receive a text message from the security detail telling me that Edward Penn has finally been located. He says he took a walk to clear his head after having been cooped up in the condo and then went for a drink at a wine bar. The stress, it seems, is getting to him. Natalie had told me that when she isn't sleeping, Jennifer cries constantly and that Edward sits just staring out the window quite a lot. The horrible thought crosses my mind that this case has to end one way or another in order for anyone to resume a normal life. For Jennifer's sake I want it to end with the Eliminator being caught. I decide to stay in the neighborhood for awhile. There's a small trattoria a few blocks away where I can grab a quick, hot meal and hang around the area.

Around eight o'clock that night, I take my last surveillance walk around Jennifer's condo. I park a few blocks away and walk the streets four blocks in each direction from the condo building. Nothing unusual is happening and I certainly don't expect any surprises. This Eliminator is too professional to make stupid mistakes that will put him in someone's radar. The night is warm and it feels pleasant to walk. I think about Jennifer and Edward stuck inside their building. It's really not a good idea for them to venture out but I keep thinking that with Adrian's crew, Will, and me, maybe going out to that local trattoria might not be too dangerous. It would certainly relieve some of the tension in that condo. Jennifer's birthday isn't for a few weeks yet and the hit, according to the contract, is supposed to be on that day or shortly after it. Except for the fact that the Eliminator is playing psychological games with his prey before the kill, I would say that she's safe for the next few weeks. Sighing I head to my ride and go home.

Back at my brownstone, I find I have a very welcome, unexpected visitor; Will's back sitting in my living room, drinking a beer and watching a Yankees game. And I feel healthy enough and more than happy to see him. From the way he presses his body against mine, I know he's happy to see me too. He turns off the TV and leads me to the bedroom.

"Baby girl, sweet, sweet Cate." Will murmurs this into my hair while we're lying in bed that night exhausted after our marathon of sexual encounters. After being separated for a few days sex with Will is like a dangerous and erotic electrical charge. I lay with my head snuggled on his chest breathing in that heady male scent combo of sex, sweat, and body heat. His hands travel up and down my back and rest comfortably on my butt. I feel him press against me and know that in a few minutes he'll be ready for another round of sexual activity. I'm relaxed and ready for action. When it comes to relieving tension, sex is pretty comparable to whacking tennis balls against a wall.

Six forty-five has Will and me rushing out the door of the brownstone together but headed to different places. The workday schedule has taken over. Will wants to get to the gym and then head home to shower before having to give a nine o'clock report on his conference. I have to get to my office by seven-thirty for a very important meeting. Through Adrian's contacts, I'm meeting a man who used to be a very successful sniper for hire. Now in his late sixties, he's retired and works as a paid consultant for security firms such as Sec.Co and even the CIA. I'm hoping he may be able to give us a few pointers on catching the Eliminator.

At the outer door to my office building I see Adrian talking to a tall, tanned, well-built man with a shaved head. I am assuming this is the former sniper; he obviously works out and seems to take very good care of his body. He does not look like the stereotype of a sixty-ish male. His body looks rock-hard.

I greet Adrian who introduces the man with him simply as Dave. Considering that he was a gun for hire, I'm quite sure that's not his real name. So many aliases in the field of death and destruction. We all go single file up to my office where I unlock the deadbolt and we enter. Adrian has very thoughtfully brought three large containers of coffee.

The man called Dave looks around my office with the practiced eyes of a true sniper; clear and concise, registering every detail. Then he turns his gaze on me and, despite the morning's heat, I feel a chill. I offer my hand and after a brief moment he shakes it.

"Cate, I've told Dave here about the problem and what's been happening. He might be able to give us a head's up on finding this guy." Adrian is a former Navy Seal, sure of himself and confident. Still his voice and manner are completely respectful toward this former sniper, a man who has played God with human life.

Dave walks over to the couch and I notice that he seats himself in a position of protection. His back is to the wall and he is facing the door. The windows are to his immediate left. He can see who or what is approaching him and, if he had to do so, could take out anyone coming from either direction quite easily.

I'm pretty sure he's got a gun somewhere on his body.

"So you're going after the Eliminator." He says this as a fact. "You're not going to see him coming, not with all the surveillance in the world. This is guy is a Coast to Coast."

He looks at Adrian when he says this as if I'm not part of the conversation. Adrian feels obliged to tell me what that means. "A Coast to Coast is a..."

I stop him mid-sentence and say, "A hockey term for a player who carries the puck from his own net all the way to his opponent's and scores. In layman's terms this guy will get the job done no matter how many people try to stop him." I smile at Dave. "That is what you meant, right, Dave?" Dave looks at me coldly. "Well, let's hope he doesn't *deke*." I add, "That word means a fake-out, gentlemen. Comes from the word 'decoy' but then being hockey fans you both would know that term."

Adrian muffles a laugh with a cough and I see him looking at me admiringly. I'm pretty pleased with myself too since hockey is not my type of game. I'm more comfortable with the terminology of baseball and tennis but I've learned to talk sports with certain types of men like Dave. This guy is pulling the male superiority crap that men of a certain age and temperament used years ago to dismiss women as inferior. I have no time for male-dominated bullshit and Adrian knows it.

In the 1950s and '60s it used to be a time-honored male mind-game strategy to form a camaraderie by talking sports in meetings where women were present. Since most women back then didn't know a hell of a lot about teams and players, male colleagues did it to exclude women from important conversations. The sports talk formed a bond even between strangers who were male thus successfully cementing a possible business deal or other work-related actions. That their female counterparts may have been more knowledgeable about the actual business didn't matter; other men were loyal to the "sports" guys.

But those guys definitely underestimated the female mind and innate cunning. Women in formerly male dominated jobs such as law enforcement, medicine, and business quickly caught on and began learning and using the sports-lingo. Talking sports is fairly easy for me now. I'll mention something, one little thing about any sport that's in season or a player who's in the news, and I immediately become an associate member of the boys' club.

"I'd watch my ass if I were you," is Dave's response. "This guy is no pussy." I shake my head at this outright ploy to shock or embarrass me.

Leaning forward I look directly at him and say, "Then that makes two of us, Dave. I'm no pussy either and I always watch my ass."

Now that I've got his attention, I tell him to give Adrian and me any strategies for finding the Eliminator. He looks from me to Adrian and mutters a coarse comment under his breath that I'm pretty sure is disparaging to females in general and to me in particular.

"So far, what's happening is good and protective. I agree with the surveillance of the victim; that's a priority right now. But finding this ghost is not your biggest problem. Stopping him from completing the mission is. Now that might sound contradictory but it isn't, not really. The ghost has to be taken out of the equation. You have to eliminate the eliminator."

"And how do we do that if we can't find him?" I lean back in my chair still locking eyes with Dave.

"I said finding him is not your *biggest* problem, honey. I didn't say not to try. He's been here; you know it. He's playing cat-and-mouse with the woman. If his job is happening soon, you can bet that he's close by. I say when the hit is supposed to take place, you bait the trap."

I stare at him for a moment before it hits me that he wants to bait the trap, as he says, with Jennifer Brooks-Warren. "You mean put my client out where he can kill her? I don't believe that's an option."

Dave looks at me with a smirk. "Let me tell you a story, little *girl*." I let the intended insult go and he continues. "My grandfather was a shepherd in Romania. Stayed out all night, rain, shitty weather, darkness as black as coal on cloudy nights, guarding flocks of sheep. Every so often, there was a hungry wolf, usually a lone wolf, who would make a meal outta one of the sheep who may have wandered a little way from the rest of the flock. Now, whether you sell a sheep for slaughter or shearing, you make money. But a dead one means a significant loss of profit to the shepherd. You got to get rid of the lone wolf." He pauses and continues locking eyes with me. "You know how shepherds get rid of a scavenging wolf in the old world countries, little girl?

"When a shepherd wants to kill the killer, the wolf who's been slaughtering his flock, he does two things. He cuts his own arm, the fleshy part just above the elbow where the blood will drip easily.

"Then he smears his own blood on a lamb and ties that lamb to a stake just outside the confines of where the flock stays at night. Now why a lamb? Lambs are babies and, when they're taken away from the other sheep, they bleat for their mothers. They'll cry all night long and the sound carries.

"Why human blood? Wolves track by scent and human blood is pungent. The sound of the bleating and the smell of the human blood sends the wolf into a frenzy and he zooms in for the kill. The shepherd takes his gun, hides a short distance from the lamb and when the wolf comes..." Dave stops and learns toward me menacingly cocking his hand into a gun pointing at my head, "BAM!"

He pulls a make-believe trigger. "HE ELIMINATES THE ELIMINATOR." I don't flinch and he leans back in his chair. "Never once heard of the wolf getting the lamb before the shepherd got the wolf."

"Adrian? What's your take on this idea? Is it worth the risk? This Eliminator seems to be one step ahead of us in everything."

"I don't like the idea. My job is to protect the victim at all costs. What if, and I don't really care for this idea either, I put one of the women on the detail in Jennifer Brooks-Warren's place. Wig, clothes, I told you we have a woman working this who's the same height and build."

Dave grunts. "Won't work. This guy is no fool. He'll know."

"Look, Dave," I say annoyed, "Putting her out there like a lamb to catch this guy is insane. We may not even see him coming."

"You won't."

Adrian and I both look at Dave. "Then what's the point in putting my client's life in mortal danger? It doesn't make sense if we won't be able to protect her."

"Again you misunderstand me. I said *you* won't see him coming."

"And?" I say impatiently. He's dancing on my last nerve.

"You won't; I will."

"You want to be in on this case? You're offering your services?"

Smug smile and a nod. "Fifty thou, honey."

"We've got to discuss this with our client. Truthfully? I don't see her as wanting to go along with this live bait thing either. I'll let you know later today what will be needed, if anything, from you but, again, I don't see her agreeing to this."

Dave looks at Adrian and says he'll wait to hear from him later. This dismissal of my authority, simply because I am a woman, is too much for me. "Hey?! Hey, Dave? *I'm* the one you're dealing with here. No one else but my client has more say as to how we proceed with this case. Get that straight. You'll hear from *me*, not Adrian, one way or another by five o'clock today."

Dave gets up from his chair and walks intimidatingly around my desk to where I'm seated. When I fail to get up but stare directly into his eyes, he leans down close to my face and says, "Honey, did you ever wonder *why* shepherds are always *men*? Simple truth? You can't trust a *woman*. Because a *woman* will try to think of another way to save the flock. She'll try to use her brain instead of her gun. You'd see lots of slaughtered sheep then, honey." His smirking smile is like ice. "As for you and your case? Your little bleating lamb is as good as dead if you don't use my idea and services." I don't flinch and he backs away. As he turns and walks to the door he stops near Adrian and says directly to him, "You have my number. Call me either way."

I want to throw my hefty paperweight squarely at the back of his head as he's walking through the door but I control myself. He slams the door as he exits and I say, "He's in it for the money, that bastard. He just wants a payday. A fee of fifty thou! Where'd you get this son-of-a-bitch, anyway, Adrian?"

Adrian seats himself on my desk and nods. "He is a total shit, I agree, but he was highly recommended. Listen, Cate, speaking of money, my company hasn't been paid a cent yet. We've been following her for a month now. No down payment sent as I requested when we met them the first time, nothing. I thought you said she was loaded."

"She is loaded. I've seen her bank records." I stop. "Come to think of it, I have to ask Myrtle if *we've* been paid anything besides the retainer fee. I'll find out, Adrian, and text you. Besides that, what do you think of that guy's plan?"

"Too risky. Like I said my job is to protect her and I don't think that I can do that putting her in harm's way. But let me think about it, Cate. We might be able to use him, let me see."

I agree and we rattle off a few other ideas. I tell him about my plan to get Jennifer and Edward out for a night and though he's a bit skeptical, he agrees that the tension in that condo is explosive.

"Benigni coming?"

"Yeah, he doesn't know it yet but yes."

"Good. Haven't seen him in a few months. We were at the police academy together. Tell him I'm looking forward to seeing him even though it's not exactly a real social event." He smiles, grabs his coffee and leaves. It's going for nine-thirty and Myrtle will be coming soon. God, I hope she brings some of Harry's cheese tarts today.

CHAPTER 18

IF WE JUDGED a person's happiness by the photos in their home or on their social media we would tend to believe that everyone led a happy life. Look at sites such as Facebook, Twitter, Instagram, and all the rest: filled with nothing but happy, happy people. The smiles, the cuteness; everything's good, the we're-happy-as-kitties-with-catnip pictures.

But the smiling faces in pictures hide life's skeletons, the darker side of our actual lives. The smiling people are just for show, nothing more. They're not real. My brownstone has pictures of me with Giles; Melissa; birthday celebrations; restaurant outings; baseball games; my parents, Nonna Rita; and Myrtle and Harry. And even though Will and I have certainly had our miserable relationship bumps, the smiling, happy, even goofy pictures of us are still there.

When I was in Jennifer's condo last week, something struck me. I hadn't really let it settle in my mind because there was too much else going on and I was fatigued and on pretty strong antibiotics. But what I noticed was a lack of pictures. Okay, maybe it's because Jennifer doesn't want any pictures from her past to remind her of how she looked; that I get. But, there are none of Edward either. This was his condo before he met Jennifer, he's in his fifties so he did have a life before they got together. You would think that he would have some mementos of his past; a few pictures from his professional achievements, relatives, friends, vacations, but not at all. The only picture I did see in the entire condo was a recent photo of Edward and Jennifer posed together. Strange.

The doorman gallantly holds the door open for me and waves me through. He quickly buzzes the "Penn residence" as he calls it and I enter the elevator for the ride to their floor. The building manager and he know some of what's going on in regards to Jennifer and they're fascinated by the details.

I'm just here to check out the premises and talk to Jennifer. I need to gauge her mental status and if necessary, suggest having a doctor come in and examine her. The kind of stress she's been under takes its toll physically as well as mentally.

Natalie, Adrian's agent, is standing right in front of the elevator doors as they open. She greets me by telling me that Jennifer is resting but that Edward is available. I glance at my watch; it's eleven forty-five. "How long has Jennifer been resting?"

"She never got out of bed today except to go to the bathroom. Been like that for the last three days. Those sedatives she takes knock the hell out of her. I don't know if that's good or bad. When she's awake she cries a lot, but, still, I don't like how the pills affect her mind. Instead of making her calm, they seem to make her almost comatose and depressed."

I nod assent. Relying on pills to get you through life is dangerous and something that I avoid. When I was conked on the head last year during the McElroy missing person's case and had to stay home for three days, I did leg-lifts in bed and squats in the kitchen to keep myself mentally alert. Will had to almost physically restrain me from doing jogs around my brownstone. Staying comatose was not an option for me and I even secretly threw away the pain meds I was given because they made me groggy. A good over-the-counter pain reliever did a fairly decent job of keeping the pain a dull ache.

"Cate, what an unexpected pleasure," says Edward rising from the loveseat to greet me as Natalie escorts me from the foyer into the living room. "Jennifer's a bit out of it today but I'll go get her if you really need to speak with her." I raise my hand to let him know that's not necessary and shake my head.

"No, I can talk to you. I'm guessing that Jennifer is using

sleep to escape reality."

Edward looks down at the carpet for a moment. "So you know?"

"Know what? That she's taking doctor-prescribed sedatives?"

"That she is changing from a woman who loved life and took great care with her appearance to someone who doesn't care about anything anymore. It's almost as if she's giving up."

"That's a fairly normal reaction to the strain she's been under, Edward. The closer we get to her birthday, the more the reality of her situation sets in. I'm working on this, Edward; I've put all other cases aside and am concentrating on finding this hit man."

I look around the living room; there's just the one picture of Edward and Jennifer that I had seen before.

"You don't have many pictures of yourself on display, Edward," I say casually. "I'm surprised. A man like you who's been honored in business and traveled the globe should have some visual memories of all that—friends, colleagues."

Edward looks a bit surprised by my blunt statement. It seems as if he doesn't quite know what to say. Then after a brief pause he smiles at me in his sad way. "If it were up to me, I would have all the pictures of my life displayed. I *did* have a life before I met Jennifer, a very rewarding and successful one. But...well, you know that she wanted to start life brand-new. She has made the decision to leave her past behind and I can respect that. At the same time, though, she didn't want to see me..." He stops as if he doesn't want to say too much.

"She didn't want to see you what, Edward? You can tell me." I press gently. "You know it will be confidential."

Edward sighs and looks out the window. "Cate, it hurts me to say this, I feel very, incredibly disloyal even saying this but the truth is that Jennifer is a very jealous woman. A month after she moved in here she asked me to put the pictures away. She cried almost hysterically when she saw pictures of me with female colleagues. It was insane of course, to be jealous of my life before

I met her but..." He sighs deeply and continues, "She did not, does not, want to see pictures of me with other people from my past life. Jennifer wants our life to have started when we met, as if neither of us had a life before. I understand her need to be the one and only in my life right now. Sometimes her need to be constantly reassured that I love her and that she is all that I want is very exhausting. Of course that will change the longer we are together and she becomes more secure in the relationship. Also, after this frightening situation is...over, I believe she will be more accepting of the fact that I know other people and want to socialize more."

"I'm sorry, Edward, I didn't know any of this."

"Please don't repeat this to Jennifer, Cate. I don't want her to be upset any more than she is."

"Of course I won't say anything, Edward." To alleviate the tension which must be explosive in this condo I tell Edward about my plan for him and Jennifer to have a night out on Wednesday. "You'll be very well protected, Edward. Adrian's people and Adrian himself will escort you. I'll be there with Detective Will Benigni who is a decorated police detective. In fact his precinct is close by. We'll make sure that nothing happens. This restaurant has a back room, no windows or door, where we can have dinner and just relax. You and Jennifer need to feel like normal people."

I don't say that Jennifer's death day isn't for a few weeks yet, the day of her birthday, and that men like the Eliminator are sticklers for that contractual detail. I just tell him that we'll take care of everything.

"Cate, Jennifer will be so happy to hear this. We've both gone a little crazy in here. A night of feeling normal will be wonderful for her, for us. I'll tell her about it when she...wakes up."

"No, Edward, let me tell her. I have to set it up and make sure everyone is on board with this. I'll speak with her soon."

As he sees me to the door I tell a little lie, "You know, I'm not into photo displays very much. The frames and all, they're just dust collectors." Edward simply smiles and shakes his head.

Going down in the elevator I think about what Edward just told me about Jennifer being a jealous woman. Somehow she doesn't seem to be the type but then who knows? Maybe there's more fire in Jennifer Brooks-Warren than I know.

Back at my office I get a nice surprise; Dr. Giles Barrett is standing outside the door to my building. He greets me with a hug and long, moist kiss. "Catherine, how are you feeling?"

"Pretty well," I say catching my breath. Giles always was a good kisser and very good at all-day foreplay. My erotic catalogue of sex-gone-by catches me unaware.

"Good, that's good. So you're feeling better then, no relapse?"

"No, I'm feeling really well. Um, do you want to come inside?"

"Actually, Cate, I came by to see if you'd like to have late lunch with me. I have a court date at five so I have a couple of hours to spend some time with you. How about Enzo's? I have a bottle of wine in my car, that special merlot you like." He pauses smiling, "Unless you have pressing work with a case...of course I'll understand."

I debate his offer. Seriously there's nothing that can't wait until later or even tomorrow. The promise of a good bottle of wine with a lovely lunch at Enzo's is very tempting. My only problem is actually being *alone* with Giles; for a while there I was making a good bet with myself that we would end up together as a couple. We probably would have too if I hadn't given in and had my sexual itch scratched by the erotically charged hands and other body parts of the devilishly sexy Will Benigni. Still...why not spend an hour or so with Giles? After all it's only a lunch. I mean, what's the harm? I sigh deeply. Jesus, I can convince myself of just about anything! "Sure," I say. "Want to walk it?"

"Yes, that would be nice." He grabs my hand and holds it warmly as we go down the street together. On the way we pass

Bo the homeless man who actually isn't so homeless; he has a small place in the basement of an abandoned building not far from my office. It's warm and protected and I know he calls it home.

"Hey! Hi!" He hurries over smiling a grin with a few missing front teeth. Some day I'd like to get him to a dentist. The problem is that he's afraid of any and all people he thinks may take away his freedom. That includes doctors and dentists. Giles walks over to him and asks how Bo's friend is doing.

"Hey?" Bo calls his friend Hey because he doesn't know his real name. Bo says "hey" a lot. When he says "hey" I never know if he's saying hello to me or wants to talk with me about his friend. "Yeah, he's okay. He's stayin' by me now, I think. Yeah, yeah he is. Came last night, yeah. He might go away again, maybe Alaska or Mexico, maybe, but now he's here."

"Cate and I will bring you both something to eat. How about two subs?"

"Okay, yeah. Hey, hey can you bring the cheese things? I like those." Giles knows he means the mozzarella sticks and says he'll make sure Bo and his friend get those along with the subs and iced teas. We wave to Bo as we continue on our way.

Enzo's is always crowded but the owner finds us a table in the back away from the noisy street. Enzo himself pops the cork on the wine Giles has brought, pours us each a half glass, and places the bottle in a chill bucket. Then he takes our orders. I decide on steak pizzaiola and a Caesar salad. Giles gets shrimp scampi and penne pasta and orders the food he promised Bo he would bring back. Enzo leaves and we're alone. Giles takes my hand. "It's good to see you, Catherine." I smile and nod.

"So how is everything? You said you had to be in court today. New case?"

Giles breaks off a piece of Enzo's delicious brick oven–baked bread and dips it into the small dish of special oil and garlic sauce on the table. "Recent case, an exhumation request from Staten Island. A man was buried a short while ago and his daughter has been crying financial foul-play. Seems that her father left a very expensive painting, *Marie Madeleine* by Artemesia Gentileschi, to a woman his daughter says influenced him unduly. Says this woman had a perverted sexual hold on her father. Anyway, the painting's last estimate was for $200,000."

"Artemesia Gentileschi was one of the few famous female artists of the Renaissance. Nice gift!" I say. "Must have been very close friends."

"More than friends it seems. The daughter is claiming that the woman introduced her father to some deviant sex games, her words not mine, and that these games made her otherwise godly church-going father into a sex slave." I lower my eyes and smile at the words "deviant sex" and when I look up, Giles is smiling at me wickedly. Oh lord!

"Excuse me for asking this, but since when did testifying about an exhumation on Staten Island become the business of the NYC ME's office? Isn't that a local decision? I know you or a member of the state staff have to be there when the body is exhumed but why do you have to testify? Is there a hint of murder or something like that?"

"Not murder—that would be easy, but no. This case came from a colleague in Staten Island. He needs confirmation about procedure. Since I'm the chief ME, he called me. Long story, the man was in politics, had been a police chief before he retired to go into the political arena. He had his share of enemies but the original autopsy report showed nothing out of order. Massive cerebral hemorrhage, nothing to suggest foul play. And the man was hardly a specimen of health; well over three-fifty in weight, diabetes, and high blood pressure. The only foul play I can see was a man who didn't take care of his health. "

"So?"

"The problem is that the daughter insists incriminating evidence, sexually explicit pictures of her dad and this woman, were buried along with her father. She claims that the pics will identify this...dominatrix. The daughter's words refer to her as a 'perverted whore'. The will was worded so as to keep the identity of the woman secret but the daughter claims that an assistant funeral director told her that right before the coffin was closed, a woman came in and placed some photos in her father's jacket pocket. She only left after having watched the coffin lid being tightly secured. Daughter wants him dug up and the photos examined. Says she feels his sexual activities or relationship with said woman may have contributed to his death. Anyway, that's all I know. I'm just there to give an opinion on exhuming the body if there's enough evidence to do so."

"Well, good luck with this one. Sounds interesting to say the least." Our food arrives and we put conversation on hold for a while. Enzo is an epicurean artist and his food presentation has to be admired. Then the delight of actually eating it begins.

Over coffee and a chocolate shell filled with ripe raspberries, I tell Giles about my Jennifer Brooks-Warren case and all the strain this impending death sentence is putting on her. He agrees that the stress of it all can cause her to become disoriented and depressed. "She shouldn't be taking any heavy sedatives, Cate. Mild ones can do the trick just as well. Depression and heavy medication are a dangerous combination. While the mind and body aren't made to withstand unremitting stress levels for long periods of time, they're also not made to tolerate prolonged strong sedation."

I tell him about my plan to get her and her fiancé out of the condo for a night and he thinks that's a good idea. "Provided she's well protected, and from what you tell me she will be, this will have a beneficial effect on her state of mind."

I have an idea. "Want to come along with us to the restaurant? I mean you *are* a doctor, maybe it would be a good idea for you to come. You once told me that in med school, you were fascinated by the study of the effects of drugs on people suffering from depression. Check out her mood and all. I believe her fiancé's doctor saw her once and prescribed some sedatives. I've suggested having him or another doctor come to examine her in her home, but Edward, the fiancé, says she won't let anyone come to see her. As long as she has her sedatives she feels she doesn't need to see a doctor. How about it, Giles?"

He doesn't answer right away, just spoons the rich concoction of chocolate and raspberries into his mouth and contemplates what I'm saying. I've always known Giles to choose his words carefully and answer with honesty. Maybe I am asking too much of him. After all there is an element of danger in the restaurant outing. Every one of us, with the exception of Jennifer and Edward, will be armed. I don't think Giles even owns a gun, let alone would know how to fire one accurately. He'll probably say no.

But his answer surprises me. "It would be a good medical experience, that's for certain. Drugs and depression can lead to something lethal. I hope her fiancé is monitoring her doses. She shouldn't have them in her possession; I'd be concerned about an overdose, accidental or otherwise." He sips his coffee and his look of concern for someone he doesn't even know touches me deeply. "All right, Catherine, sure, I'll come. You said Wednesday, right? Six?"

"Yes, six on the dot. Come early, though, parking's a bitch." I tell him who'll be there and look to see if the mention of Will's name brings a reaction but except for a small smile, he says nothing. I tentatively broach the topic of Giles and Felicia.

"How's Felicia? She really helped me that night."

"She was happy to do so. Have you called to thank her?"

I look around the restaurant before I answer. "Um, well, no. I have been meaning to, really, I have, it's just that I've been so busy with this current case and several smaller ones. You know how it is. And seriously I'm..."

Giles grabs my hand across the table and smiles. "Jealous? And that's okay, Cate. Jealousy is a very human emotion. God knows I've had that feeling concerning you and Will."

"Will? You're jealous of Will?" I guess I shouldn't be surprised but I am. Giles always seems so easygoing and laid-back. The kind of person who just understands what is and what isn't possible and goes with the flow of life. But I did hurt him; I know that.

"I *was* jealous of Will for a while, a long while I have to say.

When you and I were together I knew you still had some very strong feelings for him. And we were together for almost two years, Catherine. When you got back together with him, believe me, the jealousy was there. The irony is that Will and I could be friends if we'd met at another time and if it weren't for the fact that we both...well, you know. But, Cate, it is what it is. I'm not jealous anymore." He smiles again and squeezes my hand. "Not so much anyway. And I can take you out as a friend, a very well-loved friend and make myself be content with that. I do want you in my life." Over my protest he picks up the check lying on the table and hands the cash, plus a generous tip, to the server.

As we walk outside, still holding hands, Giles turns and says, "You've no reason to be jealous of Felicia, Catherine. She's a lovely woman, warm and intelligent, but we aren't seeing each other officially. Right now it's just a few comfortable dinners and social gatherings. Neither of us is ready for a commitment." Warm and intelligent; I feel a nasty prick of the green-eyed monster. I am such a bitch.

Back outside my office building we hand the large lunch to an anxiously waiting Bo. He examines it then holds it close to his chest as if someone might take it away from him. Life on the streets. Before he leaves to bring the food back to where he and his friend Hey hide from people and the elements, he tugs on my sleeve.

"Hey, hey listen. That lady, that doughnut lady. She was cryin', I saw her. She was cryin' when she was walkin' down the street. I like her. Maybe somebody kicked her or somethin'? Maybe she lost a puppy? You better check it out. That's what you do, right? Yeah, you do that, yeah. She was cryin'. She always gives me doughnuts! I like doughnuts. I hope she don't go to Mexico or Alaska. No, not Alaska. She's nice, that doughnut lady. Yeah, she's nice. 'Bye." And he quickly disappears down the street toward the rat-hole he calls home.

The "doughnut lady" Bo's telling me about is Myrtle. Inside my office I see Myrtle sitting at her desk with red, swollen but dry eyes and a look that warns me not to ask questions.

CHAPTER 19

"CATE HARLOW," I say distractedly as I'm checking my e-mail and instant messages. Myrtle went to the bank so I picked up the phone. I should have let it go to voice mail but there's something about an unanswered phone that gets to me. I know people who always let their calls go to voice mail and I can never understand why. Maybe that's the PI in me, who knows for sure? There are times when I want to say to complete strangers, "Answer the God-damned phone! It might be important!"

There's a pause on the end of the caller and I say, "Hello? This is Cate Harlow. Who's calling?"

"Um, yes, hello. Is this Ms. Harlow, the *private investigator*?" The voice sounds strangely familiar.

"You got it. Who's calling?"

"This is Konrad Jasinski. You gave me your card."

"Sorry, Mr. Jasinski, I give my card to a lot of people. You'll have to be more specific."

"Of course, yes, I'm Konrad Jasinski." Pause. "Luca Memorial Services? Do you remember me?"

Jasinski? Oh right. He wrote his name down on a piece of paper, which I stuck in Jennifer's file. I check my caller ID. It *is* the weirdo funeral guy. Even over the phone he gives me the creeps.

"Yes, Mr. Jasinski, I remember you. What did you want to tell me?"

"Oh, that's splendid. I had *hoped* you would remember me and our conversation about the Perfect Ruby Rest 0557 product?"

I sit down and look out the window at my small family of doves nesting in the abandoned flowerpot on my fire escape. I have to put feed out for them after lunch. I close my eyes and say, "Yes, I do remember you and that product very well, Mr. Jasinski." What I remember is how he lovingly stroked the casket as if he were its lover. "Go on."

"I'm so glad. I thought I may have dialed the wrong number." He clears his throat and continues. "Well, my call is about the Perfect Ruby Rest 0557. It is one of our most beautiful resting containers. You may remember the lovely lines and the smooth satiny finish? It is especially fit for a lady and I was wondering…" Jesus! I shiver. Is this guy trying to sell me a coffin? "Mr. Jasinski, are you giving me a *sales* pitch? Because if you are I can tell you…"

"Oh no, no, this is not a, what did you call it? Oh, yes, no, this is not a sales pitch, no, not at all. Well, not unless you are in need of one, of course. I would be glad to be of service in your time of need." His voice hovers like a hungry ghoul in a horror movie and I am annoyed.

"Mr. Jasinski, just *what* is this call about?"

"The Perfect Ruby Rest 0557. That is what I'm calling about, Ms. Harlow."

"What about it?"

"The one that was ordered for a Jennifer Brooks-Warren last week? Well, you gave specific instructions that we were not to call the lady in question so I'm calling you."

"Yes, Mr. Jasinski, but just what about the…product… warrants this call?"

"It was picked up."

"What?!" I'm on my feet. "By whom?"

"The Perfect Ruby Rest 0557, the one supposedly ordered by Ms. Brooks-Warren, was picked up last night, around eleven-thirty. I wasn't here myself but I saw the delivery book this morning that lists merchandise delivered or picked up. We at Luca Memorial Services *did not* deliver it, no. It seems as if it was picked up by a truck rental company."

"What's the name of this company?"

I hear a rustling of paper. "U-Move-It National."

A do-it-yourself haul-away company. Their trucks from eighteen wheelers to small pick-ups are all over the city. The Eliminator, from what I gather, has picked up the casket from Luca Memorial late at night when the regular manager and workers are not around. He only had to deal with one person, an office worker doubling as a night watchman. Still I may be able to find out where the casket was taken.

I ask Mr. Ghoul if he can get hold of the person who was in charge last night to come down to Luca Memorial today to speak with me. I tell him that I'll be down at his office later this afternoon. "Yes, yes, of course Ms. Harlow, I'll call him now. I'm sure when I explain the necessity of you having to speak with him, he'll be glad to accommodate you."

"Thank you, Mr. Jasinski. I'll be there at three." Damn!

After I hang up I think of Jennifer. She hasn't called me yet so obviously the Eliminator hasn't sent any message to her concerning the delivery of the casket. If there was a delivery I'd know about it, if not from a terrified Jennifer then surely from her fiancé Edward or Adrian's alert crew. I still haven't told her about the little outing I planned. I didn't want her to obsess about leaving her condo until everything was set. I check my watch; it's almost twelve noon. That means that it's been over twelve hours since someone picked up the casket. The fact that I haven't heard from her or Adrian's team is a good sign but I call her just in case.

Edward answers the phone. "Hi, Edward." I make my voice sound normal and professional. "Just checking to see how everything is. How's Jennifer feeling?"

"She seems fine but I know everything is getting to her and to me as well. Any news on your end? Are you close to finding this, this hit man?" His rich voice is pleasant but I hear a tired catch to his words.

"Actually we're getting some new intel so I'm confident that we'll find him."

"For all our sakes I hope so."

"Put Jennifer on the phone, Edward. I'd like to speak with her about all of us going out to dinner Wednesday night."

"Of course." I hear him call to Jennifer, "Sweetheart? Cate Harlow is on the phone. She'd very much like to speak with you. And, she has a nice surprise." A few seconds elapse before I hear Jennifer's voice. She sounds tired and old.

"Jennifer, I know this is wearing on you. But as I told Edward a few days ago, I have a little outing planned for you two. How does dinner out at a nice Italian restaurant Wednesday night sound? You'll be with me, Adrian and his crew, and a New York City detective. Sound good?"

There is a brief pause. "I guess. Whatever you feel is best, Cate. I just, I—I just want this over." Jennifer sounds groggy.

"Jennifer? Are you feeling all right? Do you need a doctor? I can have one come to you."

"I'm just very, very tired now, Cate. Just...tired. All I want to do is sleep."

"Okay, sure, go lie down and let me talk to Edward for a moment. Listen though, we'll make the restaurant trip a definite for Wednesday, around six. Now, put Edward back on the phone." There's a sound as if someone has dropped the receiver then Edward comes back on the line.

"Edward, Jennifer sounds groggy, how many pills is she taking? I mean, we don't want an overdose. Are you monitoring her?" Giles's warning about depression and sedatives is fresh in my mind.

"Oh yes, of course. Actually she hasn't taken anything today. Quite frankly, Cate, she's depressed and seems to want to sleep all the time. I assume that's natural considering all that she's going through. Sometimes I feel as if she doesn't know I'm here or even care that I am. Poor girl. I just wish I could be of more help to her."

"You're helping more than you know, Edward. Going out Wednesday night will be good for both of you. Hopefully this will all be over soon, Edward."

There's a pause on his end, then, "Yes. Over soon."

I hang up the phone. I have a sudden brainstorm; I need someone with charm and grace to make the evening seem normal and there's one person who has that down to a science: Melissa Aubrincourt. I immediately text her to see if she has any plans for Wednesday. I quickly explain the situation, assure her that we'll all be safe, and tell her one of Adrian's people can pick her up. Five minutes later I get a call from her saying she's available until her eleven o'clock appointment later that night and that she'll take a cab to the restaurant if I can drive her back to her brownstone later.

"Thanks so much, this woman needs a real distraction right now. And believe me, Melissa, you'll be safe, what with Will and Adrian's team."

Her sweet melodic voice says, "Oh I don't doubt my safety and it's my pleasure to help you. See you at six. 'Bye."

There's a text message from Will on my phone asking if I'd be able to grill him on bar exam questions tonight. I text him back, "Home around six, right now going to check out info on a coffin pick-up at Luca Memorial. See you later."

Meeting with the night clerk–cum–night watchman sheds very little light on the pick-up of the Perfect Ruby Rest 0557. All he remembers is that he buzzed a man in around 11:10, the man asked for the item and said he was here to pick it up for a client. A grainy old-fashioned video tape shows a man dressed in workman's gear wearing a cap, brown jacket, and heavy work gloves. The coffin is loaded onto the truck by a hydraulic lift. Unfortunately the camera only shows the bay doors and the flat inside of the truck, both of which were above the license plate area. The clerk doesn't have any more info or a decent description of the man and I suspect that he may have been sleeping when the truck arrived and the driver banged on the door. I write down all the information, thank both the clerk and Mr. Jasinski, who is creepily stroking one of the coffins again, and get the hell out of there.

In my car a quick call to the New York office of the U-Move-It National rental company yields very little information. The person on the other end says the company doesn't require that a renter states what they want to move. "It's a privacy thing, miss."

"A privacy policy that could be very dangerous," I say. "After 9/11, I would think some type of security and knowledge of what's being hauled would be appropriate. The truck may be involved in a potential crime." Getting nothing but, "I'm sorry, office policy," as an unsatisfactory reply to my statement, I ask him to send a copy of anyone who rented a truck large enough to move heavy furniture over the past week to my office e-mail.

"Sorry, miss. I can't do that either. Again it's a privacy thing. You need something from a judge in order to look at our files. Sorry." He hangs up and I immediately call Will to tell him about their "privacy thing."

"Can you get me a search and seizure warrant for a list of people who have rented large trucks over the past week at U-Move-It National? Their local office is down by the Bowery."

"This about the coffin text message you sent? The one that was ordered and now picked up?"

"Yes, can you help me on this, Will? You know some judges who have helped you in the past on your cases."

"True, but those cases were in fact real crimes; there was evidence enough to warrant a search and seizure. I need to give hard proof to any judge I approach that this is, in fact, a crime. That's the legal system as it works now."

"How about a not-so-legal type of search and seizure?" I hear him sigh and the sound of a pen tapping.

"You know I don't want to hear about illegal means. I know you're not always aboveboard with legal technicalities but I can't be a part of it, Cate. You know I won't."

"What about if this was me instead of Jennifer Brooks-Warren? Would you do illegal then? To save my life?"

The pen tapping goes into a staccato drum beat. "I'm not going to answer that because you damn well know that if your life was in danger, I would do everything in my power to save you. But this *isn't* you and as far as the legal system is concerned, it's not a crime to purchase and pick up a coffin. Sorry, babe, no. The guy you spoke to is right. You can't access a company's files to trace a trunk rental to a possible crime. Technically, no crime has been committed so the privacy policy stands. Plus, the license plate is unknown, and as I said, picking up a coffin is not a crime, so no judge is going to issue a search and seizure."

"Shit!"

"Love you too," he says casually. "See you after seven." I hang up the phone.

Dinner Wednesday night is interesting to say the least. Everyone is dressed in casual dinner style for the occasion and anyone seeing our group would think it was some type of an office party. I've thrown a green silk scarf that Will's mother, the lovely Francesca Sutton Benigni, gave me for Christmas, over a soft yellow blouse. The scarf keeps slipping off my neck and shoulders because I refuse to knot the material and ruin the scarf. Will keeps picking it up from the floor. The third time he places it back around my neck he laughs and says, under his breath, "Knot the damn thing!"

The security people, always two together, take turns standing by the only accessible door, locked from the inside, to the back room; Adrian has other agents outside checking out anyone who comes in the restaurant and both bathrooms have an agent inside. We've even hired Dave the sniper to do a two hour watch that will cost Jennifer five thousand dollars. "Not exactly fifty thou, Harlow," he'd said when I called him to make the offer. "But I'm doing it because I respect Adrian." Yeah, sure, I thought after I'd hung up. Respect has nothing to do with it. You're doing it for the money even if the amount offered is significantly lower than you'd hoped.

Will, Adrian, and Natalie sit facing the door and, even while they eat, I know all three are on high alert. Giles and I talk pleasantly to Edward about the stock market, politics and nothing important. Melissa tries to engage Jennifer into a conversation about fashion week. She's very good at this, Melissa is, sweet and relaxing. She knows how to put people at ease, probably a necessity in her line of work. Jennifer warms a bit to what she is saying. When Melissa regales us all with a funny story about a costume she wore as a young girl during Carnival time in her native New Orleans, I see a slight smile on Jennifer's lips.

There is no wine being served with this dinner; we need to be on guard and ready in the event that a problem arises. And even though my mind tells me we're safe for the time being, I feel comfortable knowing that my gun is in the back waistband of my designer jeans.

I watch Giles observing Jennifer and hear him ask her several innocuous questions. I know that he is watching her for any signs of being overly sedated. Her response to his questions is slower than it should be and she seems a bit confused when she answers. Giles looks at me and raises an eyebrow. Glancing at my watch I see that we've been sitting here for ninety minutes. Dinner is finishing up. A pastry and gourmet coffee cart is wheeled into the room and there's a sudden stirring at our table.

Jennifer excuses herself and heads toward the bathrooms. Natalie immediately follows. I get up and stretch and walk around the table pretending to check out the pastries. I keep glancing toward the rear of the restaurant where the bathrooms are. I am confident that Natalie can handle herself but it's always good to have back-up just in case.

"I'll be right back," I whisper to Will leaning down over his shoulder, "Get me a hazelnut coffee, okay?" He nods, pats the back waist of my designer jeans to see if the gun is there then squeezes my butt. I know he's checking to see if I'm armed but he's always ready to play grab-ass if he's given the opportunity. As I'm walking toward the back of the restaurant, my fellow diners are getting up to inspect the cart.

In the ladies' room I see that all is quiet; Jennifer is washing her hands in a desultory manner, seemingly spaced-out. I nod to another of Adrian's agents, a tall black woman with eyes that miss nothing. I know her from several cases where I used Adrian's agency. Her name's Lin; she's a good person to have your back.

When Jennifer's ready to leave I follow her and Natalie outside the door and watch them head back toward the table. Then I go back in and talk a bit with the security person.

"Did they bring you anything to eat, Lin?" I ask. She shakes her head. "They offered but I declined. I'm on duty so I'll grab a bite later."

We talk a bit more and I stretch my back. I'm tight from sitting for two hours and from being constantly on guard. I check my phone for any messages and find nothing there that can't wait. Then I head back to my jolly little group.

Back at the table I notice that everyone seems to be standing by the dessert cart. I don't see Edward. Will hands me a coffee. "Men's room," he says to my questioning look around the room. "Edward told Adrian and me he had to use the facilities; in other words he had to take a leak."

"Gee, thanks for sharing, Will," I say giving a wide-eyed innocent look. "Made my whole night."

"Yeah well, now you've got that image in your head. I'll have to do something to make you forget it. Later, baby." He smiles and winks at me knowing that his humor is breaking the tension I feel in a room without windows and a possible hit man lurking outside. He touches my arm as I'm about to sit down with my coffee. "Where's your scarf? You drop it?" My scarf, the beautiful green silk scarf. It must have slipped off my neck and I probably did lose it coming back from the bathroom. I tell Will

I'll be right back.

On the way toward the back I find my scarf lying on the floor. As I bend to pick it up I see Edward coming out of a corner near the men's room. He's on his phone and doesn't see me until he trips over me, drops his phone, and lands next to the wall. He looks startled. I pick up his phone to examine the screen checking to see if it is cracked from hitting the floor. I see a blur of words before Edward takes the phone out of my hand. I stare up at him as he gets to his feet, shaking his head as if he is clearing away distant thoughts, and sighs. Then he offers me his hand and helps me up. "Cate, what are you doing on the floor?"

"Picking up my scarf. Are you all right? You took a mean tumble there, Edward."

"Oh yes, I'm all right. I didn't look where I was going. I was checking the weather for the week. Bad weather makes Jennifer more depressed than usual." He stops and looks back toward the restaurant room where dessert is being served then down at his phone. "Especially...rain, yes, rainy days are the worst for her. Rain washes away everything, doesn't it?" He looks down the narrow hall again. "Let's rejoin everyone, shall we? I don't want Jennifer to worry about *me*, after all. She has enough on her mind."

Back at the table I see Will on his cell phone talking to someone at his precinct. His phone is top-of-the-line new, not the regulation standard phones issued to most cops. He paid for this himself so that he misses nothing that has to do with his job. Will's that dedicated to work but the phone also has everything that he personally wanted and is a technological wonder. He's the one who bought me my own top-of-the-line phone and I've never regretted having it. And as I watch him talking on this expensive cell, a thought comes to my mind. Even though I only had his phone in my hand for a second, I could tell that Edward's phone was a cheap one and definitely not new. Funny. I would have thought a man as wealthy as Edward seems to be would want the latest phone technology for business purposes. It's a bit strange that he...

Will interrupts my thoughts by bringing me a delicate chocolate crème concoction. "So far so good, Cate. But, hell, the night's not over yet. We still have to get Jennifer back to her condo safe and alive." He takes a bite of my dessert and then goes over to talk to Adrian. I find myself wishing that the night *was* over and that we were all safe in our respective beds. My own bed preferably including a smoking hot NYPD detective named Will Benigni.

CHAPTER 20

WITH ALL THE SECURITY surrounding her, Jennifer Brooks-Warren makes it back safe and sound to her condo a little before 9:30 p.m. Will and Natalie precede us and go to check out the condo building and condo itself, making sure there are no surprise visitors lurking in wait.

Adrian's team and I stayed close to Jennifer and Edward and got into the SUV with them. Giles left thirty minutes before we did and drove Melissa back to her brownstone for her appointment. Before he left, he took me aside and told me that Jennifer is exhibiting signs of early addiction. "Her speech is definitely slurred and she's slow to respond to conversation. I saw that her eyes were a bit glazed too. Talk to her fiancé and see if he can't get her to have a doctor come up to their place to examine her. Do you know the name of the sedative she's taking? Personally I think she's self-dosing and that's understandable in her situation but it can also be deadly. Call me tomorrow if you get a chance." And with that he kisses me sweetly and slowly on the lips, in full view of Will, and leaves. I remember what he said about being jealous of Will.

All's clear as far as Adrian, Will, and I see. We assess the situation and decide against using the parking garage and let Jennifer and Edward off directly in front of the building. They're hustled in the door and into the private elevator surrounded by Adrian's team. I stay in the lobby and, just before the elevator door slowly closes on her little group, Jennifer turns and thanks me. I wave a hand and wish her a good night.

Ten minutes later Will and Adrian come down in the elevator. They talk for a few moments then shake hands and Adrian takes out his cell phone to check with his team outside. Dave is nowhere to be seen but Adrian tells me that's to be expected. Once we were back at the condo, Dave obviously saw no need to hang around. "Just get him his five thou as soon as you can."

Will motions me toward the door and we walk out toward where he's parked in a no-parking zone. "The love-birds are snuggled safe in their nest, Cate. Now how about we go back to your brownstone and do some, uh, snuggling of our own."

In the car his arms go around me and his hands fondle my breasts. Sliding his left hand down my side and between my legs he kisses me in the hot and passionate way he knows excites me. I dimly think that he's kissing me like that because he saw Giles kiss me good-night but then I surrender to the feeling. "Let's go get naked," he says in that husky voice I know so well and which never fails to arouse me. We drive back to my brownstone with his right hand massaging the moist softness between my legs and his other hand on the wheel. Sex with a slight element of danger to it, that's how it goes with Detective Will Benigni. And I love the thrill of it.

The next morning I awake to find myself on the couch and hear Will whistling in the kitchen. Our clothes are scattered on the floor. I remember and smile. The coffee-maker dings three times and the rich smell of freshly brewed hazelnut coffee wafts to where I am lying. Inhaling deeply I grab a throw from the couch and huddle into it.

"Hi," says a fully dressed Will getting ready to pour two cups of coffee. "I was going to bring you a cup." I reach gratefully for the cup and take it to the counter to add more cream. My stove clock tells me it's just after seven. "You're up early," I say muffling a yawn.

"The city never sleeps, babe, especially New York City. Homicide happened about an hour ago near Central Park, my territory. I'm out the door in ten minutes."

"Okay, sure. Listen, I'm going to make some calls and then head to my office. Last night at the restaurant went well don't you think?"

"It's always a plus when no one gets killed. I got the feeling Jennifer was out of it, though. She barely stayed awake. What did the good doctor, the revered ME, have to say to you? Before he slipped his tongue into your mouth, that is." Will sips his coffee and winks at me to take the edge off his words. Jealousy must be catching.

"Jealous much?" I put my coffee cup down on the counter, facing him squarely and looking in his eyes.

"Of Giles Barrett?! You're kidding me, right?" I don't answer. "Seriously, Cate, why would I be jealous?"

"Because of what you just said."

He walks around the kitchen island and gently lifts my chin with his hand. "Okay maybe a little jealous of that kiss. But I'm here and he's not, so that pretty much tells me who the victor is here."

"Damn it, Will, stop being so territorial. There's no victor because there was no war. I'm not an island you two were fighting over. God!"

"Yeah, okay." He smiles at me and gives me a wink then pulls me into his arms and whispers in my ear. "So....what did Dr. Giles Barrett, esteemed doctor of the dead, say anyway?" Oh Will can be a real bastard! I decide to let the 'doctor dead' comment go and just tell him the specifics of Giles's assessment of Jennifer's state of mind.

"Pretty much what you just said about her. She's on sedatives because of all the stress and he says she is exhibiting signs of preliminary addiction. I have to ask Edward to watch her."

"Yeah, you should do that. By the way what's *his* story?

Something off there."

Edward Penn. The day after he and Jennifer came to my office I had him checked out both legally and not-so-legally; just the basics, no in-depth stuff. Nothing popped either way.

"I did a preliminary background check on him; found nothing unusual. He's concerned about Jennifer and the very real possibility of her being killed. I think the self-imposed confinement in the condo and the constant fear of death is getting to both of them. How would you feel if someone was trying to kill *me*?" He pulls me close to him. "I'm an NYPD detective, remember? I'd have no problem blowing out the brains of anyone who was after you, you better believe that." He holds me closer and kisses my hair. I hear him sigh and know he's thinking about some of the dangers I've encountered in my cases. Both of us, I know, have definite periods of danger in our jobs. Finally Will pulls away and goes to get his service revolver, which he stores in the top drawer of my breakfront when he stays overnight.

"You going to be home around six tonight?" he asks holstering his gun and putting on his jacket. He kisses me again and puts on his sunglasses.

"I should. If not I'll call or text you." Will's out the door and I head to the bathroom. As for the city that never sleeps this sleepy woman needs to shower and wash her hair before venturing out into it.

Catherine Harlow, Private Investigations is dark and quiet when I go up the stairs. It's only eight-thirty and I know Myrtle won't be in until nine. Or at least I hope she will; she's been coming in late and leaving early a lot lately. For a woman who prizes schedules, her hours have been erratic. With everything that's been going on with the Brooks-Warren case I haven't really been able to find out what's been happening in her life that has her so upset. So far, from the little bit of conversation that we've had I can rule out health and money problems. Her sex life sucks, so she says, and Harry has been going out at night and coming back late. If I didn't know Harry better I would think there really *was* another woman involved. But, Harry? I can't see him straying but then who really knows about other people's relationships? I knew a girl in college who seemed to have a perfect relationship with her boyfriend and whenever I saw them together they seemed so in love and happy. Then one night this girl ended up being held at campus security while awaiting the local police on charges of having tried to poison her boyfriend. Turned out her loving boyfriend had been beating the crap out of her for over a year and she had been a victim of both physical and emotional abuse. No one ever suspected.

My train of thought is interrupted by the rattling of keys in the lock of my office's ancient oak door. I glance at my watch; eight-fifty; Myrtle's early today. She has coffee and a bag from a local fast food place that sells dry and over-processed sugar buns. Seriously? No Harry goodies again. Disappointment at the lack of homemade food must show on my face because Myrtle says, "I wouldn't expect any gourmet pastries from Harry. Lately the man seems to have no time to do anything more than run out the door when I come home. God only knows what he's doing during the day. You probably haven't noticed but I'm driving myself to the office now. Harry's too busy." She plugs in her electric teapot and asks, "By the way, how was your dinner excursion last night? All went well for that poor girl, I hope."

Telling her that all is still status quo, no attempts to murder anyone, and no problems occurred, I check the bag and take out one of the overly sugared items. After one taste I put it down on the napkin Myrtle has placed under my Timothy's Coffee Emporium container. Pity that place doesn't sell pastries. When she turns to pour her tea, I discreetly spit the small bite I took into a tissue and dump it, along with the rest of the sugared crap, into the wastebasket. I love Myrtle and Harry with all my heart and I want everything to be the same as it always was. And to be truthful the foodie in me misses Harry's extraordinary concoctions. Harry, Myrtle, and good food: they're the safe constants in my crazy life.

"Myrtle..." I begin but she again gives me the over-the-top-of-the-glasses teacher look that worked so well for her with recalcitrant students during her over thirty years of teaching. "No, Catherine, no," is all she says but it's enough. I know she's not going to talk about any problems going on in her life with Harry. I lower my eyes and pretend to check my phone.

Suddenly I feel Myrtle's arms around me in a quick hug. "I know you mean well, honey, but you're like a daughter to me and good mothers *do not* burden their daughters with personal problems."

Myrtle carries her tea to her desk and begins checking phone messages and I sit and sip my coffee gazing out the window at my little family of nesting doves. Coffee finished I get down to business. A call to the U-Move-It National trucking company's main office sheds no additional light on my inquiry for rental records. Legal and polite requests aren't working so it's time to do some illegal research. I call one of my under-the-radar contacts for some help. But two hours later, I'm still unable to find out who picked up the coffin. The only thing my sources are able to find out is pretty much generic; average height male wearing worker's pants and heavy-duty work gloves, a jacket, and an old-fashioned cab driver cap.

While I'm putting the new info into the Brooks-Warren file I hear Myrtle angrily muttering to herself as she sits hunched forward looking at her computer screen, "Well now, *that* certainly explains it." Curious, I walk over to her desk and look over her shoulder. Displayed on the screen is an article about sexuality. *The number one reason for men past sixty to cheat is boredom in the bedroom. The need for added excitement or romance leads older men to seek a lover with new sexual ideas.* "Boredom!" She furiously clicks off the tab, gets up from her desk, and busies herself near the file cabinet. From the look in her eyes, I know enough not to ask about it. But I also know the time has come for me to step in and try to help two people whom I love dearly.

"I can't believe I let you talk me into a stake-out on Harry." Will is complaining between bites of a cheeseburger. It's getting late and we're both tired. Around seven at night I had asked Will to come with me to check Adrian's detail outside Jennifer's condo. All was well and we spent a few minutes talking with them about any possible activity on the part of the hit man. The topic of the coffin was discussed but nothing was known about its whereabouts. No one at the condo saw any suspicious delivery trucks or knew anything about the Perfect Ruby Rest 0557; there had been no delivery boxes noted of the size needed to house a coffin. Dead end there, no pun intended.

From there I drove to the Tuttles' house and told Will about my plan to follow Harry when he left their home. Myrtle had accidentally let it slip that Harry had been going out every night around eight-thirty for the last three weeks. Will wasn't thrilled about spying on Harry but I sweet-talked him into staying with me.

"Just for an hour or two, please, Will. I can't keep seeing Myrtle miserable every day."

And Will, for all his negative comments about spying on Harry, saw for himself late yesterday afternoon how unhappy Myrtle looked when he stopped by my office. He reluctantly agreed.

"This isn't a stake-out," I say defensively, taking a bite of his burger and grabbing his French fries. Harry Tuttle, along with an unidentified woman, has been in a restaurant for over two hours and I am cramped from just sitting. Thank God Will stopped at a fast food place and came back to the car prepared for a long wait with burgers, fries, and coffee. I'm starving.

"Bullshit, Cate. We're sitting in a car, watching everything that Harry does, taking notes, and making sure he doesn't see us. That pretty much describes a stake-out in detective 101. A *real* detective would know that, I should add."

"I *am* a real detective, Will, and this doesn't qualify as a stake-out in my opinion. It's more of a kind of looking out for a friend type thing."

As I say this there's movement at the restaurant door. Will sees the woman and Harry coming out of the restaurant and lets out a low whistle of appreciation. "Ouch! Harry, you old dog. He's got a hot one there," says Will admiringly. "Nice ass."

"Stop it, Will." I nudge him hard and he misunderstands why. "I mean it's not as great as *yours,* babe, but nice for Harry."

"I don't give a damn about her butt. Take your mind off the female anatomy for a few minutes and concentrate on why we're here. Can you do that?" In response I get a smile and my ass squeezed. "Will! This is Harry and Myrtle we should be concerned about here. Do you *want* Myrtle's heart to be broken after all the years they've spent together?"

He sighs and says no. "Seriously there has to be an explanation for what we see here. But, Cate, listen to me, if he *is* cheating, do you really *want* Myrtle to stay with him? She deserves better. All good women deserve better. You're the one who told me that, remember?"

Will's got me there. Even though he didn't technically cheat during our brief sojourn as a married couple, the strong potential was there and I knew it. Will knew it too and when I told him I was filing for a divorce I said all good women deserve better than to have to deal with a possibly cheating spouse.

"What should I do?" I ask as we watch Harry usher the woman into a taxi before walking to where we saw him park his car earlier in the evening.

Will finishes his cheeseburger and downs his coffee before answering. "*You* should do nothing."

Easier said than done. How can I allow Harry, whom I love as a second father, to break the heart of the woman who has always been a second mother to me? I have to do something.

"But Myrtle is miserable!"

"I know, I know, but Cate, let *them* work it out on their own. If Harry is cheating, which I'm not so sure he is, Myrtle will have to deal with it one way or another. People, even those we really care about, don't like the idea of us sticking our noses into intimate and personal business. Anyway, not everything is as it appears to be on the surface."

"This is Myrtle and Harry!"

"Whom we both know and love, yes, understood, but don't push this, Cate. Let it go and just wait it out, okay?" I don't say anything. "Cate? Promise me? You'll let it go?"

"But..."

"Christ! Come on, Cate! Be realistic here. If you push Myrtle to confide in you, you'll only make her more upset and probably angry as hell at you. Stop it and wait the damn situation out." He's not going to give up so I throw him a bone and say okay. "Are you lying to me? You better not be lying to me because your meddling will create more of a mess than the actual problem. Don't push this, Cate, let Myrtle and Harry work on it themselves. They *are* adults for Christ's sake. Give them their privacy."

"All right! Okay. Done and done. I won't get involved, okay? As hard as that will be, I promise I won't."

Will has to be satisfied with that even if he doesn't believe me and I know he doesn't. He knows me too well and knows that I'll break a promise if it's necessary. To change the subject and get him to think of other things, I snuggle next to him and squeeze his inner thigh.

"Oh come on Cate! Don't use this ploy and think that I don't know what you're doing. This is the oldest trick in the book." He doesn't resist or pull away from me but I can sense he knows my motives aren't completely sexual. After a few minutes of erotic responses, my ploy works and I feel it. He's definitely not thinking of my meddling with Harry and Myrtle.

"Time for bed, baby?" he whispers nuzzling my ear. I smile, give his thigh a squeeze, and say, "Let's go."

On the ride back to my brownstone, I calculate the best way to approach Harry to find out what is going on. I have to do it. Myrtle won't talk so maybe Harry might be my better choice to find out if there are any marital problems.

I'm pretty proud of myself for being able to distract Will's train of thought and I don't think he's going to mention Myrtle and Harry again, at least not tonight. But I'm wrong on that score. As I'm putting the key into my front door, Will touches my shoulder and says, "Just remember that meddling in Myrtle's private life can fuck up your own relationship with her royally." He looks at me sternly, his eyes warning me to keep my nose out of Myrtle's and Harry's business. "That's all I'm going to say besides get your sweet ass inside and let's go get naked."

CHAPTER 21

THE COFFIN, THAT DAMNED coffin, cannot seem to be found anywhere. Nor can the truck. My sources on the street can't find out anything about it except the sketchiest details. One of them did manage to "borrow" the list of names from the Bowery office of U-Move-It National of anyone who rented a large truck last week. No coffin pick-ups, just furniture, gym equipment, and the like. I've tracked down all but two of those people but the intel on those two indicate that they rented trucks for out-of-state family moves.

In the area around the Luca Memorial Services I spoke with the street people, those ignored members of humanity that the world conveniently refuses to see but who, themselves, see and hear everything. Still, even with a promise of cash in hand, I was unable to find anyone who noted even a partial license plate number. To them a truck picking up a coffin is not a big deal; nothing much is a big deal except surviving.

Only one woman, named DeeLee said she knew something and for twenty-five bucks told me that the plate that she saw on the back was mud-splattered and she couldn't make out any numbers or letters. I can't know if she's a credible witness because, even from a foot away from me, I can smell cheap liquor on her breath. Still, she did mention something about the driver, which might help.

"He had a nice voice."

"You heard him speak?"

"He sounded like a radio announcer. I listen to the radio when I'm hanging out by that bodega on the corner. An announcer; that was his voice."

Marc Croft? I have to ask Jennifer if she remembers the sound of Croft's voice from that night when she saw him in the bar, the night he brought Moira Hollis her dead father's finger as proof of the kill.

"What did he say? Was he talking to another person?"

She fingers the bills in her hand and then tucks them inside her shirt. "He said 'It's a shame when someone dies so young.' I didn't see anybody else. I think he was talking to himself. But that's what he said, 'It's a shame when someone dies so young.' He had a radio voice."

I tell her I'll be back in a few days. "If you remember anything else, let me know then."

"Will you pay me again?"

"Sure."

"Pay me more if I help you find him?"

"Yes, I will. I have to go now but I'll be back soon."

⁓

Myrtle has put several case files on my desk for me to check out before she can put them on the computer in the closed files as well as placing a paper copy in the locked cabinet. She asks me if I have any leads from interviewing people near Luca Memorial Services.

"Not really, no. No license plate, no real description. There was a woman who heard the truck driver say something. She said he had a radio voice, you know like an announcer on the radio. I guess she meant that it was smooth and clear."

"Or cultured and well-modulated. Dr. Giles Barrett has that type of voice, so does Will. After all his mother Francesca did send him to the best preparatory school in the city," says Myrtle, eyes on a folder while keying info into her computer. Unlike me she doesn't have to look at the keys when she types. "Sounds as if the driver was someone who traveled in a world far removed from the hard-working life usually associated with truckers and such."

"Yeah well, I would guess that the Eliminator is a world-traveled kind of guy with a very pleasant voice, Myrtle. Doesn't get his hands dirty except, of course, for murdering people for money."

I call Jennifer's condo and after four rings get a message. "You have reached Edward Penn. Please leave a brief message. Thank you." Almost immediately I get a call-waiting buzz from the same number. It's Natalie from Adrian's security team.

"I didn't want you to be concerned that the machine picked up. Sorry but I was talking with Adrian on my mobile." I know she and Adrian are engaged but they keep it very low-key and are consummate professionals for his security business. "Everything is fine here; Jennifer is sleeping again. They did have company about an hour ago, someone from the bank. We checked him out before we let him up but he's been here a few times before, so no worries. He and Edward went down to the lobby a few minutes ago." There's a pause. "Listen, Cate, you know Jennifer hasn't paid Adrian's company for our services yet, right?" Being his fiancée, I guess she has a stake in Adrian being paid. "I mean I hate to mention it but Adrian did discuss it with me. Is there any chance you can talk to Edward about this? Jennifer is in no state to be bothered with it but, well, maybe you can talk to Edward for Adrian. He's pretty well off from what I understand so he can deal with this, can't he?"

"Oh, sure, yes, I will Nat. I'm sorry Adrian hasn't been paid yet. I would think that Edward *would* take over paying bills now that Jennifer seems so out of it. I've been using Adrian's security teams for a couple of years now and he's always been more than reliable so I feel kind of responsible. Yes, I'll call Edward later." She thanks me and then says she's going to check on Jennifer.

As I put down my cell phone and turn to look out the window, I hear the very prim and proper voice of Myrtle Goldberg Tuttle say, "*Catherine Harlow, Private Investigations* hasn't seen a dime either other than that retainer check. You might want to ask about your *own* payment when you speak with Edward."

⁂

Voices, voices. I find myself trying to remember the voices of men who have had anything to do with Jennifer in recent days. I'm trying to discern any voice that sounds like a radio announcer. The manager of her condo building has a smooth voice sort of like a radio announcer, so do several male tenants I have heard speaking while I was in her building. Giles has a cultured voice, Will's voice has that definite assertive voice you get in some boys' prep schools. Edward, her fiancé, has a pleasant business voice. I am obsessed with voices as I try to find where and how the Eliminator is going to strike. What does he sound like? Jennifer is so medicated that she's no help in remembering his voice.

To get an answer from someone who has heard him speak I even call Moira Hollis to ask her if the man who eliminated her father had a 'radio voice.' I can tell that she is terrified that I contacted her. But after she understands that the call is not in any way threatening to her, she says she doesn't think the Eliminator's voice was distinctive. "It was clear but not like an announcer's."

Voices, voices; what does the Eliminator, aka Marc Croft, sound like? A few nights later, as I enter the front door of my brownstone, I find out.

"Hello, Cate." His voice is low, soft, and calm so the startle factor is minimal. Still I let out a small gasp of surprise. He is sitting in the dark in my living room waiting for me. I had assumed the programmed lighting that usually goes on well before I come home had blown a fuse. It's happened occasionally in the past. Now I know the lights must have been deliberately tampered with by my unexpected guest. My breath quickens along with my heart beat but I will myself to stay calm.

"Who are you?" is all I say as I stand in the entryway of my brownstone.

"You can call me Marc Croft, one of my many names, to be sure," he laughs. He rises from the chair in one quick cat-like movement. Flight would be futile since I've already closed the door and I can sense that he will be on me before I can swing it open again. If I reach for my gun, he'll shoot me before I can aim.

"Lock the door so we're not disturbed, Cate. We have some important issues to discuss."

All this is said so matter-of-factly that it sounds as if we are two co-workers having a serious business problem and don't want to have our meeting interrupted. He walks over to where I am standing, his soft-soled shoes making almost no sound on the wood floor. Reaching behind me he takes the Smith and Wesson out of the back of my jeans. Then he quickly runs his hands over my body to check for other weapons. His gloved hands are firm and absolutely professional even when pressing very personal parts of my body. This man knows what he is doing and I pretty much know that I am safe from any sexual assault. In a strange way I am this man's equal: a professional who has to make sure that the adversary facing me is unarmed. The difference between us is that he is a hired killer and I am not.

"Over by the couch, Cate. Sit down and keep your hands placed on your knees."

I do as I am told. When you're weaponless and your opponent isn't, the smartest thing to do is what you're told. I am still in an open area so my chances for escape are better than if he had me in a car or windowless room.

"So talk," I say with as much bravado as I can muster—after all, this man has eliminated people without blinking an eye. If I was in his way he might see me as a liability to getting his job done. Killing me would make sense.

"Jennifer Brooks-Warren."

I draw a ragged breath and ask, "What about her?"

"Don't insult my intelligence, Cate. Let's discuss why you think *you* can stop me from fulfilling my contract. You're a small-time PI. Not really playing in the big leagues."

Keeping my own gun on me he grabs the bottle of Chivas Will left on the side table last night. "Mind if I have a drink? I don't usually drink on the job but I don't see you as a threat. You're not a real opponent."

He opens the bottle and takes a healthy slug from it all the while keeping his eyes on me. Jennifer was right about his eyes. The headlights from a passing truck illuminate the far side of the room and I can see his hard blue eyes. Ice-cold, she had said. Blue, ice-cold eyes. A killer's eyes.

He sighs and takes another swig before putting the bottle back on the table. "I don't understand why you'd try to take me on, Cate. You're not, as I said, big league material. Oh, you're tough enough. In a way, you remind me of my Victoria. Jesus, but *that* woman was big-league all the way. Why'd you take this Brooks-Warren case?"

"I'm an investigator. Taking on cases is how I earn my living." I feel oddly calm talking to him. His manner of speaking is mesmerizing. Quiet, husky, male voice; even though I know how very dangerous this man is, he doesn't sound threatening. His voice is actually soothing. That's to his advantage; his victims are taken off guard by that lulling voice.

Voices.

"Stick to following teenage lovers, cheating spouses, and employee background checks, Cate." He laughs softly. "Or stay with finding missing persons and pedophiles. That seems to be what you're good at."

He's referring to the McElroy case from last year when I helped find a boy who had been missing for ten years. That case had inadvertently led me to a pedophile monsignor and Church cover-ups in a New Jersey archbishop's office. The monsignor I nabbed was now spending some quality time in prison and the archbishop had been relieved of his ecclesiastical duties. Job well done there at least. But then, I wasn't facing a professional killer in that case.

"This business with Brooks-Warren is beyond your prowess."

"Maybe," I say, "Then again, maybe not." I change the subject. "Who's this big league Victoria? Another person you killed? She proved to be your match and so you had to kill her?"

"Quite the investigator, aren't you? Ah, Victoria. She was most certainly my match and she is dead...*because* of me. But... I didn't kill her."

"What happened?" I try to sound concerned because I want to keep him talking.

Ignoring my question, he grabs the bottle again. "Want some?" he says holding it out to me. "You look like someone who enjoys a stiff drink."

"No." I shake my head. "I don't drink on the job either and *you* look very much like a threat to me."

That gets a short sardonic laugh from him. "Smart woman, Cate. Keep alert. Don't let your guard down for one second. I like that about you." He puts the bottle down.

"You don't know me well enough to like or dislike anything about me."

"I know enough about you to know that you almost got killed last year during your missing person's case; got smashed in the head and kidnapped, but still managed to solve the case and bring a pedophile to justice. Brava to you, Cate Harlow. By the way, I hate child molesters. Those bastards I have killed for free." Another long look at me. "You drive a SUV because it makes you feel safe on the roads, your best friend's name is Melissa, a lady in a profession called the oldest one in the world. She's very hot, by the way." He laughs. "And I also know that you can't quite make up your mind which man you want to fuck, stalwart NYPD homicide Detective Will Benigni or Dr. Giles Barrett, the head of the city's morgue. It's an interesting coincidence that both men are somehow involved with dead bodies, isn't it? That turn you on? So you see, Cate, I do know a lot about you."

"You certainly did your homework, didn't you?"

He ignores my sarcasm.

"I am going to say this once, Cate. I get paid to do a job, it gets done. Stay out of my way or you could get hurt...badly."

I make a stab at rationality. "No exceptions? Come on, Marc, you can make a change in your work ethic." He laughs when I call him by his name. He knows what I'm trying to do. I want to make this conversation as personal as possible. First name basis and all, as if we're going to be friends.

"This Jennifer Brooks-Warren has changed her life dramatically. She is *not* the person she was two years ago; not only not physically the same but emotionally as well. You can keep her money, believe me. She's told me so. She has a new life, she's about to be married. Let it go."

"Married?" He seems surprised. "Now *that* is a very interesting turn of events." He laughs again. "Getting *married*." He looks at me calmly and shakes his head. I hear him curse under his breath.

"Yes, getting married. Let it go. You have the money. Call it off."

He curses again then gives me a cold, chilling smile. "You're right. She *has* changed; she's very different from who and what she was two years ago. And about to enter *holy* matrimony, well...damn!" He pauses as if he's calculating an option. "You know something, Harlow? I'm a sucker for love." The way he says that chills me even more. "And...since you asked *so* nicely, Cate, I think I will release her from *her* contract. Of course I'll keep the money. It's sort of a professional agreement fee if you will. Sure, why not? Consider her released. Happy now?"

He's being sarcastic. This sounds too easy, too pat. Something's not right and he knows I realize that. "You'll release her? That easily, huh? Why do I get the feeling that she's still not safe from you? I guess this time you'll be sending her a note about leaving her alone then?"

"Probably not. I'm not big on written material. Your detective skills are really not working overtime here, Cate. I said I can and will release her from *her* contract. No problem there. Done."

He laughs, a bit sadly I think. "But, you see, Cate, there's one small problem. This isn't about *her* hiring me anymore. There's still a contract out on her, a new one with quite a hefty payout. Someone else, it seems, wants her eliminated. It's a lot more money than the paltry ten thousand she paid. Once I get paid, this new contract will be fulfilled, believe me."

Another person? Someone from her past, someone who knows she has money and is going to marry into even more money. Who? That man Kevin from whom she stole money or some relatives who feel they have been wronged? A man or woman she didn't tell me about? Maybe Jennifer hasn't been completely honest with me about her past or even her present.

"Another contract? Who wants her—" I don't get to finish my question. He shushes me the way a person might gently shush a talkative child.

"Close your eyes, sweetheart." The hit man walks over to where I'm sitting. The adrenaline rushes through me at his approach and I am instantly on the alert.

"If you're going to kill me, I'd rather keep my eyes open and maybe get in one good kick before I go." All I get as an answer is a soft laugh and my Smith and Wesson, empty of bullets, dropped in my lap.

"Stay away, Cate. You're not on a level playing field. Stick with what you know in your world and stay out of mine. By the way, your sniper buddy? He's dead. Call it collateral damage. You didn't really think that that old sniper could take me out, did you? Foolish mistake, Cate."

Dave dead? No wonder Adrian and I didn't see him after the dinner. The Eliminator is that good that he was able to kill the sniper and none of us, a top-notch security expert, a decorated NYPD police detective, and me, a pretty savvy PI, suspected anything. He must have been very close to the restaurant where we assumed Jennifer was safe with all the security. He is a White Death!

I get up quickly and swing at his face but, before I can stop him, he grabs my neck firmly and, with a practiced touch, presses down on a sensitive pressure point. The next thing I know I wake up, alone on the floor of my living room, my gun and the bullets next to me. I feel as if I am just coming out of anesthesia, groggy and unsure of where I am. Damn the Eliminator is good! Out cold for, I check my watch, fifteen minutes.

I stand shakily and list slightly to my left. Then holding on to furniture I walk to my kitchen to grab a bottle of cold water from the fridge. I drink most of it then put my head in the sink and pour the rest of the cold water over the back of my neck and my face.

It's only later, when I'm sitting down with my eyes closed, that I think of something about Marc Croft. His voice—that woman on the street, the one near the Luca Memorial building, said he sounded like a radio announcer. Croft's voice was clear and soft, but he lacked the distinctive voice of a man who speaks for a living. His voice had a very slight mid-western sound. If this woman hadn't heard Marc Croft, then who had she heard saying, *It's a shame when someone dies so young?*

The pressure point knock-out from Marc Croft aka the Eliminator has left me feeling as if I have a hangover. I take a shower hoping to lessen the drunk feeling. Later I drink bottle after bottle of cold water. In a couple of hours I feel better, not one hundred percent okay, but better.

Going to my computer, I sit down, open a confidential file named Duchovny and write down everything that I can remember about what Marc Croft said. I even put in the part about a woman named Victoria who seemed to be an important person in his life.

After I'm done, I walk over to the comfortable lounger that faces the window and put my head back. Mouse and Little Guy come out from wherever they were hiding and hesitantly walk around the living room. They jump up onto the lounge chair and begin a soft self-soothing purr. I like to think that they're happy I'm alive. So I sit with a cat on either side of me and look out at the cars going by in the night. Sitting there I make a decision: I will not tell anyone about what happened here tonight, especially Will. If he knows, he'll start his own search for the Eliminator and that could throw my whole case off. Thank God he has a law review class tonight. I'll handle this myself. The locks on my doors and the security lighting system can be fixed before he comes over tomorrow night. What with the long hours of my day, and the emotional drain of having a very unexpected visitor, I fall into a dreamless sleep and don't awaken until almost eight the next morning.

CHAPTER 22

THE FOLLOWING AFTERNOON, still a little groggy, I'm down by Luca Memorial Services. I decided to do a sweep of the area, talking to the street people down there one more time, to see if I can glean any other information concerning the coffin pick-up. My security system is being fixed by the company that had originally installed it. I tell them nothing about it being disabled; let them think the security lighting failed because of some glitch in *their* system

As I'm walking around talking to the street people and writing notes, I get a call from Jennifer's condo. I put my phone on speaker so I can hear without holding it to my ear. It seems that Jennifer has received a text message from the Eliminator: *"Your special gift has already been picked up for you. It's very comfortable. Happy birthday!"*

"I'll be over within the hour," I say juggling phone and notebook. "Everyone is to just hang in there. No one is to leave the building. Got it?"

The woman to whom I paid twenty-five dollars for information last week has been standing next to me and asking if I can give her any money for a sandwich. I put my phone in my pocket and take out a five. "Don't spend this on any more booze," I say sniffing her alcohol-tinged breath. She smiles slyly, stuffs the bill in her shirt, looks at me and says, "So you found him, huh?"

I'm cornered by a man who saw the exchange of money. He says if I give him money too, he can tell me where the aliens have landed. I take out another five, tell him to go buy the aliens lunch, and turn to leave. The woman touches my arm, "You found him! Right? Right?" She follows me as I'm walking away. "You *found* him." She grabs my wrist and nods.

"Sorry?" I'm distracted and need to get to my car, which is parked two long city blocks away. With only one thing on my mind, I'm not listening to what she is saying.

"You know, that guy! That *guy!*"

I'm about to sprint away from her but the woman won't let go of my wrist. "I can't talk now," I say. "I have to see someone right away. This is urgent."

"That man? You're going to see him?" Sometimes the inhabitants on the street live in dual universes; she's probably talking about someone she knows or met and thinks I know.

"Look, I'll be back, okay?" I say finally releasing her strong grip on my wrist. "You can tell me about this guy then. But right now I have—"

"Okay, but I'm glad you found him. I helped you, remember that. You owe me money now." She stands there nodding at me smugly. "You said you'd pay me more money if I knew anything else about that man who took the coffin."

I stop and turn. "Wait a minute. Who do you think I found?"

"The guy with the radio voice." I look at her without answering. "That guy, the announcer guy," she says slowly as if she is talking to a child, "you were just *talking* with him on your phone. You found him, right? Now you have to give me money."

Some of the street people have followed her and she turns toward them saying that I'm going to pay her because she helped me. I pull her away from them and make her face me. "Are you sure, are you absolutely sure a voice you heard just *now* is the same one you heard when the coffin was picked up?"

"Give me the money first," she says defiantly.

"I'll give you the money when you answer my question. Are

you absolutely certain you heard the same voice on my phone that you heard that night?"

She looks at my face. "Lady, didn't you hear me? I just said so. I said that you found the radio voice man."

I hand her two tens, all I have left in my wallet. Then I close my eyes and sigh. The call was a conference call, a four way conversation. The "radio announcer voice" she just heard belongs either to the verbose and windbag building manager, the well-spoken security expert Adrian, or to the elegant Edward Penn. All three with "radio voices". Shit!

"What are you going to do, Catherine?" Myrtle is incredulous at what I am telling her as she sits on the couch in my office drinking a cup of tea designed to help women over a certain age lose weight.

"I'm working on it, Myrtle. At present, I have no idea. It could be any one of them." Having returned a short time ago from Jennifer's condo where I read the text message she had received, I am at a loss as to how I should proceed.

"Edward Penn, that distinguished good-looking man, her fiancé? The one with the beard?" asks Myrtle. "Do you really think he could be behind this murder-for-hire?"

"Maybe he wants her money. She *is* loaded."

"Do you *really* think that, Catherine? If that's the case, well... that bastard! Wanting to have that poor woman murdered for her money?" She looks at me and shakes her head disbelievingly. "Personally, I don't believe it's true. From what I understand, regardless of the fact that we haven't been paid a cent since she wrote us that retainer check, he's wealthy himself. He doesn't need *her* money." Myrtle sips her tea and shakes her head. "And Adrian? You've known him for several years, haven't you? It is possible that it's the manager of the building. I haven't met *him*. What's your gut instinct say about all this? You always tell me that it never fails you."

"Well, it seems to be failing me now," I slump down in my

derful and concerned. And he insisted that I move in with him. He said that the hit man might be more cautious about doing anything if I wasn't alone. Edward even made all the arrangements to have my condo rented out. Then there was that message from the...the...hit man." She chokes on the words and I hand her a bottle of water to sip before continuing.

"Remember I told you that Edward went to the police when I received that first cryptic note about twenty-five being special? After he came back to the condo, he said that he felt they weren't concerned enough to really be of much help. So he told me that he would find a good private investigator for me and he did." She looks at me and smiles. "You."

I asked a few more questions about Edward and their life together. Later after she had left *Catherine Harlow, Private Investigations*, I called Wells and Cummings brokerage firm to get a confirmation that Edward was indeed associated with the firm. The person who answered confirmed that, yes, the name Edward L. Penn was a legitimate name on their letterhead. "Anything else I can help you with?" she said sounding bored and in a hurry to do something else. I said no, nothing else thank you, and she said, "Okay-thank-you-for-calling-Wells-and-Cummings-have-a-nice-day" in a rush of words and hung up. Wells and Cummings must have hired someone's needy relative as a receptionist. As I placed my phone on my desk, I silently thanked the gods for Myrtle and her crisp professional style and crossed Edward off my list of possible suspects.

Now I look at the file on the Brooks-Warren case and search for something in the questions and answers about Edward that I might have missed. Nothing pops. Is it possible that Edward somehow managed to contact the Eliminator and offer him more money to kill Jennifer? I muse. But that doesn't make sense. The Eliminator was going to kill her anyway, right? So why offer more money to do a job for which the person had already been paid?

Then there's Adrian, a man I've known for five years, a man

who went through the police academy with Will; is there something sinister that I don't know about him? But what? Is he a secret mercenary? I know very little about his personal life or even where he is when he's not working a job for me. But still, nothing makes sense and I want to discount Adrian as a suspect just on the fact that he always seemed as legally upright as Will. That's not a good reason however, and until I can prove otherwise, everyone is a suspect.

And that building manager, a man who seemed a little too interested in the building's tenants. Is there a connection there with Jennifer? Is that annoying, rather mousy man, a hit man? Three men, three voices, all clear and well-spoken; whose voice is the one the homeless woman, DeeLee, heard the night of the coffin pick-up?

I set my desk phone to record the voices of the three men, one of whom is a potential murderer, and make the first call to Adrian. My question concerning security for Jennifer and Edward has him talking about the problem for a good ten minutes. Then I call Edward and have him detail Jennifer's depressed condition. It's amazing how willingly people will talk when asked simple questions. Next I call the manager of the condo building, am put on hold, and listen to Stevie Nicks sing "Rhiannon" while waiting for him to pick up.

"Sorry Ms. Harlow. I can talk now, very busy day, new tenants, and all. How can I help you?"

"Yes, thank you for speaking with me. Just one quick question. Have you seen anything at all that you might consider to be suspicious this morning?" He talks for half an hour.

Now that I have the voices of all three men recorded all I need is my "hearing" witness. Myrtle agrees to stay late tonight while I go to search among the street people for my source.

"What else do I have to do, Catherine? It's not as if someone is waiting to have dinner with me," she says obviously referring to Harry and his nighttime excursions. Seriously, I have to get involved in the Myrtle and Harry caper as soon as this Eliminator case is tied-up.

The streets around Luca Memorial Services are filled with commuters leaving stores and office buildings. As for the street people, except for a few of them begging on the sidewalks, they are invisible. I can't find DeeLee anywhere, which means I have to search the alleys and the basement stairwells of empty buildings. That means rats, roaches, and risk, the three nasty R's in the life of a New York City private investigator.

I ask people slumped in corners of buildings and in makeshift, cardboard shelters if anyone has seen DeeLee. Either they say no or I get no answer at all. Several drunks offer me a sip from their bottles. "Have a drink with an Iraqi war vet, pretty lady?" says one haggard young man wearing a camouflage shirt. He must have been a good-looking man before going through hell; his looks remind me a little of Giles. "I got some good weed too. Come on, sit with me and I'll tell you war stories that will scare the shit out of you." I politely decline and feel sad. The street people, each one with their own story of how they got here, they get to me every time.

"DeeLee," I call out in an alleyway where I see several huddled bodies. No answer. I continue to several dark stairwells where I see rats scuttling down the stairs. The stench of urine and feces burns my nostrils. I go down a narrow passage between two buildings and shine the flashlight embedded in my new phone. "DeeLee? Have you seen DeeLee?" I ask several women slumped near a window. One of them rouses herself enough to look in the direction of my voice.

"You can't be here. This is Big Annie's alley. You are not one of my people," she says moving forward menacingly. She's a big woman. I stand my ground and ball my fist behind my back.

"I'm just looking for DeeLee, that's all. I mean no harm to anyone. I'll leave if you tell me where I can find DeeLee."

"You a cop? I can smell cops."

"I'm not a cop. I just need to talk to DeeLee about something that happened down by Luca Memorial Services. It's important and could save a woman's life."

Big Annie looks me over assessing whether I'm a threat to her alley. She must decide that I'm not because she says, "Go check La Quinta bodega. They dump their food out at five. It's DeeLee's turn to wait there by the dumpster today and bring the food back here."

La Quinta bodega is on the corner of a block full of dilapidated buildings, most with broken windows and boarded-up doorways. The bodega lights are on outside but I don't see any surveillance cameras. I follow the smell of discarded food around to a narrow alleyway and find the dumpster. DeeLee is perched precariously on a broken vegetable crate, the top half of her body invisible inside the dumpster. Besides the odor of stale food I distinctly smell alcohol. "DeeLee?" I say this softly so as not to frighten her and make her fall backward. "DeeLee? It's me the woman who spoke to you about the..." I hesitate and try to think of something that will spark a memory in her liquor-addled mind, "the radio voice man. Remember me?"

She lifts her body up, her arms full of opened Styrofoam cartons oozing tossed barbecue and salad-bar remains. The smell is overwhelming. DeeLee carefully steps back off the crate and one carton falls from her grasp spilling chicken wings and ribs. Once down, she places the other cartons on the ground and scoops the contents of the spilled one back into the container. Food is food and if you're starving, some dirt isn't going to stop you from eating food from the ground.

"DeeLee?" I say again, fishing money out of my back jeans pocket. All I have left is a five and three ones but it's better than nothing. I'll buy some burritos for her and the people who are waiting for her to return with dumpster dinner. "Remember me?"

Stacking her cartons one on top of the other she eyes me with suspicion then nods. "You're the one who found that radio voice man. You owe me money." I watch her stuff the dumpster cartons into a large plastic garbage bag.

"Yes, I do owe you money but you have to come with me to get it."

"Why?" She shifts away from me.

"Because you have to listen to the voice again. It's on the phone in my office. I need you to come with me back there and I promise you I'll pay you a lot more money. I'll even get dinner, a real dinner for you."

But she isn't having any of my offer. "Yeah, no. I have to get this food back to Syl and Louise and Big Annie. They're waiting for me. Tonight's my turn to bring food."

"Listen, DeeLee, I'll buy fresh food for them too. Even before we go back to my office, I'll get some burritos from that food truck down the block. We'll bring them back to your friends and after you identify the voice at my office, I'll buy a whole bag of food and you can bring it all back here. Come on DeeLee, you can trust me."

She looks me up and down the same way Big Annie did before answering me back in the alley. "If I come with you, you got to leave something with Big Annie so she knows that you'll bring me back here." She points at my wrist. "You got to leave her your watch."

I glance at the old Tag Heuer, an heirloom I inherited from my Nonna Rita, knowing that I probably will never see it again if I leave it with Big Annie. This watch and a gold bangle bracelet she brought with her from Italy were the only expensive pieces of jewelry she owned. For me it isn't about the expense, it's the emotional value attached to it. Nonna Rita gave the watch to me when I entered college. I hesitate and sigh deeply. The exchange better be worth it. Finally I say, "Deal. Let's go, DeeLee."

CHAPTER 23

AFTER DELIVERING SIX burritos and the contents of the garbage bag back to Big Annie's alley, DeeLee and I drive my Edge back to the office of *Catherine Harlow, Private Investigations*. The stench of body odor and alcohol makes driving with the windows open a priority. I would like to take DeeLee to a women's shelter so she'd have access to a shower, shampoo, and clean clothes but I know she'd never allow that to happen. I can't help but think about the people who live on the street. The plight of the homeless is a shameful blight on our society; so much more should be done to help them. They fear cops, social workers, and hospitals because they don't want to lose their freedom. They prefer, and I can't say I really blame them for this, living precariously on the streets rather than living in supervised shelters. It's a no-win situation.

My personal connection with the homeless began with Bo, the man who lives near my office in the basement of an empty building. I give him a weekly twenty dollar bill and I know Myrtle brings him food from her home and buys him snack food as well. I count Bo as one of the lucky ones because he has people who look out for him but what about those like DeeLee and her friends? They pretty much fend for themselves.

Once inside my office I tell Myrtle to call Enzo's and place a large order for ten subs and iced teas. Then I hand DeeLee a burrito and a bottle of water. Myrtle brings over a box of cookies and DeeLee eyes her suspiciously. "Is she a social worker? Some nosy social worker gave cookies and hot coffee to my friend Carl. He went to the shelter with her and we never saw him again."

"No, this is Myrtle Goldberg Tuttle. She's my assistant and she will be staying here with us while you listen to the voices. Myrtle, this is DeeLee." Myrtle extends her hand and, after a second, DeeLee shakes it. She sits down across from DeeLee who is tense at first and then relaxes. Myrtle has always had a calming influence on agitated clients. The windows are closed so that the noise from the traffic passing in the streets below is muted and the air inside my small office is rank with odor and heat. I need this to go as smoothly and as quickly as possible.

After she's finished with her food, I tell DeeLee that I'm now going to play the recording of the men's voices. "I numbered the recordings one, two, and three, okay?" Only Myrtle and I know the order of the voices. "Here's a pen and paper. When you hear the same voice you heard last week down by Luca Memorial, write down the number."

"The radio voice man?"

"Yes, you said you heard him on my phone two days ago. Think you can remember his voice now?"

She looks at me through narrowed eyes as if I am the dumbest person in the world and says, "I told you that already."

"Okay, good. I will play each one twice." I push the button to playback the conversations. "Now listen carefully. This is number one."

The atmosphere in the room is tense as DeeLee listens intently to each man's voice. Not wanting her to feel pressured, I deliberately don't look at her but keep my eyes focused on the phone. Myrtle stands up and walks to the window looking down into the approaching night.

"Okay." DeeLee looks at me and says, "The radio voice man. I wrote the number down like you said. Here." She hands me the paper with the word "TWO" in big letters. Myrtle looks at me expectantly. I show her the word and she draws in her breath.

The radio voice man, the man who picked up the coffin, the one who said, *It's a shame when someone dies so young,* has been identified.

Number two is Edward Penn.

⁓

As much as I believe DeeLee when she ID'd the voice, I have to have proof that the coffin was actually picked up by Edward Penn. If it is Edward, what's his role in this hired kill? Jennifer Brooks-Warren positively stated that she, and she alone, had the contract put out on her life. A contract that was to be fulfilled on her twenty-fifth birthday. How does Edward Penn figure into this? It doesn't make sense. I have to think this through.

Myrtle comes along for the ride when I take DeeLee back to Big Annie's alley. Before we left, I had explained to her about having to leave my watch with Big Annie as insurance that I'd bring DeeLee back safely. Myrtle raised an eyebrow and pursed her lips but said nothing.

Three large bags of food and canned sodas from Enzo's are in the back seat next to DeeLee. She's anxious to get back and share her goodies. "Big Annie's gonna be so proud of me," she giggles. "I never get a whole bunch of food like this!"

I'm lucky this time and find a space closer to the alley where we all get out and help DeeLee carry the bags. Once in the alley, and before DeeLee can share the bounty, Myrtle asks where she can find Big Annie. A jumble of clothing detaches itself from the other women and says, "I'm Big Annie." The woman is almost as tall as Will. She looks broad but that might just be because of the layers of clothes and blankets she wears. Big Annie towers over the five foot two Myrtle. "I'd like to speak with you," says Myrtle primly shaking hands with her. "It's very important." Big Annie leads Myrtle farther down the blackness of the alley.

They seem to be gone for quite a while. I put my hand on the back of my jeans where I have my gun and wait tensely. Come on, Myrtle! What are you doing back there? A few minutes later I breathe a sigh of relief as I see Myrtle walking toward us. Big Annie is following her. "Let's go, Catherine." As we leave I see Big Annie handing out food to the other women but keeping the bags between her and the building, guarding her stash for tomorrow.

Even though I parked close to the alley, the walk back to the car creeps me out and I'm on alert for any danger. Once inside the car with the doors locked and with me maneuvering out into traffic Myrtle touches my arm. "Here. I retrieved your watch."

"What?" I glance at her hand holding the pretty Tag Heuer. "How?"

"Oh, it wasn't so hard. When we shook hands I slipped her a twenty dollar bill to get her to talk with me. Then I simply told Big Annie that I would make a deal with the bodega you mentioned. They'll supply those ladies with all their daily leftovers and twice a week they'll give them fresh salads. The leftovers will be suitably wrapped in plastic containers, no Styrofoam, and can be picked up by the back kitchen door. With that deal, it was easy to negotiate for your watch. I know how much you treasure anything from your grandmother, Catherine. By the way," she continues, "we'll pay for the fresh salads out of petty cash. I'll call La Quinta tomorrow and get everything started. I am quite sure that they will be very happy to do this community service for the homeless. It's good PR for the store and I'll make sure they know that."

"You slipped her a twenty?" is all I can think to say. I am flabbergasted.

"Yes, I did, Catherine. I *have* learned some things working for you and one of them is that people are more willing to talk if you grease their palm."

You go, Myrtle! When we stop at a light, I reach over and give her cheek a kiss. Then I put Nonna Rita's most beloved piece of jewelry on my wrist and drive on.

Before I leave for home that night I call Adrian and tell him to make sure Natalie or another female member of his security team is with Jennifer at all times. I don't tell him my suspicions concerning Edward; solid proof is needed before making an accusation.

"Okay Cate, I'll tighten the detail. It's getting close to her birthday, so this is a wise move."

The following morning I set my investigative skills on discovering everything I can about Edward Penn, something I failed to do when I met him. I could kick myself for not being more thorough. The first thing I have to do is check out Jennifer's story about Edward being on the board of Wells and Cummings. Arriving with my Brooks-Warren file at Wells and Cummings, which is an austere building on Water Street, I feel out of place and totally under-dressed. Well-tailored suits and expensive outfits are worn by any and all who are entering the building. Even though my one concession to the corporate world was to wear a lilac Stella McCartney top, my jeans and sneakers make me stand out as "not one of them." But who knows? Maybe that's an advantage on my part.

The preliminary phone call I made to the brokerage house inquiring if an Edward Penn was a member of the board notwithstanding, I enter the foyer of Wells and Cummings on the twentieth floor, flash my ID, and ask to see someone who might know about Edward Penn. "This is a legal matter," I tell the flustered young receptionist behind the front desk. Then comes the lie, which flows so easily from my lips, "The police have been informed concerning this matter." Maybe not officially informed, but I did tell Will where I was going and that I just might say that bit about having informed the "police." "Sure, no problem," he said. "Just *do not* use my name since this isn't one of my police cases. My captain would go after my badge if he thought that I was involved in something that is not official business for the precinct. Got it?"

"Yup, got it. I won't use your name or badge number," I answered. Not unless it's absolutely necessary, I thought.

The receptionist disappears behind an inner sanctum of expensive doors for a few minutes. She returns with a member of the board, who ushers me into a spacious office with a commanding view of Water Street and its surroundings. "I'm Harlyn Vanders. How can I be of help?" says this well-dressed woman as she offers me a seat.

In a conversation that takes less than a half hour I find out that the Edward L. Penn on the board of Wells and Cummings isn't the Edward Penn who is engaged to Jennifer Brooks-Warren. In fact the Wells and Cummings Edward Penn, a founding partner, has been dead for thirteen years. When I question why Mr. Penn's name is still on the letterhead thirteen years after his demise, Harlyn Vanders smiles and answers, "It is customary to keep the founding partner's name on company stationery, Ms. Harlow. It honors the member's legacy and is a courtesy to his or her family who naturally still have stock in the company."

When I show her the picture of Edward with Jennifer she says he's definitely not a member of the board and isn't the Mr. Penn whose name is still on the brokerage letterhead. Their receptionist gave me the right info when she said an Edward Penn was on the letterhead; she just neglected to tell me the man bearing that name was dead.

"Any other way I can be of service to you?" She looks discreetly at the digital clock on her desk.

"Uh, no, thank you, Ms. Vanders. I have all the info I need." On the way out of Wells and Cummings I call the bank where Jennifer has her account and make an appointment with her bank business manager.

Leaving Water Street, I drive to the precinct close to Jennifer's condo. Edward had said that he filed a report with the police before he and Jennifer came to seek the services of a private investigator and Jennifer believed him. So did I. He lied. When I get to the precinct where Edward said he had gone for help, I find out that no one knows anything about him or any report being made. "The only contact we ever received relating to this case came from you today, miss," a weary-eyed desk sergeant tells me. "There's no report about someone trying to murder this Jennifer Brooks-Warren and there's no report filed by an Edward Penn. We never received a call to send officers to that building, either. Sorry."

Edward has been lying all along about being in contact with the police. He never talked to the cops in the lobby of the condo building. I've been so focused on the Eliminator that I failed to notice anything else.

Walking to my car, I trip over a piece of broken sidewalk and drop the Brooks-Warren file, scattering all Myrtle's neatly typed pages on the ground. I begin to gather them but an errant breeze scatters everything away from me. A kid handing out flyers bends down to help me and gallantly hands me the scattered papers and the manila file. I thank him with a smile and he winks at me, nodding to the bundle he has handed me.

Parked outside the precinct I begin to put the papers in order by date and notice something that wasn't with the original sheets; a flyer advertising a Male Strippers Club has been placed between two file pages. I take it out and begin to crumple it when a thought hits me. This advertisement was easily placed inside the file without my noticing a thing. The kid wasn't *helping* me as much as he was taking the *opportunity* to slip an advertisement in with my papers.

That note Jennifer received at her condo! *"Have you made arrangements yet?"* What had Edward said about finding the note? *"Jennifer received a note from The Eliminator. It must have been left at the front desk of our high-rise last night. The manager gave it to me when I went down to get the paper."* But the manager never gave him the note at all. Edward had the note on him all the time!

The manager told me that he had handed the mail and a circular to Edward who had then dropped it all on the floor. Edward Penn bent down to retrieve the dropped papers and that's when he had the opportunity to place the note in with the mail.

After picking it all up, he deliberately held the envelope up so the manager could see it. Anyone would assume the note had been hidden in a circular and had fallen out when the mail was dropped. Of course! The question is, why? Is Jennifer's fiancé somehow working with the Eliminator? Marc Croft did say to me that he, himself, wasn't into writing notes. Is Edward writing cryptic notes to terrify Jennifer on his behalf? What exactly is going on here?

I glance at my watch. It's time for me to drive to Jennifer's bank and have that meeting with the business manager handling her affairs.

Edward Penn is a devious son-of-a-bitch. I find out that he has tried withdrawing money from Jennifer's account on numerous occasions. That the business manager is an astute man and wary of someone like Edward Penn is to his professional credit.

"Your credentials have checked out, Ms. Harlow," says the manager, a sixtyish gentle man in charge of a section called Personal Wealth. "The recommendations of certain law enforcement agencies are also highly praiseworthy of you. You're bonded and secure. This is why, as a fiduciary, I am willing to speak with you in so blunt a manner." He adjusts his glasses and moves some papers around before he begins. I take out pen and notebook and wait expectantly. "A month ago, Mr. Edward Penn came in requesting to withdraw $100,000 from Ms. Jennifer-Brooks-Warren's account. Of course, we refused to do so. His name is not on the account even though he has tried several times to convince Ms. Brooks-Warren to have a joint account. He then requested a loan using the Brooks-Warren account as collateral. Said that his fiancée had given permission in a written note. However, the signature purported to be Ms. Brooks-Warren's was unverifiable. Of course we said no. Speaking to the account holder was an absolute necessity at that point but we were unable to speak with Ms. Brooks-Warren for confirmation at the time. He said that she was ill and unreachable. That naturally made us very suspicious of his request. I must tell you that he was very angry at not being able to get any money." He looks at me for a long moment then leans forward. "Now, I don't know if I should be telling you this. Please understand, Ms. Harlow, what I tell you must be kept in the utmost confidence until our investigation is completed but I feel this information may shed a new light on your case."

"I understand and you can count on my confidentiality."

"There's an in-house investigation going on right now concerning one of our bank officers. It seems that he may have broken a fiduciary trust. I have good reason to believe that he may be involved with Mr. Penn in an illicit transaction."

"May I ask in what way?"

"He seems to have been paid by Edward Penn to supply him with pertinent information about our customers. It is possible that this officer alerted Mr. Penn to Ms. Brooks-Warren's substantial fortune which came from her father's $1,200,000.00 life insurance policy. Unfortunately, during the course of our investigation, we are finding out that this is not the first time this man has given financial information to Mr. Penn. It seems that in the past, two other women who have accounts with our bank were in the same position as Ms. Brooks-Warren."

"They were wealthy, too?" I continue to write down what he is telling me.

"Not only well-off, but alone. No family, just completely alone, the same as Ms. Brooks- Warren. It seems that Mr. Penn is what my generation calls a shyster. He plays the concerned older man wanting to protect young women, tells them he's worth a fortune but says he doesn't like to discuss his wealth—that sort of thing. Of course, at some point in the relationship, there always seems to be a scheme where a man such as Mr. Penn says he needs ready cash for a deal of a lifetime but his assets are all tied up. Nine times out of ten, the woman will readily advance the cash to him and will never see him again."

I nod. "He plays on their vulnerability and their kind hearts."

"Exactly. A very sad state of affairs." I get up, thanking him for his time and his honesty.

"I hope all goes well with your investigation, Ms. Harlow."

"Yours too," I shake his proffered hand and smile. "Nail the bastard, will you?"

"*You* nail that bastard Penn for me. Ms. Brooks-Warren deserves better." And on that note I leave. I have all the info to confront Edward Penn and get Jennifer out of that condo into a place where she'll be safe from both the Eliminator and Penn.

It's beginning a light drizzle as I leave the bank. Just before I get to my car, my phone beeps once alerting me to a text. The message I receive from the security company is brief. "Cate, this is Adrian. Received your text that the Eliminator has been apprehended. I'm confirming your message that our services are no longer needed and I've pulled my detail. Great work, Cate. Just to let you know, we still have not received any payment. Send me a message or call me about our bill." Someone sent a text to Adrian telling him the Eliminator has been caught and to pull his security people off the job? That doesn't sound good. Jennifer is unprotected and in danger.

I no sooner put my phone into my back jeans pocket than it beeps with another message. An e-mail from TRUST flashes an urgent message on my phone screen.

"Duchovny has no part in what is going down now - ur client in danger - there is another killer "

Another killer? Only one person comes to mind.

The devil himself, Edward Penn.

CHAPTER 24

EDWARD PENN doesn't even flinch when I come into the room. The manager overrode the security code, which allowed me to take the private elevator directly to Edward's condo when I told him I had reason to believe that Jennifer's life was in immediate danger. I see wine in a beautiful cut crystal decanter on the table next to him. I feel as if I am in a 1930s movie; the apartment is so well appointed and classic with the main character, Edward, in an expensive-looking tracksuit and soft leather slippers, looking regal and relaxed. Everything is elegant. The only disconcerting and out-of-place items in the room are a pair of mud-encrusted work boots and heavy-duty work gloves tossed near the fireplace. He's reclining on a new, expensive-looking leather couch. His right arm rests casually on an overstuffed pillow and in his hand is a silver handled Derringer. The irony isn't lost on me that the Derringer was once called a 'gentleman's gun'.

"Where's Jennifer?"

"Come in, Ms. Harlow. Please come in," he says pointing the gun at me. "I see that you've managed to let yourself into my abode unannounced. Jennifer is not here at the moment. I myself have just returned from a rather unpleasant but very necessary...errand...and decided to have a glass of Petrus Pomerol, 1998. I understand that you like a good merlot. Pity that I can't offer you any of this excellent vintage but I am in an indulgent mood and by that I mean that I feel like indulging *myself*."

"Quite an expensive indulgence, Mr. Penn. About two thousand a bottle if I'm correct."

"Ah, you know your wines, Ms. Harlow! Now how does a lowly private detective with a less-than-stellar income come to know about fine wines?"

"It's a hobby. We lowly PIs have to have something to occupy our time when we're not chasing scum like you."

"Oh hardly scum, my dear lady. I have the best of everything and I live like a lord."

"On money you scammed out of emotionally needy women. You paid that bank clerk to give you the names of single, wealthy women who had no family ties. I'm sure you have the same deal with other dirty, little sneaks whom you pay well at various banks and brokerage houses. You've been scamming women out of their money for years, haven't you?"

"Guilty!" He laughs and takes another sip. "Little simpletons who *need* a man such as myself to help them learn how to spend their money."

"But there's one thing I don't understand, Edward. I would count you as a basically use'em and then lose'em kind of Lothario. You get them to give you money for one scheme or another then leave them. Why did you want Jennifer killed?" He laughs heartily as if I've told him a hilarious joke.

"Ah, now you know my deepest secret! Yes, why indeed! I'll tell you, dear Cate. You're correct in saying that I get the money from wealthy women and then leave them high and dry. It's a wonderful little scheme and has always worked well. But, sadly, it didn't work with Jennifer. That needy little *remade* woman wasn't as easy as my other targets. She held onto her money and doled it out a little too slowly for my taste. Maybe she inherited her old man's parsimony. I fear I have rather expensive habits and I like ready cash, something my other women were more than willing to give me. But that plastic swan who used to be an ugly duckling actually was smarter than I thought. The only thing I was able to do was to get her to make a will leaving everything to me; even that was a challenge.

"I thought that meeting Jennifer was heaven sent. Alone, no family, and when she told me about the contract on her life; what luck! I knew she was a perfect mark. If she was killed, no one would miss her. I could wait; the hit man was scheduled to strike on her birthday. The months leading up to her demise were rather tedious, though. For all that she said she was a whore in high school, sexually she was very naïve. No sexual adventures for her, none of the kinky things that *I* want done in a sexual encounter. Obviously she was only a quick, excuse my vulgarity here, but she was only a quick fuck for hormone-raging teenage boys. To make life a little more interesting while I waited, I started sending her little messages that she, and you, assumed were from the hit man. I had a copy made of that old picture of her and sent it with the first note. What fun I had while I was waiting for her demise and making plans for my future!" He laughs cruelly. "But then, unfortunately, I found out that my nice little plans for the future were about to be changed, dear Cate. I heard from the man who was contracted to kill Jennifer."

"If I may be so bold as to ask, how were *you* able to contact the hit man anyway? Jennifer and I had no luck with that whatsoever."

"Oh," laughs Edward when I confront him with that question, "*that*. Actually Jennifer was more successful than she thought. Her own ads and the social media pleas eventually paid off. He *did* contact her. I took the call when she was…sleeping. Of course, I made sure to take *all* her calls so that I would know all her financial business. When I answered the phone he said very abruptly, 'This message is for Jennifer. Tell her the contract has been canceled, fee retained.' I was stunned and suddenly angry. All these months waiting and waiting were wasted. He canceled the contract. Just like that. No fucking honor among thieves or murderers I guess." Edward settles himself more comfortably before continuing.

"I blurted out the first thought in my head. 'You mean you're *not* going to kill her? Why not?' He laughed at me and said if *I* wanted to have her eliminated it would cost more money. I immediately offered him twenty thousand dollars for a new contract. He laughed again and upped it to one hundred thousand, that shrewd bastard. He obviously knew about her will and what I would inherit from it. Her monetary circumstances had changed significantly since she had first contacted him. I had no choice but to agree. Why should I save her life? As I said Jennifer wasn't exactly forthcoming with large cash amounts and even with her glamorous new looks, she was a pretty boring, clingy person. Being with her would simply drive me crazy. I like new vistas, new women, exciting, aberrant sexual adventures. Why, Jennifer would have expected me to be faithful! I need my freedom.

"As for his fee, hell, I thought I could borrow the money against Jennifer's account. After all, as her sole beneficiary, I would certainly have her money after she was bumped off." He stops and flashes me a sinister smile. "Do you know that Jennifer would have left most of that lovely money to a stupid women's shelter if I hadn't convinced her to make a new will?"

I am so tempted to slap that self-serving smile off his face. "A new will that she obviously signed while you had her drugged. Notarized no doubt by your cohort from the bank, the man who has come to the condo several times."

"Bingo, Ms. Harlow, bingo! You are sharp, aren't you? Oh I had her nicely sedated when she signed that crucial piece of paper. Actually I'd been giving her drugs for quite a while, always at strategic times. Of course before we arrived in your office that first time, she had been off the drugs for a week. I had to have her rather alert with no hint of sedation. You're sharp-eyed and would notice her groggy demeanor. All you saw was a woman who was tense, tearful, and jumpy; all natural reactions for anyone who fears for her life.

"Ah, well, now where was I? Oh yes; I made arrangements

to have her, what's that word he used? Oh yes, *e-l-i-m-i-n-a-t-e-d*. Jennifer would know nothing about any cancellation of her original contract and neither would the police, those security people, or you.

"After her elimination, I *would* say murder but that's such a nasty word, I would play the grieving fiancé, robbed of a life with the only woman he had ever loved. Her money would set me up quite handsomely for some time to come and of course I would have my freedom. Brilliant idea on my part."

He licks his lips after taking a long sip of the Petrus Pomerol '98. Edward Penn looks me up and down then laughs. "Most women are not like you, Ms. Harlow; you're skeptical and hard to fool." He sits back and laughs. "But, getting back to my proposed contract with the hit man, there was a nasty little fly in the ointment. My request for a loan was denied. The best-laid plans and all that bullshit, you know? This hit man wanted the money for the new contract up front. Imagine! I didn't have that kind of money and since the bank refused to lend me the amount, I was in quite a difficult position. What to do, eh? So...I took matters into my own very capable hands. After all, I already had her pretty well drugged, I was sending her ominous mail and messages to scare her witless." Another sip. "Actually you almost caught me the night of that pathetic dinner you arranged. I dropped my burner phone right after I sent that last text to Jennifer. Yes, dear girl, I did it all. *I* was the one who ordered the fucking coffin, a fancy coffin too good for a backwoods girl really! By the way, is it still raining? She so hated rain! But, as I told you, rain washes away everything!

"You," Edward smiles warmly at me as if reliving a memory of a pleasant meeting, "hiring you was the best idea I had. I convinced Jennifer to hire a private investigator, I said *I* would find someone. I did my research, Cate dear, yes I did. You were perfect. You seem to have an affinity for helping poor whiny women. It must be your goal in life to help those stupid bitches who seem so incapable of helping themselves. There was the Reynolds woman crying 'My baby, my baby!' and you took her case and found her daughter who was kidnapped 22 years ago. Mother and child reunion!" He begins to sing the beginning of the old Paul Simon song by that title. "The news loved that one. And then there was that sad-faced woman, that what's-her-name McElroy woman, another little mouse; you found her missing brother for her, kid sexually abused by the parish priest or someone. Such drama! That was all over the news media. You specialize in scared, helpless women so I thought why not throw one more your way and keep Jennifer busy while I plotted my next move? Jennifer was a weak, scared shitless bitch."

He said *was* as in *is no more*. "Where is she, Edward? Where's Jennifer?" I feel my heart start to race. Edward Penn simply sips his wine and says nothing. "Where *is* she?"

"My dear girl! Such drama from someone who always seems so cool." He laughs again. "Anyway, I have no fear. She's somewhere you will never find her." He checks his watch.

"Actually she may already be gone." He laughs at his little joke. "And you will never leave here alive, Ms. Harlow. The story will be that you came here and were killed by the very same hit man who was hired by stupid Jennifer. I will be the one who finds you. Shock, terror, oh dear me and all that crap." He looks at me menacingly. "Now dear, Cate, slowly remove your gun from the waistband of those divinely tight jeans you're so fond of wearing and toss it over here. Be careful, dear, don't make any sudden moves."

I have to take a chance. Will would say I'm reckless but I have to do it. In one smooth move I take my Smith and Wesson out of my waistband holster, aim it downward, and fire it at the floor behind me, startling Edward. Stepping quickly forward I kick the silver Derringer out of his hand. He tries to reach for the heavy crystal decanter to use as a weapon but I'm quicker than he is and in a second I am aiming my gun at him. "Don't do it, Edward. You know I won't hesitate to shoot you." Then, before he can react, I jab my gun hard into his groin.

"Ow, you bitch! You fucking bitch!"

"Where is she, Edward? Where? Tell me now or I swear I

will shoot and blow away whatever manhood you've got there. The blood and flesh will spatter all over the very expensive upholstery on your new leather couch. And the best part about all that? You'll still be alive, Edward. I won't kill you, I'll neuter you one ball at a time; I'm that precise a shot, you bastard. Trust me, I'm very good at what I do." Actually shooting any man in the testicles will more than likely do more than neuter him; the loss of blood will kill him. But all Edward needs to know is that I *will* shoot him there.

"You'll never find her, you bitch."

"Where is she?" I jab harder.

Edward gasps for breath through the pain. "Buried alive in the type of coffin perfectly suited to her needs."

"Where? Where's the coffin?"

He coughs and smirks. "Now where do we put coffins, dear? In the ground, *deep in the ground.*"

I twist the gun harder and he screams. "In what ground? Where did you bury her? When?"

For a few precious minutes he's unable to speak then, when he hears me cock the gun, he mutters, "It was…around…six, six this evening. Unmarked grave, there're so many of them. Over 800,000. You'll *never* find her." Then he passes out. I check my watch; it's just after 6:30. Calling Will, I hurriedly tell him about Edward and Jennifer's possible murder. "I'll send patrol cars right now and I'm on my way." I hang up and look around for something to restrain Edward until Will and his people get here. I put the Derringer in my pocket and hog-tie Edward up tightly with corded drapery tie-backs.

He buried her alive! Edward buried her alive! But where, where? There are so many cemeteries; where would he be likely to bury her? I have to try to find her. With no idea where to look, I race down toward my car thinking of cemeteries in the local area. I'm forcing myself to think as rationally as possible. Okay. Buried. Had to be in secret. Wouldn't want any witnesses. I don't believe that he had an assistant. Secret, secret. He said "so many unmarked graves, over 800,000." Where?! I stop and lean next to a car, then hit the Google search button on my phone. Clearly and slowly I say, "Unmarked graves, 800,000" and a robotic voice comes back with

"Hart Island, New York." He didn't go for a local graveyard. Hart Island, there's a Potter's Field located on Hart Island, a small island in New York City at the western end of Long Island Sound.

It has quite a history; I remember learning about it in high school. It's on the easternmost part of the Bronx borough and had been used over the years as a Union Civil War prison camp, a lunatic asylum, a tuberculosis sanatorium, a boys' infamous reformatory, and finally a potter's field.

Indigent people and a lot of inmates from Riker's Island are buried there. I also remember with dread that the island is a restricted area under the jurisdiction of the New York City Department of Correction. No one can visit Hart Island without contacting the prison system first. I hit my speed dial to call Will again.

"Hart Island. Okay, Cate, I'll deal with the bureaucratic bullshit. Where are you?"

"Near the parking garage."

"Get back to the building and meet me outside. We have to get to heliport NK39 at One Police Plaza. Two other officers will be with me and I'm getting an emergency STAT Flight from Westchester Medical to follow us. I'm contacting Hart Island authorities now."

I race back to the building doing a quick calculation of how long a person can last inside a coffin before the air runs out. My God! A closed box under maybe six feet of dirt. How long would the small amount of air last? How much air! How can that be calculated?! Think Cate, Jesus Christ, think! I punch in Giles's number. The call goes to voice mail. That means that he's either in autopsy or in a conference. I call the morgue.

"Office of the Medical Examiner."

"Dr. Giles Barrett. This is Cate Harlow."

"I'm sorry, Ms. Harlow, but Dr. Barrett is not available."

"This is an emergency. Get Dr. Barrett now. It is a matter of life and death."

"But..."

"Now! Someone will die if you *do not* put Dr. Barrett on the phone!"

Two long minutes go by and then I hear Giles's soothing voice. "Catherine? What's going on?"

"I need some information. How long can a living person survive in an airtight coffin buried underground?"

"I don't quite understand. What...?"

"He buried her alive, Giles! Edward buried Jennifer alive. I think she's in an unmarked grave on Hart Island, in Potter's Field. Now tell me how long does she have?"

"I don't know for certain, Cate," he says as calmly as possible though I hear a touch of fear in his voice, "but I do remember a lecture I heard in med school on controlling breathing. The lecturer talked about an escape artist who was placed in a lead-lined box. He said that there's only about two to three hours or so of air in a sealed box. The air supply could last a little longer only IF a person could stay calm enough to keep their breathing slow and not use up the oxygen too fast. But it's a Catch-22. As the oxygen levels get lower, the heart rate speeds up in an effort to get more oxygen to the body, which will, in turn, speed up the breathing causing the air to run out faster. Through controlled breathing the escape artist had lasted almost three hours. The average person would panic. Plus, this escape artist was in constant contact with his assistants by a communication device placed in the box. If he was in trouble they'd get him out fast."

Jennifer is alone with no one to help her and death is the only possible end. Shit!

"Catherine? Listen to me carefully. There is something that could possibly be in Jennifer's favor. If she was drugged, if Edward drugged her to put her in the coffin, her vital signs will be lowered; her breathing and her heart rate will be shallower and slowed down considerably. Please call me later, Catherine. Let me know...either way. Good luck!" I see Will's unmarked car screeching to the curb and put my phone in my pocket. *Oh God, I hope he drugged her!* I think, getting into Will's car and racing, sirens blaring, toward the heliport.

※

Hart Island is a thin half-mile long strip of land at the yawning mouth of Long Island Sound. It is a dismal place at any time of the day but coupled with dark clouds and a steady drizzle it resembles a landscape right out of a vampire novel. People buried on the island run a wide gamut from indigents to prison inmates to the misinformed public. One third of its inhabitants are infants because their parents couldn't afford a burial. Then there were those families who didn't understand what the term 'city burial' meant on a death certificate. Many of the dead here were homeless, many others were simply unclaimed. Giles once told me that it is a sad truth that if a body remains at the city morgue for more than a few weeks that the corpse will automatically be sent for burial on Hart Island. A team of inmates from the state prison system do the honors of burying the indigent, the unwanted, and the lost.

"Here," says Will just before we land. He's handing me a HAZ-LO tactical police flashlight and a state-of-the-art police mobile phone used by rescue teams. "We're going to scan the island and hopefully the second team will be here soon to help us. Harbor Patrol is sending a crew as soon as they can. We have to split up to be able to cover as much of the area as possible." Pointing to the phone he says, "Stay in contact with me as much as you can. If you see anything at all, let me know immediately."

"What about Edward Penn? Your officers get anything out of him about where he buried Jennifer?"

Will shakes his head. "Not yet but they're working on it. He claims he doesn't know what we're talking about and that you attacked *him* because he failed to protect Jennifer when the Eliminator grabbed her. He swears the Eliminator told him he was going to bury her but that he, Edward, has no idea where. The guy is trying to lawyer up but so far we've been able to keep the call from going through. We're claiming technical difficulties with the phone service. He's in a holding cell downtown complaining about internal genital injuries he says *you* inflicted. You really jam your Smith and Wesson in his balls?" I nod. "That's my Cate," he says admiringly.

After landing on Hart Island we fan out in all directions to look for a fresh grave. There are really no guards on the island; just a harbor patrol that goes by every hour or so. The island is so isolated that they follow no real set schedule. We've got a scent dog with us but, as one of the officers said to Will and me in the police copter, if the coffin is lead-lined the dog won't be able to sniff out anything. God help us if that top-of-the-line Perfect Ruby Rest 0557 is lead-lined.

Even though the island is relatively small I quickly lose sight of Will and the other two officers. Only their flashlights are visible for a while, unearthly lights moving across the island. I stop near a plain white grave marker. Damn!

The rain has created a misty fog that hangs over the island adding to the eerie, chilling look. I cannot see where Will and the other two officers went; even their lights aren't visible any more. I hear intermittent barking but can't know if it's the police dog or one of the wild dogs on the island. I feel desperate and hopeless. Over by the broken fence I see movement and then several creatures, maybe rats, scurrying across the wet ground. I don't really want to know what they are, I just want to find Jennifer alive and get the hell out of here. A gull flying across the water's edge gives a screeching cry and I jump at the sound.

Even with the flashlight to guide me I slip and slide in the soaked soil. At one point I fall flat and the mobile phone goes skittering off down a small hill into a muddy trench and out of sight. I shine my light down the slope but see nothing. Going to get it is not an option; I don't know how deep that hole is and I can't risk falling into it. Besides, time's running out; I have to find that new grave.

Suddenly I see a figure walking toward me out of the mist. I breathe a ragged sigh of relief and yell out, "Will!" But it's not

Will or either of the other two cops who came with us. It's another man wearing what looks like the type of backpack worn by combat soldiers or survivalists, and he's carrying a shovel. One of the group of convicts who do the burying on this island? Jesus! I put my hand on my gun. No, he wouldn't be here alone; there would be guards and other prisoners with him. It has to be some type of a custodian who is employed here or maybe one of the Harbor Patrol agents. Still...keeping my right hand on my gun I pull out my PI license with my left and run toward him.

"Sir? Over here!" The figure walking toward me stops. "Sir? Do you work here? I'm a private investigator, there are police and a detective on the island searching for a grave dug this evening. There's a woman buried alive here. Help me!" The figure turns away from me and hides his face. "Hello? Can you hear me?" I run over and a familiar voice says, "I can hear you just fine. Stay where you are." It is the voice of the man in my condo; the Eliminator, Marc Croft! His right hand holds a gun and a canteen hangs from the utility belt he's wearing. I move toward him in spite of what he said and the fact that his gun is aimed in my direction.

"Jennifer is buried alive somewhere on this God-forsaken island. Edward buried her here. He said you wouldn't kill her because he didn't have the money you wanted."

"I don't bury people unless they're already dead. Quick kills are what I do."

"Help me find her then. She's going to die! There can't be much air left; he buried her an hour ago."

"Since I am not the one who is killing her, I should say that if she dies, she dies. But her death *would* be a travesty. This woman didn't deserve this type of death; no one does."

"You're carrying a shovel. Why did you come here?"

"To undo a wrong."

I see him looking around with some type of a hand-held device that I know is a thermal scope. I had intended to buy one for my own use after reading an article on how an infrared scope was used by the Los Angeles County sheriff's department to find a lost hiker. The trouble was I couldn't afford it and decided that it had to wait. It seems that the Eliminator doesn't have the same money problems; he has all the latest equipment of the spy trade. "Your companions are scattered all over the island and that's good. Good for me, good for you," he looks at me with those cold eyes, "and good for her." He holsters his gun and I take a quick look all around me.

There's no one that I can see. Will and the others are not in sight. I'm alone and I need help now; I don't give a damn if it's a hit man or the devil himself who helps me. I feel a desperation verging on hysteria.

I take a deep breath. "I can't stand here talking with you; we're wasting precious time. We have to find her. My God! She's going to suffocate!" He doesn't move. I need to get his attention. "Victoria!" He turns and faces me. "When you were in my brownstone you mentioned a woman named Victoria. You felt responsible for her death. How did she die?" I say this quietly watching his reaction. "You said you didn't kill her but that she died *because* of you." When I say this I see his hands grip the shovel hard. "Don't let this woman Jennifer die because of you. Please, help me find her. I know that's why you came here, I know there's more to you than just being a killer."

The Eliminator advances toward me and smirks. "You misjudge me, Cate. I am an *assassin*; that's all I am. I said I do quick kills but I also do torture and take body-part trophies when necessary to prove a kill. Don't nominate me for sainthood; I am no more than a cold-blooded killer." I have my hand on my gun but I see something in his face that makes me know I have nothing to fear from him. His jaw is clenched with determination and his eyes hold an intense anger in them. But just for a brief, very brief moment when I said the name Victoria, I saw a look of sadness, a vulnerable emotion of which I didn't think he was capable. It quickly passes but that look gives me an edge and I continue to press my point.

"You said you came here to undo a wrong. All right, then let's do that, let's undo that wrong, whatever it was, together.

Don't tell me what it was, I don't have the time to find out. Just help me find Jennifer's grave before it's too late. I'll help you all I can but I don't know where to look. Tell me what to do."

"Look for a fresh grave," is all he says as he begins to walk away from me again. I look around. The rain has made a mudfield of the surrounding area and I don't know where to begin. "Wait! They all look fresh! The rain," I am panting with fear for Jennifer's life as I approach him, "The rain makes everything look as if it is all freshly dug up." I hear that bastard Edward saying, *"The rains washes everything away."* This burial was planned for a rain-soaked day.

The Eliminator turns again facing me and his cold blue eyes look directly into mine. I don't know what he sees there, my fear for Jennifer, my desperate determination against the odds, but he sees something and my instinct tells me that that something is all I need to gain his help.

"No, you wouldn't know, you're not trained to look for new graves. I am." He looks around and points toward a corner lot. "Look, see that one over there by those stones? That small mound of earth on the side?" I strain to look and see what looks like a ball of mud slightly higher than the ground around it. Is that the grave? I start to run over to the muddy mound but he grabs my arm and stops me.

"That's not the one you're looking for; that grave was dug a few days ago. The mud is packed down but it's hardened. It's fresh but not as of today. I'm just showing you an example. The ground always tells secrets, you just have to know what to look for."

"How will I know if a grave has been dug today? How will I know it's fresh?" I am having trouble breathing because I know Jennifer won't be breathing if I don't find her within the next thirty minutes. Marc Croft patiently explains and it seems to me as if he's wasting precious time.

"One, you'll see marks of dirt packing to conceal the grave, probably quick packing as the killer wanted to get out of here as soon as possible. He wouldn't take the time to police his brass."

Police his brass—it's a military term as well as police slang for cover your tracks, hide the evidence. I've heard Will use it. "Two, look for a disturbance in the *surrounding* area; deep drag marks, grass or vegetation moved around, a scattering of stones or gravel in one area. Those are the signs of a fresh digging. If you look you'll find where he buried her."

"What about tire marks from a truck? The coffin had to be driven from a boat to here."

To answer he points to all the crisscrossing tire marks in the soft ground. "Too many to follow. Not all the marks you see are for coffin delivery."

I begin to sweat and panic. "Everything looks the same to me."

As I'm talking he's looking around, methodically canvassing the area, missing nothing. He is wasting so much time! Suddenly he points and says very quietly, "It's in that plot by the two crosses. Come on."

"Are you sure? How do you know it's the right grave?"

He looks at me with his cold, steel-blue eyes and says softly. "I *know*." I guess when digging graves is part of your business, you pretty much do know a fresh grave when you see one. I don't question him again, just silently follow at a run to where he's pointing.

The ground is soft with rain. My feet sink deeply into the wet soil and make a sucking sound with each step. Oh God, oh God, oh God! Shit! Goddamn it! I'm screaming prayers as well as curses in my head. Jennifer, please be alive! Please let that bastard Edward have drugged you enough so that you don't wake up and know that you're inside a coffin! Don't let him have drugged you so much that you're already dead! Please be alive!

The plot of land is small and, as I get closer, looks as if someone had recently packed it. Throwing his backpack on the ground, Marc Croft points out covered up drag marks leading up to the plot. At the grave site he begins to dig the soft wet ground. Down on my knees I begin to scoop mud with my hands forcing myself to dig carefully making every dig count. Without missing a beat the Eliminator says, "There's a trowel over by that marker to your left. Get it. You'll dig faster." I turn, see it, and slip and slide my way over to it in the mud. Back at the grave I dig frenziedly with both the trowel and my hands. Time and the digging seem to be going in slow motion.

"I don't think it's too deep," he says. "As soon as I get her out you're going to have to call those cops you came with for help."

"My phone, I can't. I dropped the phone down a slope into a trench back there." I point to the area where it slipped out of my hands. He looks at me and shakes his head but continues digging.

"We'll have to use mine then...if it's necessary. The police and I aren't exactly a good mix." He's like a machine digging robotically. I've never seen a man work as non-stop and fast as he is working. My hands feel numb and I taste blood where I bit my lip in my frustration.

"She's about three or four feet down, no deeper. I can almost guarantee it. He's not the type of person who would take the time to do a proper job." The way he says proper job, as if he has firsthand knowledge of just how deeply to dig when burying a person, sends chills through me.

A pile of mud is building next to his side of the plot. The Eliminator is methodical. His pile of mud grows slowly and steadily. I dig like a dog going after a groundhog, flinging mud and stones everywhere and I feel as if I am sinking into a mud hell. Then, without warning the rain-soaked ground where I'm kneeling gives way. I fall hard, deep into a muddy hole. A sharp pain shoots through my right knee as it hits something hard. Marc Croft comes over to my side and pulls me up one-handed out of the mud-filled abyss with no effort whatsoever. He pushes me aside to peer into the hole then begins a renewed marathon of digging. "Get the trowel, dig with me. There's something in here."

I try to stand but my knee buckles and I fall back down. Crawling over to the trowel and back to the hole I begin digging again. Time seems to stand still again but in a few minutes

I hear a *thunk* as the Eliminator's shovel hits something solid. He grabs the trowel out of my hands and leaning into the hole begins to scrape the soaked earth from whatever is in there. I drag myself over and am instantly heartsick. The wooden box he's found is not the Perfect Ruby Rest 0557; it's a plain solid wooden crate. We have the wrong grave! "It's the wrong grave, we've been digging the wrong grave! You said it was the right grave, you son-of-a-bitch, you said you knew! This is a goddamned cheap packing crate, not a coffin." I struggle to my feet and stand on my left leg. "We have to find…" but the Eliminator isn't paying any attention to me. He's using the butt of his gun to break open the crate's lid. "Why are you wasting time?!" I limp over to him, fall to my good knee, and grab his arm. "She's going to die if we don't…" He shoves me back hard and I land on my side in the mud.

"She *is* going to die if I don't get this lid *off*."

The box is square and looks old. Edward buried Jennifer in a plain crate that looks as if it held furniture. Of course, that new couch he had delivered last week! He must have kept the box just for this burial. But where's the coffin? Why a box and not the expensive Perfect Ruby Rest 0557? Edward's words *"Too good for a backwoods girl"* and *"A coffin suited to her needs"* come into my mind. But I can't think about that now; I have to concentrate on getting Jennifer out of that crate. "Let me help you," I say as calmly as I can. "Please, I can work with you and then we can…" But he doesn't let me finish my sentence.

"You want to help me? Stop talking and stay the fuck out of my way. Your help is a liability and I don't like liabilities; they mess up a job. I usually get rid of liabilities." Subdued, my heart pounding, I kneel as close as possible to him without being in his way and watch breathlessly as the Eliminator works to free Jennifer. Hurry! Jesus Christ, please hurry up. It is all I can do not to jump in and break the lid with my fists.

Without looking at me he says, "Take your off sweatshirt and the top you have underneath."

I'm stunned. "What? Why?"

"I need the sweatshirt to wrap her in. She's been underground; her body temp will be low."

"Okay, but why my top?"

"The mud has seeped through the slats. She'll have mud in her nose and mouth. You're wearing a cotton top and I'm going to need something soft to scoop the mud out so she can breathe. Any more questions?" His voice is low but filled with anger. Not wanting to be a liability, I hurriedly take off my hoodie and toss it to him. "Now give me the top and come here."

I hesitate, but only for a moment, then take off the lilac Stella McCartney top, a birthday gift from Melissa, and slide over to him. Feeling vulnerable in just jeans and a bra I kneel next to him on my uninjured knee. "You want to help? Then do exactly as I say and nothing more. Take out your gun, Cate, and don't get cute with it. I can kill you with my bare hands if you try anything." I do as he says. "Hit the wood with the butt of your gun, help me crack these thick wooden slats open." Again I do as he says and begin to smash the butt of my Smith and Wesson against the slats. I see blood on his hand as a jagged piece of wood slices across his palm but he seems impervious to the cut. Through the small opening my gun has made, all I see is mud and grass that have slipped through the slim openings. The mud may have suffocated her. I keep banging that gun with all my strength like a hammer

Then, suddenly, with a monumental effort, Marc Croft pulls a large piece of wood away and I see her. Jennifer Brooks-Warren, the beautiful woman Myrtle thought was a model the first time she saw her in my office, is lying in the crate, death and mud covering her. There is no movement.

The wood creaks an unearthly sound as the Eliminator uses the trowel as a crowbar to loosen the other slats. Then he reaches inside and presses his fingers expertly against the pulse point on the side of her neck. He moves his fingers around to the other side of her neck and I draw in my breath waiting for what seems like an eternity. His shoulders sag a bit as he curses and wipes his bloody hand across his forehead. He sits back on his heels, closes his eyes, and lets the steady rain fall on his face.

She's dead. I sink back onto the ground and put my head in my hands. Jesus Christ! I couldn't save her. Even *his* superhuman efforts couldn't save her. Dimly I'm aware that her body is being lifted out of the box. Oh God, Jennifer, I am so sorry, so sorry. I failed to protect you. I am so very sorry!

She's dead.

CHAPTER 25

"SHE'S ALIVE."

"Alive?" I scramble to my knees and look at Jennifer lying absolutely still, Marc Croft leaning over her. "She's alive?"

"Just barely alive, but she's got a pulse."

Marc Croft has Jennifer on the ground and is gently but firmly cleaning the goop of mud and grass out of her mouth and nostrils with the soft material of my top. From a bottle in a holder he has attached to his belt he pours water over her face. Then he begins to do CPR. I kneel next to him and watch as he tries desperately to breathe life back into Jennifer's still body. "Breathe, come on you poor foolish woman, breathe!" I hear him say, cursing. "Breathe!" Slowly and rhythmically he gives her mouth-to-mouth, trying to resuscitate her limp body. Speaking to me he says, "Know CPR?" When I answer yes, he simply says, "Good. Take over." He gets his backpack and pulls out a monitor of some sort. Glancing at him I see him check two small paddles and some wires. He also takes out a syringe and a small bottle.

I do chest compressions the way I've been taught, left hand flat on the chest, right hand pressing down on the left. One-two-three, one-two-three. Breathe, Jennifer, breathe! One-two-three. Marc Croft brings over the device he had in his backpack.

"If we can't get her heart to start pumping, we'll use this portable defibrillator. Ever use one?"

I shake my head no. "In your line of work you might want to learn. Get up now, I'll take over." I shakily move to the side to give him room and he kneels over Jennifer's body. His hands, much bigger and stronger than mine, perform measured chest compressions. After what seems like an agonizingly long time, I hear a hissing sound coming from her throat. He pours just a bit of water in her mouth and it gurgles over the side of her lips as he turns her head to the side. She's silent.

"Wrap your sweatshirt around her shoulders," he says, pulling off his own shirt and wrapping it around her legs. I see scars on his chest and back. He was tortured at some point in his life. Seeing me look at them he says, "Comes with the job, sweetheart." Then he turns his attention back to Jennifer. "She was drugged before being put in the ground. I'm going to inject adrenaline. If it works, and in my experience it usually does, we won't need the defib." He fills the syringe with a clear liquid and expertly jabs her in the chest causing her to gasp loudly and open her eyes. Suddenly she begins to struggle, hitting awkwardly at Marc Croft. An unearthly scream issues from her as she turns in her struggles and sees the wooden box. "No, no, please, no-o-o-!"

"It's okay, you're alive," says Croft holding a thrashing Jennifer next to his chest. Turning to me he says angrily, "I think she was semi-conscious when he put her in that box. She knew what was happening to her." Jennifer's thrashing slows down and she begins to sob. The Eliminator cradles her as if she were a child. "Shhh. You're okay, you're alive. Shhh. All over now."

Hearing this soft, kind voice issuing from an assassin makes me shiver. What a scene we make! Covered in mud and grass. Me in a bra and jeans, the muscled but scarred body of Marc Croft, the man who was hired to kill Jennifer Brooks-Warren, holding, rocking, and soothing his once-intended victim as if they were lovers. Time seems to stand still as I survey the unbelievable scene in front of me.

Disembodied voices carry from a distance away and Croft glances around. "I see moving lights way over by the north side, Cate. That would be the cops. We need help with this. Call out to them. They'll come. Walk forward so they can hear you. I can't leave her. Go!"

Pain shoots into my knee as I stand up and limp toward where Croft is pointing. They're so far away their lights look like fireflies flickering on and off. "Help! Help us! Over here!" I yell as loudly as I can, waving my flashlight back and forth. "Help! Here, here!"

I glance around at Marc Croft who has wrapped the sweatshirts around Jennifer more snugly and is holding her head as he dribbles water into her mouth. "Bring them over here, Harlow. Hurry!"

Turning toward the lights I limp toward them as fast as I can, screaming louder and waving the flashlight in a wide arc. Suddenly I see one of the lights in the distance flashing a code back at me that acknowledges my position. They're coming closer.

"Over here! Over here! Please hurry!"

"Cate?" Will's voice comes out of the fog toward me. "You okay?"

"Yes! We've got Jennifer! Hurry! She's alive but she needs care!"

Within a few minutes Will and his emergency team surround me. "Help her. We found the grave and we got her out. She needs immediate medical care. Marc has given her preliminary care. We need more help. We..."

"Who's we?" Will looks at me standing there shaking with exhaustion and pain, my top half dressed only in a bra, and he takes off his jacket to cover me.

"Marc and I. He saved her. See? Marc, tell..."

I turn around to see Jennifer lying on the ground swaddled in two sweatshirts, the EMTs hurrying toward her. Marc Croft, aka the Eliminator, is nowhere in sight. "He was right here. He was here!" I turn looking in all directions but the foggy mist is all I see. The Eliminator has disappeared into thin air.

Will is surveying the scene as the EMTs tend to a still-sobbing Jennifer. "There's no one here, Cate." He walks over to where Jennifer was buried and looks down into the hole at the shattered box. "How did you get her out of that grave?"

I pull Will aside away from earshot of the medical personnel. "Would you believe me if I told you it was the hit man who helped me?"

"The Eliminator? He was here? With you?" I nod. "Why didn't you call me?"

"I dropped the phone down a slope and it slid into a trench. I was afraid that if I went after it, I'd slide into that damn trench too. But, Will, the Eliminator knew just how to save her. He's a survivalist; he knew where to look for the grave and what to do."

As Will takes out his police phone I grab his hand and stop him. "No, don't. Don't go after him. He saved her life. Edward tried to kill her, not this guy. It's a long story but he did help *me* and she's alive because of him. Let him go," I sigh and steady myself by leaning on Will. "You'll never find him anyway."

He thinks about it for a second then puts his phone away. "How badly are you hurt?"

"I'm not, not really, just jammed my knee. I'm fine." The EMTs have put Jennifer on a stretcher and I limp over to her. "You're going to be okay, Jenn. You're safe now." She grabs my hand and just stares at me. I don't think she recognizes me but then her eyes seem to re-focus. In a barely audible voice she whispers, "Thank you, Cate."

One of the EMTs gives me an ice bandage to wrap around my knee. Other officers from Will's detail arrive as Jennifer is being taken to where the helicopter waits and we watch her go off.

"We're going back by Harbor Patrol. They're at the dock. I've already radioed them," Will tells us. He consults a map on his phone, finds the coordinates and all of us slowly walk down to a small dock by the river's edge.

―≈―

Jennifer has been taken to the emergency trauma center at Westchester Medical. Will receives a call from the center and he puts the caller on speaker phone so I can hear. A Dr. Bishop alerts us that Jennifer is drifting in and out of consciousness, is severely dehydrated, and has been heavily drugged. "It's a touch-and-go scenario, Detective," says the doctor on the other end. "The next few hours are critical." Will thanks him and asks to be kept updated. He also gives the doctor my number with instructions to call me with the same updates.

Will drops me back near Jennifer's condo where I am parked. A ticket is prominently displayed on my windshield for parking in a restricted area but Will grabs it and says he'll take care of it. We smile at each other wearily, both of us remembering the ticket I got last year and how Will refused to fix it for me. I'm exhausted. "Want your jacket back? I have an old tennis shirt in my car."

"No, keep it on. You look cute." Will winks at me. "See you tomorrow, babe. I've got to finish up the paperwork on this case at the precinct and then head over to the law library. It's been an interesting day. Lunch tomorrow?" I nod. "Dessert later at your place?"

"Sure."

"In bed?" That gets a laugh from me. He'll never change and I'm glad. Ignoring the mud covering me, Will grabs me and pulls me tightly against him, kissing me long and hard, his tongue exploring the inside of my mouth. "Cate, my gutsy, reckless, Cate!" he murmurs with his face nuzzled against my neck. His hand gently cups my right breast and his tongue massages the hollow by my throat. What is it about danger that makes us want to have sex? Is it an affirmation that we're still living, that we survived an ordeal?

I hear a discreet cough and a voice saying, "Umm, excuse me. Detective?" It's one of the cops who was with us on Hart Island. Will reluctantly breaks away from me, adjusts his pants, and becomes all business. "I, uh, checked any boats that may have come from the Hart Island area plus the city docking ports, sir, and there's no viable info concerning the man PI Harlow was with on Hart Island. No one seems to have seen him either coming or going to the island. It's almost as if he was a ghost."

I lean back against my Edge breathing heavily from the exhaustion of the last fifteen hours as well as the erotic kissing encounter with Will and say, "He *is* a ghost, officer, he's the White Death. You'll never find out anything about him." Then I climb shakily into my Ford Edge, say goodnight to Will and the young cop and drive back to my brownstone.

Three days later the Jennifer Brooks-Warren case has been filed in the closed case folder on my computer. Because she insists on my doing so with all my cases, a paper copy has been given to Myrtle to be put in the locked filing cabinet. She once told me that she likes having back-up copies in case of a computer crash. "You'd lose all your work, honey!" she said. "Then what?"

Edward Penn is at Riker's Island and has retained a public defender as legal counsel. He's claiming innocence of course. That's not going to help him. My statement concerning what he said to me regarding his attempted murder of Jennifer, as well as his death threat to me, will pretty much seal his fate and he won't be going anywhere for a long time. When she's well enough, Jennifer will testify about being drugged and buried alive at Edward's hands. I hope he rots in Hell.

Jennifer is still hospitalized and I'm not sure that she knew who I was when I went to see her. The doctors told me that she will recover and that I saved her life. Of course I know better. She wouldn't be alive if Marc Croft hadn't been there. It's a shame that he can't take the credit for saving her. I hope he's well.

For some reason I don't want to be alone right now and that's especially true at night. I keep seeing that box in the ground and the way Jennifer looked when Marc Croft pulled her out. Will came over last night with some good Thai food and after we ate I asked him to sit with me on the couch and just hold me. We fell asleep in each other's arms and I felt safe for awhile. Life and death are too closely tied to our jobs and we both know it. I hope Jennifer finds someone like Will someday, someone who will make her feel safe too.

CHAPTER 26

EVEN THOUGH I know that Myrtle is glad that Jennifer was found alive and will make a full physical recovery, I haven't seen her smile in over a month. I am determined to find out what Harry has been up to and why his actions seem to be making Myrtle so miserable.

Early in the afternoon, while Myrtle is busy with some *Catherine Harlow, Private Investigations* billing, I slip away from the office and go to see if Harry is home. When I get to their house, and even before I knock on the door, I can smell the delicious aroma of freshly baked goodies. Oh Harry! Can a man who makes such heavenly food concoctions really make a mess of a once-happy marriage? God, I hope not!

"Catherine! What a nice surprise. Come into the kitchen and sit down. I have some nice fresh coffee and pastries. How's everything going?"

"Oh, you know, all work and so on. But I just finished a case so I thought I'd come and pay you a visit." He smiles at me and pats my shoulder absentmindedly then walks over to his baker's oven. I don't know exactly how to begin so I take a deep breath and jump right in. "Harry? I've got to ask you...what in the hell is going on? Myrtle is getting sick over what she thinks you're doing."

"Doing?" He smiles at me a bit distractedly. "Here, have a cannolo, I just made them. It has chocolate crème filling."

I take one, bite into the heavenly crème inside the hard shell and find that I have a hard time swallowing. I can't even enjoy Harry's gourmet pastry now.

"It's good, Harry, but listen to me. Myrtle's worried about what you're up to, whatever it is that you're up to."

"Worried? Why would she be worried?"

"You *know*, Harry! All the secrecy and all the late night goings-out. The phone calls to the, um, *that* woman. The bottle of Cialis you're hiding in your underwear drawer. Your wife is sick over it."

Harry looks sick himself. "You mean…you mean *she found out*?! No, no this is terrible. I didn't want her to find out like *this*."

"Well, of course not, I know that you…"

"I was going to ask you to help me with this. You're like a daughter to us. And it isn't going to happen for another week yet anyway. I wanted to keep it a secret for as long as I could."

"I'll help all I can, Harry. I love you and Myrtle, but maybe you should reconsider…"

"I wanted it to be a surprise!"

I simply stare at him. Who surprises their spouse with the announcement of an affair?

"She's got to come to the restaurant, Catherine. Regina Margherita? I want you to bring her there next Saturday. And I want her to meet this woman, Alex, who is responsible for all this. She's made me feel so good about what I'm doing."

"Harry!"

"What? This woman is fantastic and Myrtle will grow to love her!"

I decide to let Harry know that I followed him and saw him with this woman. "Listen Harry, you should know that Will and I did a little surveillance on you. I did it for Myrtle. We know where you've been going. I haven't given my findings to Myrtle yet because I wanted to see if I could talk some sense into you but what you're doing is not a secret now. You've got to stop it, Harry!"

Harry walks over to the countertop by the stove and begins putting the cannoli into a cake box.

"You *spied* on me? Really, Catherine, I wouldn't have expected that of you. We're family. You don't really..." He sighs and shakes his head. "Anyway, I can't stop, Catherine, I *won't* stop. Alex is the best at this. This is something that I've been planning to do for so long. I need to do it. Besides Myrtle *deserves* this; she needs to know how much..."

"Omigod Harry! Stop, stop, stop! Why do you want to hurt her? If you want to leave and be with this other woman, then just go. Don't drag it out."

Harry stops what he's doing and very calmly turns to me. "Leave who? What other woman are you talking about, Catherine?"

"Alex!"

"Alex? What about Alex?"

"You're leaving Myrtle for Alex!"

"What?!" Harry stares at me as if I've gone crazy. "Catherine, oh my God, no, Catherine sit down, please. This is all wrong."

Sinking into a kitchen chair, I mutter, "You better believe it's all wrong."

Harry sits across from me and removes his glasses so he can pass a shaky hand over his face. He takes a deep breath and faces me.

"First things first, Catherine. I am *not* leaving Myrtle, not for anyone. I love her more than you can ever know. We've been together since we were twenty years old."

"So this Alex woman is just a middle-aged fling for you?" I say indignantly. "If that's the case why do you want Myrtle to meet her?"

"Catherine, stop jumping to conclusions and use your detective's skills here. There was no fling, there *never will* be a fling for me. Think clearly and calculatingly, dear girl. What's next week?"

"June. What does that have to do with all this?"

"What happens in June? What event do I celebrate every June 9 without fail? This year is even more special than ever."

I put my brain into PI mode and suddenly realize what I failed to see. I was worried about Myrtle who was certain that Harry was cheating on her and so I only saw the situation as a friend would. Of course. What an idiot I am to have failed to understand! June 9th is Myrtle's sixty-fifth birthday, but I still fail to see what a birthday has to do with Harry and another woman.

"All right, Myrtle's birthday is coming. But who is this woman Alex? What's she got to do with the birthday? And why did Will and I see you embrace this woman a little over a week ago outside of the Regina Margherita restaurant?"

"I was simply thanking her. Alex Marsden is the city's most elite party planner. She's planned an elaborate dinner and birthday party for Myrtle. And it's a beautiful semi-formal affair, you know how much Myrtle likes to get dressed up. Oh my God, Catherine! How could you think I would want any other woman besides my beautiful, intelligent Myrtle?!"

Chastised I just sit there with nothing to say except that I'm sorry I jumped to conclusions. I put my hand on Harry's and we sit there for a while both of us feeling a bit foolish. Then Harry smiles wanly at me and says, "Catherine? Can you help me get Myrtle to her surprise party without spilling the beans?"

"I don't know. She's pretty upset. She thinks you're cheating on her."

"You'll think of something, please do this for me, for Myrtle and me. I love her so much. Maybe your lovely friend Melissa can help."

I nod and ponder how the hell I'm going to get Myrtle to that party, even *with* Melissa's help.

"I think you *should* meet Harry, Myrtle," I say. Melissa and I have been talking to her for over an hour with no results. She's obstinate as hell. Having called Melissa earlier and explained everything about the Harry-Myrtle business, she willingly came over late in the morning to offer her help. Her entrance into my office was like a breath of fresh, lilac-scented air.

"What?! Meet him so he can tell me that he's leaving me for another woman? No, I can't. Absolutely not." She shakes her head vehemently. This is going to be tough.

"I'll drive you there. I'll be with you, Myrtle; you won't be alone. But I seriously think you should be going to the restaurant. It's a very upscale restaurant: women are dressed in cocktail dresses looking fantastic. Meet him, okay? Talk to him...and Myrtle? Wear something sexy. Make him see what a gorgeous woman you are."

"You want me to meet Harry and possibly this, this *other woman*, his *mistress*? Catherine, I thought you were on my side in this!"

"Myrtle, I'm on both your sides. I love you and Harry and I think there's a chance that you may be wrong about his cheating. Just come with me and see what Harry has to say. Let's both get dressed up and look great, what do you say?"

"I say absolutely not, Catherine! No!" She looks from me to Melissa defiantly. "Now if you'll excuse me, I noticed this morning that we're out of yogurt; I have to restock." And with that announcement, she grabs her bag and exits the open door. Melissa throws her hands up and says, "This is not going to be as easy as I'd thought!" We plot strategies until Myrtle comes back a half hour later.

A pot of tea is waiting for Myrtle when she steps through the door after her self-imposed errand. Melissa helps Myrtle put away the yogurt and then settles her on the couch with a nice cup of tea. She leads the conversation away from Harry and engages in girl-talk. But when she looks at me and smiles, I know she's going in for the win.

"You know what you need, Myrtle? A girls' day of beauty!" In a gentle and charming way she convinces Myrtle to get a massage and have her hair and nails done. "I know that always makes me feel better. I know the perfect place. Let's do this together." She takes out her phone and calls a salon she patronizes. Within a few minutes she has set up an appointment for both Myrtle and herself. "We're in luck! Henri has an opening in half an hour. This will be fun! You need a day off and I'm sure Cate won't mind, right, darling?" She looks at me pleadingly. She's so convincing I just stare at her for a few minutes.

"Oh! Yes! Of course. Go! There's nothing here I can't handle by myself right now."

Myrtle isn't completely convinced. "Oh, Melissa, I don't know. There are things that need to be done here."

"I just made the appointment, Myrtle darling. It would be rude to cancel."

"Well...I guess it would be all right. Are you absolutely sure you don't need me, Catherine? What about the rest of the billing?"

"I'm sure you can do that tomorrow," says Melissa taking charge and looking at me pointedly to agree.

"Tomorrow is fine, no problem. Don't worry, Myrtle, just go with Melissa and enjoy!"

After a few more minutes of gentle persuasion, Myrtle says that maybe it will be good for her to be pampered. As they leave I hear Melissa suggesting a little shopping trip after their day at the salon. "I need your help picking out an outfit, Myrtle. You have excellent taste. Will you come with me to Bloomingdale's?"

◆

They return to the office very late in the afternoon looking fabulous and carrying several bags from Bloomingdale's. Melissa has worked magic with Myrtle's mood. Besides buying something for herself, Melissa has picked out a low-cut form-fitting dress, which will show off Myrtle's ballroom dancing toned body beautifully. Myrtle changes in the bathroom and models the dress for us. She looks great!

I see that she has convinced Myrtle to meet Harry at the restaurant on Saturday. All the while they were in the salon, she let Myrtle pour her heart out and offered a sympathetic ear. She also gave her some good advice. "Walk in like you're royalty, Myrtle, look Harry in the eye and tell him you want an explanation concerning his late night activities over the past couple of weeks. You're a strong woman, darling, let him see that. Put up a fight for your man. Don't let this other woman win. You're too good to be treated so shabbily."

And after much convincing on the part of Melissa, Myrtle decided that she was right. "I am a strong woman. I will meet Harry and get to the bottom of his shenanigans. If he's cheating, then, well I have to know. After all the years I've invested in this marriage, I won't let him go so easily." She stops and looks at herself in the mirror. "But let me tell you young women that as far as that trollop is concerned? If Harry *is* cheating with her, I will rip her hair out! At his age, really!"

The party was a success with a very attractive Myrtle marching determinedly into the restaurant intending to confront a cheating Harry and his "trollop" only to be greeted by shouts of "Surprise!" and "Happy birthday!" She was flabbergasted when Harry Tuttle, resplendent in a silver tux, came over to her and hugged and kissed her in front of everyone and then introduced Alex. Prepared for a fight, Myrtle truly was speechless.

After the cocktail hour she and Harry disappeared for a walk around the outside of the building and came back twenty minutes later with their arms around each other. They came up to me together and thanked me profusely for caring enough to meddle.

"Meddle? That's Cate's unofficial middle name," said a very handsome Will handing me a cranberry martini with a strong shot of Grey Goose vodka. He was wearing a dark gray suit with a dark blue shirt and blue striped tie and pretty much took my breath away. We matched. I looked damned good myself in the indigo blue short cocktail dress I had worn when Will and I had dinner with his mother last year. It was nice to take it out of my closet and show it off again.

Giles was there with Dr. Felicia and we were all cordial to

each other. Will and Giles even joked about the whole Tuttle comedy of errors. I walked past Myrtle's table and overheard her and Alex deep in conversation about Alex's twelve-year-old son who was having a problem with math. Myrtle was offering her experience of thirty-five years as an educator and Alex was listening intently. As Shakespeare said, "All's well that ends well."

After the party we drive Melissa home. Before getting out of Will's car, she asks me to come to her brownstone the next morning. "Come over to my place for coffee and brunch."

"Sure, yes, I can be there around ten. We haven't had a nice long chat in quite a while."

Will and I drive home emotionally exhausted but happy for Myrtle and Harry. Once inside the brownstone Will suddenly grabs me and kisses me deeply before feverishly undressing me. "Promise me you won't ever change, Cate."

"What brought this on?" That deep, tongue thrust kiss has me dizzy with anticipation of what comes next. He gently holds my face in his two hands and looks earnestly into my eyes.

"You know how I told you *not* to meddle? To let Harry and Myrtle work it out on their own? Well, I'm telling you now to keep meddling in the lives of those you care about. You're a royal pain in the ass, you can drive me crazy with your slightly illegal actions, you stick your nose in where it doesn't always belong, and there are times when you act without thinking and put yourself in way too much danger. To top that off, you're severely domestically challenged." He laughs. "But, babe, you're fiercely loyal and anyone you love knows that you've always got their back and are looking out for them. So, I'm telling you now, just this once, don't ever change. Keep on being *you*, exactly the way you are."

It's as close to an apology as I'll ever get from Detective Will Benigni and I begin to say as much but he lays me down on the soft carpet and his tongue begins a slow descent from my neck downwards, touching special places on my body that leave me too breathless to speak.

CHAPTER 27

THE TWIN AROMAS of good coffee and Creole seafood quiche greet me as Melissa opens the door to her beautiful brownstone. She gestures me to sit in the kitchen and gets right to the point. "I need your help, Cate. Do you remember that friend of mine who died not too long ago?" I nod.

"His daughter is in the process of having his body exhumed and that can spell disaster. She is that vicious a person." Seeing my look of concern she quickly says, "Not for me, disaster for this gentle man whose forty year political and humanitarian career will be sullied and he will be made a mockery of a human being. He was a man who had certain...sexual preferences that I was able to fulfill. There are pictures of him with me fulfilling his fantasies." She holds her head high and fixes me with a challenging look.

"Melissa, you know I've never asked about how you earn your money or what your profession entails. The truth is I don't care. Our friendship is what matters, not what either of us do to pay our bills. I don't have to know anything that involves you personally if you don't want to tell me."

For an answer Melissa hands over a manila envelope. "No, it's better if you do know what this entails. Actually, you need all the info I can give to you to be able to work the case. The pictures in here are duplicates of the ones buried in my friend's jacket pocket." I begin to open the envelope as Melissa continues. "I don't care what anyone knows about me. I am who I am, Cate; I make no apologies for that. If you feel uncomfortable then I'll have to find someone else to help me. But I want you to know something; I chose *you*, not because we're friends, I chose you because you're the best at this private investigation business and right now I *need* the absolute best to deal with this issue."

The pictures that were buried with Mr. V. are very erotic to say the least but I don't change expression as I look at them. This is real porn with real sex toys. They show the usually elegant Melissa in a very different light as a dominatrix, carnal and frightening, and Mr. V. as her slave. Melissa is right about ruining her client's legacy; if these pictures of him were ever leaked to the public, the memory of him as a compassionate politician and humanitarian would be completely erased. The public would judge him wrongly as a perverted old man.

"Melissa, I have to ask one question: Why did you put the pictures in his jacket pocket?" Her eyes well with tears before she answers. "It was his request. He knew he was ill. The last time I saw him, he told me that having the pictures buried with him was what he wanted. How could I not honor that wish? I had no idea his daughter would find out." She takes a deep breath to control herself before continuing in a soft but firm voice.

"I need you to stop this woman, Cate. This man, this kind, gentle man does not need to have his wonderful political legacy destroyed by a vicious scandal." She pauses. "There's one thing you should know. I believe his daughter is hiding a secret of her own that she doesn't want to come out. Something her father told me about a possible affair. She's principal of a private high school for girls and a stickler about morals. She's been quoted at educational seminars about how she lives her life according to a strict God-given moral code and expects the same of her faculty and students. In my experience, someone who shouts that loudly about morals has very few of their own."

I nod; I've met too many moral crusaders who have been

true degenerates. "Anything else you can tell me about her?"

"I know her son married into a very well-to-do family with social connections. My client said that his daughter was in awe of them. I also know that her husband has a criminal record for gambling and that her father kept him out of jail."

Suddenly I remember what Giles had said about that exhumation case on Staten Island. Is Melissa the woman who was given an expensive painting? "Does any of this have to do with a certain Artemisia Gentileschi painting worth over $200,000? Giles is being consulted about an exhumation. The person who is insisting on having a body exhumed claims a Gentileschi painting that was given away as a gift is rightfully hers."

She nods. "He wanted me to have it. He said that the painting always reminded him of me. I have it in a bank vault. I'll never part with it."

"Okay, Melissa, you've given me a lot to go on. I'll tail her and find out any secrets she has hidden. This is all I need."

Taking a deep breath, Melissa gets up and pours coffee for us both with a shot of Sambuca on the side, something we both need. We silently agree to drop the subject. Then we settle down to more coffee and quiche and talk about last night's party.

The next day I do a complete background search on a woman named Laurie Clerke. Within a week I have all the info I need and am ready for action.

Finding out the dirty, distasteful secret life of one Mrs. Laurie Clerke, principal of Lakefield High School, proved easier than expected. Mrs. Clerke leaves the building at four on the dot every Thursday. Her afterschool trips on those days take her to a seedy motel on the New Jersey side of the Lincoln Tunnel. There she meets a married teacher employed at the same school and they spend several hours inside room 229. That they don't completely pull the vertical blinds together is a plus for me and I take shot after rapid shot of their "activities." After their second Thursday tryst, I have more than fifty pictures of them doing the nasty.

My meeting with Laurie Clerke takes place three days later. Inside the closed door of Mrs. Clerk's office I confront her with pictures of her marathon sex-capades with the married teacher from her school.

"Yes, I can see that the pictures are upsetting to you. Here are the others. I understand your shock, I mean, seriously, Laurie, these don't exactly show you in the best light now, do they? Especially the one where your butt is in the air and your mouth is on his...well we won't go into that.

"Now let's get down to business, shall we? You're not going to have the body of your father exhumed and expose his private life to the world. That painting you so covet? You're going to forget about it. If you even attempt to have him dug up or locate that painting, these pictures will go out. They'll go to the son of the man you're having the extramarital affair with and then his family. Oh, and I don't think that you'll want your daughter to see you like this, or your son and his wife or his very wealthy in-laws, right? No, of course not." I smile at the woman in front of me. "And your husband who has a criminal record and is known for having such a short fuse that you fear him enough to have your bills from Macy's and Bloomingdale's sent here to your place of work rather than face his fury. Imagine his anger when he sees these!

"You can keep these pictures if you want. You know, as a sort of memento? I'd just be very careful *where* I kept them if I were you. I have copies in three different locations as a security measure. Oh, and Mrs. Clerke? Speaking of being careful, I'd be very, very careful of ever calling anyone a perverted whore again if you know what I mean. Those pictures of you prove that you have firsthand *personal* knowledge of what those words mean." I hand over the last two pictures. "Especially in these back and front pictures here? I think your kids would definitely call that perversion."

I walk out the door, smile at the secretary and whistle all the way to my car. Case closed.

CHAPTER 28

"HELLO AGAIN, CATE." Marc Croft is standing in my living room in the dark. I put my hand on my gun. "Christ! You!"

"Let's keep this friendly now, Cate. No need to try to play hero. Besides, realistically you'd be dead before you got to point the gun at me. Sit down and let's talk."

The room is dark but I see a glint of silver and know he has a gun fixed on me.

"I'm not going to harm you in any way. I'm simply here to congratulate you on a job well done. And I got to keep the money, ten thousand from Brooks-Warren. Plus I helped myself to Edward Penn's vast collection of diamond jewelry scammed from his other victims I'm sure. They will bring in a nice payday. I'm content, Cate, I really am."

His voice is low and smooth but I remain standing. "And I'm truly glad that Jennifer is alive. Come on now, Cate. Sit down a while. I want to talk to you."

"What about? I was kind of hoping I'd never see you again? I did have my locks changed and a new alarm put in."

He laughs. "My God, Cate, I can get into anywhere I want. No locks or alarms can stop me from getting to you or anyone else. I'm a consummate professional. Now you should know that."

"Great, so for the rest of my life I have to be concerned about coming home and finding a professional killer sitting in the dark in my living room? What a way to live!"

"Ah no, sweet lady, after tonight you will never see me again, that I can promise. I have other things I want to do. I'm going to disappear for a good while. I've got quite a stash of money to keep me going. Don't forget that, in a strange way, I helped you find Jennifer Brooks-Warren. That should earn me at least an hour of your precious time. Detective Benigni is at his precinct, Dr. Barrett is dining with colleagues; both of the men in your life are occupied. You'll have to settle for my company tonight. Now, sit down Cate. I won't tell you again." He smiles but his eyes are hard. "Let's talk. I want to tell you about Victoria. You're so very like Victoria. Not a killer, of course, unless the situation warrants it; I bet you could kill if you had no other choice. I know you must have thought about it."

He's right. I have thought that if it would save an innocent life, I would be able to kill another person. I'd *like* to think I'd find another way. But then, who really knows? I've never been in that situation and I hope that I never am.

"You're strong, the same way Victoria was strong. But you're vulnerable too; you care too much about helping people. Victoria couldn't afford to care. Your vulnerability works for you but it destroyed Victoria. So let me tell you about her."

"Victoria? What about her?" I ask moving to a chair nearest the door.

"I want you to know how she died. In a strange way Victoria saved your client or at least the memory of her did." He looks straight at me, those piercing cold, so very cold, blue eyes that have seen so much of the dark side of the world. "Just like your client, Victoria was buried alive but unlike your client I wasn't able to get to her in time to save her."

I let my breath out slowly. "Why was she buried alive?"

"We were on a mission; we did a lot of missions back then. Victoria was a skilled infiltrator; she could get you in and out of a place without anyone knowing you had been there until after your job was done. We were a good team; so good that it was almost as if we could read each other's minds. We didn't have to talk to communicate, we just knew what had to be done and we did it.

"You're not supposed to fall in love with your mission buddy," he laughs abruptly. "But I did. Oh, we fucked, of course we did. Sex was a given. It happens and usually it's just a way to deal with the stress of dangerous missions; it doesn't mean anything. Danger heightens your senses to an incredible degree. The unbroken rule is that you don't cross the line; you don't fall in love because that becomes the real danger. If that happens, you become human and you begin to look after your partner more than you're supposed to do. You tend to get sloppy with the rules, jeopardizing missions and your own life."

I think about the way Will and I kissed with such deep, urgent passion after the ordeal on Hart Island. We could never be partners on patrol; we'd always be distracted with worry for each other. "What happened?"

"Our last mission together was in South America. Victoria got us in quietly and quickly the way she always did. It wasn't even a major kill. Some petty official was trying to make a name for himself by attacking the central government. This guy wasn't so clean himself; he was into the drug trade. We needed to eliminate him and get out. We'd done so many missions like this one, no one foresaw any major problems." The Eliminator shifts in his seat and doesn't speak for several minutes. "The guy's brother was an enforcer in a local drug cartel but he wasn't supposed to be a threat because intel had checked and found out that he would be in Venezuela the night of the kill. For some reason I'll never know he didn't go to Venezuela and he found out very quickly what had happened to his brother. He was soon out for blood, our blood.

"According to set plans, mission members split up after a kill. We did just that and went separate ways intending to rendezvous at a small plane hidden in a jungle area. We had less than two hours to get to the plane and we both knew that if we were caught we'd be in the hands of a man capable of the most hideous tortures. Victoria made it but I didn't. I was shot but managed to escape and hide out in the jungle. But Victoria didn't know that; she thought I was captured and she knew what was going to happen to me." His voice becomes low and cold.

"She should have just left, saved herself; the mission was over, the order was to leave and get out. She was safe, alive, but she went back to find me! Victoria, my strong, brilliant Victoria loved me enough to go back into that hell-hole and try to save me." He stops, and even in the half-light I see him shaking his head in disbelief, remembering what she had done. "She was captured, which is something that never would have happened to her if she was thinking the way she'd been trained to think: survival at all costs, no mistakes allowed. But she was only thinking about saving me. Her feelings and her fear for me made her a vulnerable target.

"After they captured her, the brother of the man I killed decided on what he felt was the most appropriate punishment for someone who had helped kill his brother. He taped her mouth shut, then buried her alive under six feet of dirt and rocks."

I feel sick to my stomach. The cruelty of humanity never ceases to scare me. "Did you know what happened to her?"

"No, not immediately. I hid in the jungle for more than twenty-four hours before I knew she'd been captured. A local hunter had seen it all, my escape and her capture. By the time he found where I was hiding, the cartel members had moved on. He took me to where they had buried Victoria.

"She'd been under the ground for over a day and I knew the chances of her being alive were non-existent. Still, I didn't want to leave her there so, with his help I dug up her grave. When I found her body her sightless eyes were open in terror and her nails and fingers were shredded raw from trying to claw her way out of the dirt. I was too late to save her."

I need to ask a question that is burning to be answered. "And the man who did this? Please tell me he's not alive." He shakes his head. "With what you know about me, Cate, do *you* think I would let him live?"

"No, I don't. What happened after you found Victoria?"

"I took her body back to the plane and flew her stateside, to Florida, where I was met by a woman and two men who helped orchestrate our mission. They helped me place my beautiful, foolish Victoria in an empty mausoleum in an abandoned church yard. I couldn't bear to put her back in the ground. Then...I went back to Colombia.

"It took me almost a month before I could find the cartel enforcer but when I did, I made sure that his death was more brutal than what he had done to Victoria. I kept him alive for three days. Let's just say he suffered...a great deal. After his elimination I hid out in Florida and drank two years of my life away, guilty for not being able to save Victoria. Eventually, the guilt dulled, I stopped trying to destroy myself and I went back to doing what I do best: killing." He gets up. "So that's the story of Victoria. As far as my helping you find Jennifer, well, you can read a lot into my story or nothing at all. Never forget for a second that I am not one of the good guys; I'm a highly skilled assassin, a killer and I enjoy my job. Let's just say that I was able to do for Jennifer what I couldn't do for Victoria. After tonight I'll never mention the name Victoria again. It's too painful. But for some strange reason that I can't explain, I wanted *you* to know who she was."

He walks over to me. I jump up from my chair and he laughs. "Don't worry. You'll never see me again. One loose end to tie up and then I'm gone." Marc Croft, the assassin, the highly paid killer-for-hire, the Eliminator, unexpectedly grabs me tightly and kisses me gently on the mouth. "Good-bye, Cate Harlow, Private Investigator. Stay safe."

Then the ghost, the White Death walks out of my door and out of my life.

I write down all the details I remember about my last visit from Marc Croft and put it in a password-encrypted file on my computer. This is one file that I do not intend to share with anyone. It's for my own personal info and I hope I never have to add anything to it. I don't think I will; somehow I believe that Marc Croft will keep his promise that I'll never see him again. I have to trust him on that.

Later that night I'm on the computer writing up the last few notes for Melissa's private investigation when I hear my front doorbell ring and my named called. "Cate?" Will's voice carries through the front door and I get up to open it. He kisses me and hands me take-out from his favorite deli.

"Hey, baby." He hugs me and kisses the side of my neck. Releasing me he takes his service revolver and badge and places them in the top drawer of my breakfront. I notice an envelope sticking out of his jacket pocket as he takes the jacket off, loosens his tie and tosses the jacket and the envelope onto an armchair.

"Got any Chivas?"

"In the china cabinet. Pour me one too." Hitting *save* on Melissa's file, I log off listening to Will open cabinet doors and rattle glasses. Today is the day the results for the Bar were due to come in. I'm dying to know what's in the envelope.

Carrying two glasses and the bottle of Chivas, Will comes back into the living room. Handing me one of the two glasses he carefully pours the liquid first into mine and then into his own. We clink our glasses together in a silent toast. He looks so serious and not at all happy. I hear him blow out his breath before he downs his entire tumbler and immediately pours himself another. The deep exhales are the only fragile side of Will I know. He's fearless and professional on the job but personal issues bring out the stressed deep breathing I know so well. I reach over and grab his hand.

"Results are in for the Bar, baby." He doesn't smile. Shit! He didn't pass! I feel horrible for him.

"Bad?" I ask putting my own tumbler down on the coffee table ready to offer hugs, kisses, and any other physical acts he wants for comfort.

"Bad?" He laughs and drains his second glass. "Bad!" He mutters the word again. Oh boy, I can feel the tension in the room.

"Well, how...bad? I mean you know that you can always take it...again and...I know that you might see this as..."

"I passed."

"What?!"

"I passed the God-damned thing. I passed the Bar with fucking flying colors!"

I don't know whether to smack him or hug him. He passed! But he doesn't seem happy about it. Maybe he's in shock or just so tired from all the studying and the grind of taking the actual exam.

"But that's great, Will. You passed the Bar. That's quite an achievement, don't you think? I'm so proud of you!" I decide to hug him. "Did you call Francesca? She will be over the moon with this news."

He exhales deeply. "No, I didn't call her and I'm not going to call her, not right now."

I sit down again and sip my drink. Will drops onto the couch exhausted, like a man who has run a marathon.

"Well sure, I mean, you want to savor the moment for a while, I understand. You can always call her later tonight or tomorrow even." He doesn't respond. "I'm just so glad you decided to tell *me* that you passed."

Will moves closer to me and rests his arm on the back of the couch. "I told *you*, Cate, because I'm going to tell you something else. I'm *happy* I passed, don't get me wrong on that score; it feels good to have passed the state Bar. I accomplished something that I needed and *wanted* to do." He takes a deep breath and exhales slowly. "But...right now, I don't know what I want to do *with* it. I don't know if I really want to give up doing what I've been doing for twelve years. I'm not ready to walk away from being a detective." He sighs deeply again. "Truth, Cate? I love being a NYPD detective; it isn't just a job to me, it's so much a part of who I am. I don't know if I'm ready to *make* this dramatic a change and I don't even know if I *want* to be a lawyer full time. Do you know what I mean?"

I understand exactly what he means. I gave up a job that had a steady paycheck and set hours to become a private investigator where as far as money goes, it's feast or famine, and twenty-four hour days are all too frequent. But as crazy, sometimes frustrating, and dangerous as my job can be, I love what I do and wouldn't go back to sitting in an office translating legalese for anything.

We sit in silence for a while both of us lost in our own thoughts. A second tumbler of Chivas has added to a nice relaxed, mellow feeling. Will takes out his phone. Taking me into his arms he whispers, "Remember this?" and presses the music icon. *In the Still of the Night* begins to play, the soft sweet voices of Fred Parris and the Five Satins blending seamlessly. Even though the song was recorded in 1955 before either of us had been born, it played a part in the hot and heavy sex life of Cate Harlow and Will Benigni. Will played it the night we first made love in his loft apartment. It helped a very hot man seduce a very overwhelmed with lust me and I gave into an entire night of unbelievably intense passion that left me breathless and eager for more. Will loved the song because they sang the lyrics, *"I re-mem-ber that night in Ma-a-ay..."*; May is the month we met.

Now as I hear the familiar harmony I feel my body responding to Will's passion as he easily removes my clothes and touches places with his hands and tongue that drive me to breathless ecstasy. When we're both naked Will lays me down on the thick area rug and we make love over and over again as the music replays. The slightly salty taste of his skin and the heat from his body merging with my own gives our lovemaking a sensation that we are alone in a beautiful erotic world of our own creation. We slip in and out of sleep and awaken to explore each other anew. Life is good.

⚘

I'm making coffee the next morning when Will gets a call from a fellow officer. "Right. Got it. Let's see if we can keep this in-house for now. Media doesn't need to have knowledge of this right away. Thanks for the head's up."

"Will?"

"Edward Penn was found dead in his cell at Rikers last night, his throat expertly slit from ear to ear. Officers questioned at the prison said it looked like a professional hit but gave no details as to how the murder may have taken place. No one, it seems, heard or saw anything, no sound, no notice of unknown persons. A typed note next to the victim read: *'Services rendered, for payment received'*. I asked that this be kept quiet for now but you can be sure it will get out. Anyway, his demise, such as it was, saves the city of New York the price of a trial." I shake my head in agreement and think about the Eliminator tying up one last loose end.

What had Marc Croft said? *"I get paid for a job, it gets done, one way or another."* Looks like he takes it seriously. In a twisted, strange sort of way he fulfilled his contract with Jennifer Brooks-Warren and served his own brand of justice to Edward Penn.

Melissa gives me a hug and her dog Dixie does a little dance in front of both of us. "I'm going to New Orleans for a while, Cate. I need to get out of New York City for a bit and see my Tante Anjali. Are you sure it's no bother to watch Dixie for me?"

"Of course not. Little Guy and Mouse already love him, right Dix?" My cats may not exactly love Dixie but they accept him as a friendly guest. Both cats have let Dixie know which areas of my brownstone are off-limits to him and which are common ground. Just like humans, cats and dogs can get along very well if they respect each other's privacy.

The black standard poodle named Dixie looks at her, then at me and gives a little bark of happiness. Melissa smiles. "I've told my clients where I can be reached and one or two may be coming to New Orleans for a visit." She knows I understand who she means when she says "clients" but our friendship is a solid one based on discreetness and loyalty. I just nod.

Life is pretty much back to normal, if I can call *my* life normal at any time. Harry and Myrtle are back together in their comfortable and happy marriage which is good. They went away for a nice long weekend and Myrtle came back happy and all smiles. I didn't ask but I strongly suspect that a certain little pill put both Myrtle and Harry back on the sexual track. I'm glad for them; healthy sex is good at any age.

Harry's pastries are a daily delight at the office of *Catherine Harlow, Private Investigations*, making me play tennis two extra days a week to be able to fit into my jeans. But all's good.

The infamous, untraceable coffin Edward purchased from Luca Memorial Services was finally found. Edward had sold it to a funeral home in New Jersey. By the time I traced it to its location, the Perfect Ruby Rest 0557 had become the final, comfortable, and very expensive resting vehicle for one ninety-eight year old Miss Frances Polanca. I took a picture of this "lovely, lovely model" and sent it to the ghoulish Mr. Jasinski at Luca Memorial who confirmed that it was indeed the Perfect Ruby Rest 0557 picked up by a person we now know was Edward Penn. I paid my respects to Miss Polanca and her family then hurriedly left for NYC glad to be done with coffins and burials for a while.

Jennifer Brooks-Warren was released from the hospital three weeks after we found her and soon after that she came by to give me a check for my services. She told me that she sent a check, plus a bonus, to Adrian. Jennifer had no idea that Edward wasn't paying the bills. Her business manager at the bank is taking care of outstanding bills and making sure to clear any credit damage caused by Edward Penn in her name.

She will not talk about what happened to her but I know that she's glad she didn't have to testify at a trial about her ordeal. Edward's demise removed that burden from her. Her statement to police about what happened was sufficient. She did tell me that she is seeing a therapist. "It's something that I wish I had done before I met Edward. My lack of self-esteem is a major issue in my life. I allow men to take advantage of me," says this incredibly beautiful woman. "Physical changes don't change who you are or the problems inside you. I need to work on that." Amen to that. Work on the inner self first and then deal with everything else.

After some sleepless nights and a good, honest talk with Myrtle, I made a final decision concerning what I should do about Moira Hollis. Having checked out Moira's story about having an abusive father and her virtual abandonment by her mother and siblings, I found that she had told me the truth. She also told the truth about Anthony Cole. They had dated and, according to sources, were seriously involved. Anthony Cole did work for Damian Hollis and he did suddenly just disappear. He was never found, no body, nothing. It is entirely possible that her father had him killed.

I came to believe that it would serve no moral purpose to have her arrested for the hired murder of her father more than two years ago. Even though I felt that my decision was the best one, I needed affirmation that I was doing the right thing. I wanted to run it past Myrtle, someone whom I see as a paragon of virtue. How would she view my decision? What would she think of me if I didn't inform the police in Virginia about this murder? How would she view letting a woman who had hired a hit on her own father, bastard though he was, go free?

I found out that that peerless diamond Myrtle Goldberg Tuttle can be very practical when it comes to what's really right or wrong; she agreed with me one hundred percent. As she said, "Sending that poor woman to face justice now would be the same as beating a child for standing up to a bully. Besides, Catherine, I have a feeling she lives with the fear of what she has done and that's punishment enough. She certainly can't tell anyone and she can't seek help from a therapist and confess what she's done, so she has to keep all the feelings bottled up inside herself. You did say that the man was a monster to her. I think, I really do think, that you should let this one go.

"As I told you a couple of weeks ago, I've learned a few things working here, Catherine. When it comes to the law, it isn't always a question of black and white. There are some much-needed gray areas that should be explored before a choice is made concerning what's truly wrong and what's right. Moira was the victim in more ways than one." She places her hand on mine. "This is the right decision, honey."

She's right. Moira Hollis had certainly suffered enough. She had endured life with a cruelly dominating father, been abandoned by a frightened alcoholic mother, and left to fend on her own by older siblings who just wanted to get as far away as possible from a painful home life. She also knew in her heart that her father had gotten rid of the only man who had really loved her. In the great scheme of things, the loss of one Mr. Damian Hollis only means that the world has one less nasty bastard living in it.

Melissa has been in New Orleans for a month and has kept in touch mostly by text and e-mails. She has called me to talk a few times and has also left voice messages so that Dixie can hear her voice. She seems relaxed. Seeing her Tante Anjali, the woman who raised her, is, she says, wonderful. Her last text said she'd be back in New York City in about two weeks.

Giles and I continue to have lunch at least once a month. We're friends although there are times when I feel Giles would like us to be more than that. Truthfully, he'll always be someone who makes me feel warm and sexy whenever we're together. He's still seeing Dr. Felicia but he insists that neither one of them wants a serious commitment. I hate to admit that the little jealous spark inside me is glad to hear him say that. I feel bitchy about that but at least I'm honest with myself. Giles and I had something very special for a time there and it's a sweet memory.

Will told his mother Francesca that he passed the Bar and she, Will, and I, along with Myrtle and Harry had a small celebration at Regina Margherita instead of the super large one Francesca wanted to throw for him with family and friends. He was adamant about no one knowing he passed the Bar until *he* was ready to tell everyone. "It's my accomplishment, let me savor it alone for a while with the people who mean the most to me," is what he told Francesca.

Will still hasn't made a final decision on exactly when, or I really think, *if*, he'll be ready to leave the NYPD Detectives Bureau and start a new career as a lawyer. Right now I think we both like life the way it is; we have our careers, we're together two or three times a week, and everything is smooth. Life is, indeed, very good.

My cell phone beeps as I'm walking back to the brownstone after taking Dixie for her nightly stroll. It's Melissa. "Cate! How are you?" Her voice is melodic and sweet. "How's Dixie?"

"Hi Melissa! Everything's good, we're both well. How's New Orleans?"

"That's what I'm calling you about. How would you and Will like to come visit me here?"

"Well—I—I—I...I'd love to do that," I hesitate, "New Orleans would be nice but, seriously, I can't afford to take a vacation now, Melissa. Neither can Will. We're both kind of swamped and money is a bit tight, at least for me, at the moment. Thanks but..."

"I've already purchased the tickets," she says brightly. "First-class for you, Will, and Dixie."

"Oh, we can't let you do..."

Melissa stops me and I hear a change in her voice. She sounds scared."Please Cate, please say yes. I, well, I really need your help."

"My help? I don't understand. Is something wrong?" Her elegant voice breaks again. "What is it, Melissa?" I'm on alert and Dixie turns toward me as I stop walking.

"My Tante Anjali has been arrested for murder. You *have* to come to New Orleans to help her!"

Read the newest *Cate Harlow Private Investigation* available June of 2016.

"This third book in the Cate Harlow series is a perfect blend of mystery, magic, and astute storytelling. And the hot sex scenes between Will and Cate are a definite plus. Stunning! New Orleans, a murder mystery, and Cate Harlow go well together. *UNREPENTENT: Pray for Us Sinners* is another jewel in the Cate Harlow Private Investigation series for author Kristen Houghton."

—Greg Archer, *The Huffington Post* Book Review

Unrepentent
PRAY FOR US SINNERS

A Cate Harlow Private Investigation

Kristen Houghton

© copyright 2015 Kristen Houghton all rights reserved

Cate Harlow's best friend, the lovely "lady of the evening" Melissa Abrincourt, asks Cate and Cate's ex-husband, NYPD Detective Will Benigni, to come to New Orleans. Her beloved Tante Anjali, the woman who raised Melissa, has been arrested for murder and she needs their help.

What Melissa doesn't tell her is that Tante Angali is a sorcière, a witch, and that she wants Cate to conduct a private investigation into the murder of a voodoo priestess who has been accused of modern day slavery and sex trafficking.

As a sorcière, a "gifted person of magic," and powerful voodooienne rival of the murdered woman, Tante Anjali is the prime suspect. She was found in the murdered woman's garden with the murder weapon, a bloody knife, in her hand. Though she claims to be innocent of the murder, Tante Angali will not disclose why she was there or who else may be involved.

Will is along not only for his expertise as a NYPD detective but for his newly acquired law degree. Although he's reluctant to do so because of lack of experience, Melissa wants him to help defend her aunt in court, something he strongly feels he's not prepared to do. As he tells Cate, "I'm not a member of the Louisiana Bar. I don't want this to turn into a New Orleans version of *My Cousin Vinny*."

The case becomes even stranger for Cate as her own private investigation into the murder takes her into the mystical and frightening heart of New Orleans voodoo magic and a possible connection to witchcraft in her own family.

AUTHOR'S NOTE

Though the character of assassin Marc Croft is a fictional one, it is a fact that these professional ghosts exist. Many work in the field of espionage, some are soldiers-of-fortune, others work for organized crime, but all sell their skills for profit by eliminating people for a hefty price.

The Tor and the Dark Web are anonymity networks designed to keep identites and locations completely secure.

Hart Island does exist and is situated in New York City at the western end of Long Island Sound. It houses the largest Potter's field in the United States, with over one million unclaimed bodies and indigent dead buried there. It is a restricted area under the jurisdiction of the New York City Department of Correction and is closed to free public access. The City of New York currently offers no provisions for individuals wanting to visit Hart Island without contacting the prison system.

ACKNOWLEDGEMENTS

A special thank you to authors Carole Nelson Douglas and Jeani Rector for their positive support and their excellent advice, and to Courtney Davison for all her help and incredibly skillful editing.

Thank you to all readers who have become faithful fans of Cate Harlow and company. Rest assured that they will all be back in book three of *A Cate Harlow Private Investigation*.

CPSIA information can be obtained at www.ICGtesting.com
Printed in the USA
BVOW08s1331060616

450918BV00004B/29/P

9 781633 931695